ADVANCE I
YOUR TOMORI

"Dosunmu's writing paints a raw and honest picture of the struggle modern woman navigating a patriarchal society. The novel beautifully contrasts the modernity of Lagos with antiquated societal norms, a theme that is especially poignant in a world where women's autonomy is increasingly under threat. This novel will resonate with lovers of contemporary fiction and anyone tired of allowing others to define who and what they should be."

—*Booklist Online*

"Oyindamola Dosunmu weaves an emotionally complex and intellectually rich narrative... The novel is not a traditional narrative in the usual sense— there is no straightforward plot to follow. Instead, it functions as a layered, stream-of-consciousness meditation on what it means to live through trauma, cultural dislocation, and the passage of time... A novel that challenges conventional form and dares to ask difficult questions about memory, motherhood, and what it means to survive yourself."

—*San Francisco Book Review*

"Set against the shimmering backdrop of contemporary Nigeria, *Your Tomorrow Was Today* is a fascinating exploration of autonomy, family, and what it truly means to heal in a society that deems women selfish for doing so. A love letter to women courageous enough to be 'selfish' anyway."

—*Reader Views (5-Star Review)*

"*Your Tomorrow Was Today* is a beautifully crafted novel about healing, choice, and the strength it takes to write your own future, and it's a must-read for lovers of literary fiction with heart and cultural depth."

—*Readers' Favorite (5-Star review)*

"*Your Tomorrow Was Today* is guaranteed to be a book that will touch you regardless of gender, interests, or philosophy. Written with rare emotional precision, it is destined to be one of the most talked about books of 2026."

—*Littafi Reviews*

"An unforgettable debut—bold, moving, and necessary."

—Jeyran Main, *Review Tales*

Your Tomorrow Was Today

A NOVEL

Oyindamola Dosunmu

Silver Drive Press

Library of Congress Control Number: 2-488-122 Dosunmu, Oyindamola.
Your Tomorrow Was Today: A Novel / Oyindamola Dosunmu. pages cm
ISBN 979-8-9991626-2-5(Paperback)
ISBN 979-8-9991626-3-2(Hardcover).

World Literature / Africa / Nigeria FICTION / Family Life /
Siblings FICTION / Literary FICTION / Own Voices FICTION /
Feminist FICTION / Women

Cover design by Anze Ban V.
Interior formatting and design by Laura Antonioli.

First Edition: 2026

YOUR TOMORROW WAS TODAY

ONE

Present Day, 2024, Lagos, Nigeria.

Karen Ezeani's plans for the evening did not include Mama dying.

She shifted to adjust her willowy frame by the transparent door to the balcony, cradling a glass of bourbon—her refuge when she felt troubled. She could not bring herself to enjoy the drink, yet she was drawn to it for no reason other than it seemed to possess the inexplicable formula to dissolve knots of anxiety. Karen's face contorted as the amber liquid touched her lips, and she drew a sharp breath. The smooth texture trailed a fiery path down her throat, prompting her to tighten her grip on the glass. She waited for the sensation to settle before daring another sip.

Her gaze settled on floodlights on the Ikoyi Link Bridge, a good mile away, brightening the dark skyline. For a minute, she was lost in the steady glow of white light, lured further into her thoughts.

A few hours ago, she had sauntered into the living room, wrapped in a woolen bathrobe, lethargic from a long shower. Barefoot, she reveled in the soft carpet beneath her feet, comforted by the familiar shades and planes of her home in contrast to the work trip to Ghana: the faint smell of sandalwood, pale orange hues from the evening sun reflected off cream walls, stark white sheets of her carefully laid bed—crisp and neat—half-finished books in a wicker chair. Mundane details she would otherwise have ignored now held some significance in the wake of her distress.

She turned away from the hypnotic allure of the lights, swallowing a lump in her throat—not from the bourbon, but from a twinge of shame at her annoyance when Mama's name had beamed on her phone screen. She had stared at the vibrating gadget for longer than necessary before sliding the green button.

To her surprise, Uloma's sobbing filled her ears once she picked up the phone, replacing the rich tenor of Mama's voice she had expected.

"*Eh*, Adesuwa, oh! Mama is dead, Mama is dead, oh!"

Karen's brows furrowed. "Uloma, what happened?"

"Mama, Mama is dead." Her cousin sobbed, "Mama is gone, Adesuwa!"

"What did you say?" Her eyes widened in shock, numbness seeping into her. "Uloma, Mama, what happened to my mother?"

Her cousin's loud sniffling filled the heavy silence.

Karen's voice trembled. "Uloma, what did you say?"

"Mama died this morning, Adesuwa," Uloma wailed in Igbo. "*Ewoo*! Mama, *eh*!"

Her legs gave way beneath her, and she grabbed the dining table's edge for support as though the earth had tilted.

The line made distorted noises until the static dissipated into sounds of shouting and weeping. The cacophony of anguish at the other end of the call reverberated from a distance. Karen's mind pivoted into a comatose, awake yet dreamlike frenzy as if plunged into a trance. Her eyes were fixed on the long arm of the wall clock, watching, yet unaware of its clockwork movement ticking away the minutes. Mama died. Karen squeezed her eyes shut, counting from one to ten. Her eyes brimmed with tears, and she squeezed them shut again, but they spilled from the corners of her eyelids. Karen gave up, her glazed eyes settling on her other well-manicured, quavering hand as the news from her cousin continued in a loop. She pressed the cell phone closer to her ear to keep it from falling through a trembling hand, feeling the device warm against her skin.

"I went to give her medicine, oh!" Uloma continued sobbing, lamenting until a woman's voice filtered into the call.

"*Ndo*," the woman consoled Uloma, hissing and gnashing her teeth.

A jarring sound from the neighbor's stereo knocked her out of her daze, and the music she had hummed along to in the past threatened to grate her nerves. She loosened her grip on the phone, her hand stinging from a cramp, wiping the other hand on the bathrobe.

"I should have known!" Her cousin choked out another wail. "I should have known, oh! Mama said she felt sick yesterday. If only I knew, *eh*! Mama, *eh*! Why, Mama?"

At last, her body resumed its sensitivity to feel and to be aware. Karen listened to the younger woman weep. Uloma, the offspring of Mama's younger brother, Mama's closest relative, had lost her parents at the age of seven in a fatal accident on the way home from a wedding in Abia State, and she had lived with Mama since. For her part, Karen's mouth had gone dry, but she swallowed what little saliva she mustered. Wrapping her free arm around her stomach, she clutched at the familiar guilt that pooled into a painful cyst when she thought of Mama— images of her mother playing in her mind like still frames from a silent movie; she squeezed her watery eyes shut at intervals, determined that no tears would escape. She did not want to cry; she would not, not after alienating herself from Mama.

Stung by the news, the guilt, everything at once, she gathered the strength to disconnect the call, setting the offending device on the dining table in clunky movements and wiping both hands on the bathrobe in repeated swirls.

Hard as she tried, it proved impossible to curb her body's natural response, and pain had to run its course. Her breaths turned into short-winded gasps, each inhale and exhale cutting through her nose. The trembling in her hands grew worse with each passing second, and she clenched her fist, welcoming the smarting from embedded nails in her palm. The tears she had reined back rolled down her cheeks in vengeance.

Karen sat for a long time, her tears now suspended, as her gaze remained locked on a point in the bare wall, anchored to emptiness as though tethered by a rope. She sat until her shoulders slumped further in fatigue; her body, limp and exhausted from the sudden onslaught of emotions, demanded rest. Her movements to the bedroom were in a blur; she stripped off her bathrobe in mechanical motions, aware yet unaware of her actions, pressing a nude body between cool sheets, haunted by Mama's saddened eyes.

TWO

The next few days buzzed with activity as employees flocked in and out of various departments at Wemco Oil's headquarters, situated along the affluent part of Osborne Road. The building stood at an imposing height of eleven floors, with its tall glass windows tastefully designed to refract the blaze of the Lagos sun. Karen's office, located among senior management offices on the eighth floor, had a gold-plated door plaque inscribed with her name and title.

Her office occupied moderate space, with two black sofas by the windows overlooking a road below and a bank opposite. Magazines arranged into a tower in stylish disarray lay on a round wooden stool. The awards often caught visitors' attention, boasting of her professional accolades. The sun-kissed objects against a white-painted wall made an impressive sight. The gleaming trophies lined up on an inconspicuous gray cabinet mounted on the wall across from the office sofas, positioned at an angle that caught streaks of sunlight.

Karen threw herself into work, burying thoughts of her mother's death beneath mountains of projects and approaching responsibilities with precise urgency. Despite her unwavering efforts, guilt—insidious and persistent—seeped through the cracks and crevices of her daily routine, stubbornly lodging at the back of her mind and mocking her. She clicked away at the computer set up on an adjoining desk. Sitting on the plush leather swivel chair, shipped from a custom manufacturer, she directed meetings and entertained investors with the slick wine cooler, which chilled her expensive wine collection.

She had sent money to Uloma for the burial expenses and whatever the *ummuna*, the elders, would require for the rites. Despite that, her hope that she had done enough was fleeting. Dreams of Mama—Mama and her soulful eyes—heightened into an intimidating presence, jeering at her. Nothing assuaged the crippling guilt and stifled thoughts of betraying regrets, driving her harder at work. In truth, Karen did not work as much as she liked. She handled the technical aspects of her job because Rita, her assistant, who occupied a cubicle on the partitioned floor across her office, managed the administrative tasks and correspondence.

On Wednesday afternoon, the sun burned hot outside the central air-conditioned building. She sat cross-legged among other managers in the large conference room on the sixth floor. Tijani, the Head of Product Operations in Lagos State, delivered a report on the department's activities during her trip to Ghana. Rita sat beside her, her head bent to the side, as she jotted down meeting minutes while Tunde, the second-in-command after Tijani, listened as the man spoke. Her mind buzzed with Tunde's nearness, and she watched him from the corner of her eye, catching his sidelong glances and the lopsided smile that appeared each time he met her hooded gaze.

Her lips threatened to form into a smile, but she tightened them, staring pointedly at a ray of sunlight piercing the long table, trying to concentrate. However, her mind had a will and settled on reflecting on Tunde. It had become a tacit agreement that she never called on those trips. She did not want him to think they had a relationship, though they had long blurred the lines.

Karen straightened in the seat, fighting the urge to sigh at her thoughts. She had chosen not to dissect the intimate experience they shared, knowing it was unethical on her part to be in a sexual relationship with a junior colleague. Nonetheless, the attraction was heady, euphoric, as if they were engaged in a riotous affair—the pining, the subtle glances across the table, the way his eyes sparkled when she spoke to him in a room full of people.

At the thought of Tunde, her chest would sizzle like a pot of boiling water, sizzling with emotions that threatened to come out. He had a way of making her feel vulnerable; a simple look seemed as though he would peel back the careful layers of civility she masked over her rot. She often struggled to push him to the back of her mind and, with tremendous difficulty, not to claw at her chest and rid herself of the sensations altogether. No matter how arduous she could be, she never tied herself to him or claimed him as hers. He knew she liked it that way, yet he focused on her. The thought often confused Karen.

He had asked her to marry him once, and a wave of unease had consumed her, so much so that she satirized his request because it sounded incredulous in her ears. Marriage. It left a bitter taste in the mouth—the thought of giving herself to a man in permanent legality. Marriage encapsulated the business of being vulnerable and gradually subservient. Redirecting the dreams and ambitions of many women into another human being, her sense of self eroded into an echo chamber of her husband's ambitions. A man who could one day throw devotion back at his wife, forcing her to reckon with the husk that remained of herself. She saw what this marriage did to her sister, what it did to her mother—the same marriage. No. She did not speak to Tunde for a month, at a profound loss for words.

Tijani threw her a look with his kind eyes in a face adorned with long tribal marks, her cue to comment on his presentation, which she did without a hitch. The managers murmured among themselves as she spoke while their assistants jotted down her observations. The staff feared her; they knew she was ruthless, yet could not understand why she had to be.

As the meeting drew close, Saheed, Head of Client Relationships Service, stood, emphasizing his burly build.

"I need a few minutes of everyone's time." He clapped until the managers quieted down. "I just want to share something quick with Mrs. Ezeani."

"*Ms*," Karen snapped, bracing herself for the lengthy rant Saheed would subject her to. They never got along. She found him overbearing, always searching for opportunities to assert his dominance. The antagonism between them raged over the years; his need to assert dominance over female colleagues clashed with her sense of autonomy, compelling her to resist his browbeat attitude. Karen watched Tunde from the corner of her eye before settling on a smirking Saheed.

The man began at a snail's pace. "Last Tuesday, after work," he paused. "A client, Chief Boniface—Ms. Ezeani, you know him, correct? The man with two filling stations along Lekki-Epe Expressway—"

She pursed her lips, tapping her feet under the table.

"He called me while I was with my family," Saheed said with a bitter expression, surveying people across the table. "And he complained a lot about the attitude among Ms. Ezeani's team members. In fact—In fact," Saheed repeated, "He threatened to terminate his partnership with us. Mind you, this is not the first time I've heard this about Ms. Ezeani's team."

Disapproving grunts came from some managers, and Saheed continued.

"I had to beg him. I left my house to meet him at the Ikoyi Club that evening so that I could beg him. Ah!" Saheed raised his head to the ceiling, his finger resting under his chin and a distant look in his eyes. "I almost knelt at Ikoyi Club. Can you imagine?" He glanced at his colleagues.

A murmur spread across the room.

"I'm sure madam didn't like that," one of the managers piped, chuckling.

"My brother, she didn't, *o*." A smug expression spread across Saheed's face. "Tayo, one of your people, delayed approving that transaction Chief Boniface submitted long ago." Saheed snapped his fingers to emphasize how long. "We can't afford to delay these things. My team already has their hands full, and there's only so much we can do after we bring in a client."

The other managers nodded.

"Tayo spoke anyhow to the Chief, *kai*. He told him to wait until morning before he could work on the account. Can you imagine that nonsense?" Saheed frowned.

"How do you want Tayo to have handled it?" Karen crossed her arms. "I'm not excusing his tardiness, but you don't expect him to return to the office after the close of work."

Saheed sputtered, a muscle in his jaw ticking. "Is he the president who must do his job whenever he likes? *Abi*, does his father own Wemco?" He regarded the managers on either side of him before focusing on her across the table. "We've all had to go the extra mile for clients, which is why people come to us. *Abeg,* some of us worked our way to the top, so we can't afford to do anything anyhow."

His words stung. A cold tide of revulsion swept over Karen, setting her lips into a thin line. She lifted her chin as everyone turned to her, refusing to show her hurt. Saheed was itching for an argument—it showed in his wide stance and how he glared at her with eyes black in contempt as he sat down.

The other managers scrutinized her, poised to dissect her words, to trivialize her defense into the emotional ramblings of women.

"If you have a problem with Tayo refusing to work after closing time, I suggest you take it up with Majekodunmi." Despite her annoyance, she kept her voice even, but it came out high-pitched in her ears. The fact that she had to mention her boss's name to shut him up—because her voice bore no weight with these men—fueled her anger, reminding her of her station as a woman. Karen let out a jagged breath and dropped her gaze before saying bitingly, "I don't expect my team to work themselves to death to please anyone."

The man snickered at the mention of Majekodunmi's name. Karen dressed him down with her eyes, daring him to speak. A harsh reality existed for women—an unsettling knowledge that irked her: having to prove her worth at each task, an unending cycle fueled by the unrelenting provocations of male colleagues whose qualifications were comparable to hers.

"It's okay, Saheed," Tijani interjected arbitrarily. "It's one of those things that we take in stride as managers. We are here for one goal."

"I'm not blaming anybody, *o*," Saheed put his hands up in defense. "As a mother to the team, it's expected that she mentors these young ones correctly."

Karen raised an eyebrow, letting out an excruciating exhale. Mother to the team? It had a belittling undertone. It was no secret that they gossiped behind her back. Nigerians were often too bold, needing to voice their displeasure or condescending pity in an attention-seeking way. So the managers and junior colleagues alike wondered why a thirty-four-year-old woman would choose to remain unmarried, vocal in their disapproval, evident in how they spoke to and studied her, arriving at the same conclusion: She struck them as too difficult to control. Too hard. They said no man wanted a problematic woman; she behaved arrogantly, consumed with leading, not serving, and not malleable. Being nice never got her anywhere; she let them gossip; it would always be what humans loved to do.

The meeting ambled on after an apprehensive pause until another presentation from a man whose buttons seemed as though they would pop open from his white shirt. She reached for her phone, quelling another wave of irritation:

Karen: My place on Thursday night?

Karen texted under the table, a mask of indifference belying her actions as another colleague prattled on. She smiled, watching Tunde from beneath her lashes as he reached for his phone. His features were not classically handsome, but his allure made Karen's heart flutter whenever she was around him. She saw him hover for a moment before his gaze dropped to his phone, and she caught her breath as the sunlight formed a halo around him.

Tunde: Yes. I can't wait. Eight?

Karen turned away from Tunde to face the pimpled man speaking, gritting her teeth as a shiver coursed through her body.

Karen: Ten. I have a meeting right after work.

Tunde: Ten is good. Great.

The message came in immediately, and her heart flipped in anticipation of their time together.

THREE

Stephanie laughed in a cheery, rippling tone that subsided as she regained composure. Tunde sat across the table at their usual relaxation spot, Taste of Naija. The bar filled the ground floor of a two-story house, which had been converted into shops, hidden among Victoria Island's commercial district offices. The Taste of Naija premises appeared deserted during the day, with a lone security guard patrolling the compound, but it sprang to life as workers trooped out of the offices after work. The bar remained a favorite in Lagos because it specialized in tasty grilled catfish and hosted local musicians. Stephanie was no exception, dragging Tunde as often as they had the time.

Behind a booth, a disk jockey played old-school Nigerian music for the Monday evening blues program. The sound of neighboring generators rumbled outside, unnoticed by its patrons, and a Nollywood movie played at low volume on the television propped behind metal bars on another wall. Aside from their table, a party of ten gathered at two tables pushed together in garrulous clinks of drinks and arguments over soccer. Three businessmen sat at the room's far end, speaking in muted tones in contrast to the festive crowd. The accent lighting reflected on multiple spots in a flurry of drama, with the smell of grilled fish and spices wafting in the air.

"I can't believe that happened," her voice shook with remnants of laughter.

Tunde smiled and tugged a piece of catfish from the tray between them. His smile reached his eyes, injecting a sparkle into them from the glow of the lights.

Stephanie eyed a red blot on the checkered tablecloth, squashing a wistful longing to frame his peaceful expression under the lights so she could keep him close to her forever. Her heart fluttered, and she concentrated on chewing a piece of fish to stop her lips from curving into a sheepish smile.

"How's it working for Mr. Majekodunmi? I heard he could be eccentric." Tunde poured more beer from the bottle.

"Is it today?" Stephanie hissed, her gaze settling on a uniformed server at another table. "He isn't that bad, *sha*. He's an acquired taste." She sipped from her glass of wine. "Did you apply for the position I told you about?"

"Ah, yes, I did before you mentioned, but I don't think I stand a chance, Steph." He frowned.

"So, why did you bother applying if you felt so pessimistic?"

"Well, you know how these things are. They have someone in mind already for positions like this."

Stephanie sighed and shook her head, a braid plopping down her shoulder. "Yeah, but I don't think he's decided."

He leaned back in his chair, his eyes narrowing as he stroked his beard.

"Besides, Majekodunmi is part of the board. *Abi*, are they not the ones hiring? You worked with him on a project before." She snapped her fingers, trying to recall which project. "He may be a nutjob, but he remembers competent people. You know, with the elections, a new administration starts. Your dad was a top player at the party. Don't you think that would work in your favor?"

"You think I have a shot?" Tunde asked, ignoring his companion's exaggerated eye roll. "It's weird to be considered because of my father's connections. I'm also shopping at other companies, anyway. I've been with Wemco for a while. Maybe it's time to spread my wings."

"You have a shot; you're not an unqualified candidate," Stephanie forced a smile. "Why are you always putting yourself down?"

He shrugged. "There's talk about Majekodunmi mentoring Karen for the position." His face warmed at the thought of Karen, and his lips stretched into a brief smile. Tunde cleared his throat, swallowing as the warm glow in his chest hardened into a frigid grip from yearning for his lover as a man would while recounting a sensual rendezvous.

Her mind scrambled to a stop, and she caught her breath at the fleeting smile that crossed Tunde's face. Stephanie regarded him with narrow eyes, counting how often Karen's name tumbled out of his mouth. A cold hand closed over her heart, and she gulped her wine, pushing down outlandish thoughts. After all, it had to be impossible; the office had a strict policy against intimate relationships among staff members, especially colleagues with an existing power dynamic. Karen's leadership position placed her ahead of Tunde in age and experience.

The sudden noise from generators outside forced her out of herself, and a couple entered, dressed in matching Ankara prints.

Stephanie steered the conversation ahead to dispel her unease. "Are you surprised? Karen is Majekodunmi's work daughter." Her eyes flashed in displeasure. "*Haba*, does she deserve promotions more than others? I can't understand that woman." She clapped her hands, sending a tiny piece of fish flying to the table. I've never seen that kind of greed. Does she want everything for herself?"

"Easy, Stephanie," Tunde smirked. "Why are you upset? Well, she's an impressive lady. You can't deny that."

"Well," Stephanie drawled, mimicking his tone, "I don't like her, *sha*. Remember when she asked why I'm a Stephanie since I'm Yoruba? Very rude."

He grinned. "To be fair, that was your boss's comment, and she only chipped in."

"Doesn't make it right. Karen's such a yes-man to him."

Tunde gave another noncommittal shrug and tore off a piece of fish.

She returned to the half-eaten catfish, convincing herself she must be crazy to assume that Tunde and Karen were more than colleagues. She had known Tunde since their undergraduate days, and although they never spoke, she was aware of him. An intense warmth bubbled within her the first time their eyes met, and it struck her as odd, yet satisfying, as though they were bound in a secret conversation. From then on, she was drawn to him, searching for him at school with a fierceness, longing to hear him laugh or speak in his soft baritone voice. They had run into each other in the same office building. She had stood before him, her heart thudding with surprise, and a warm feeling pooled in her chest as he smiled at her, his lip curving upward to bring life to his dark eyes.

She had learned that a nameless stranger existed in his mind. No matter how she poked and prodded, he went as far as to confide that the woman was older. As a woman cursed to unrequited love, she hated that someone else softened his expressions, someone else unraveled under his touch. That day marked a fundamental shift, forcing her to address her tumultuous feelings for Tunde, realizing she had loved him since that first day in undergraduate school. Stephanie had licked her wounds with a tub of chocolate ice cream in the privacy of her room, accepting the passive role of being his friend, although her feelings cut away at her.

She let out a calming breath and stuffed another piece of catfish in her mouth, quelling the sudden urge to cry.

"I spoke to Boma the other day," Tunde broke the silence. "He's such a goofball!" He laughed. "He's forever making jokes about us."

"Well, Boma will never change," Stephanie answered in a light voice that belied her turmoil. "You must love me so much to follow me from school," she finished with a derisive laugh.

"Of course I do," Tunde mirrored her tone, missing the blush across her face as he turned toward a harassed waiter for the check. "You're a great person; who wouldn't? I'm surprised we didn't speak in school. I wish I met you sooner."

"Your loss," she replied softly, her eyes drawn to the fizzling bubbles in her wine glass.

FOUR

Present Day, 2024, Arondizuogu, Nigeria.

It took a while before Omo and her daughters settled into the house of her deceased mother. The old two-bedroom bungalow stayed packed with visitors from the village and relatives from other parts of the country who came to plan Mama's burial. Everyone in the family and community loved Mama, and Omo's heart was full of gratitude. Upon their arrival at the paint-chipped homestead in Arondizuogu Town, Imo State, there was a great fuss over the children who had not visited since last Christmas. Still, it was not the same as Mama's effusive fawning over them. Their grandmother waited with a bowl of steaming Eba and Ofe Onugbu, a paste made from cassava and accompanied by coco yam-thickened soup laden with fresh bitter leaves from her backyard. The glimmer of grief she carried rekindled into an all-consuming fire so that she could not reel in the tears when they came.

The evening sun glowed a deep orange, making her smile as she thought of nights when Mama was with her on the veranda. Omo closed her eyes, pretending that her mother sat on the empty stool beside her as she sat alone in the backyard, imagining the young moringa tree at the far end of the crumbling fence transformed into the mango tree of her childhood, its fruits supple and waiting to be plucked. Her heart soared, but she snapped her eyes open to the shadowed reality of Mama's death. Omo sighed and turned her attention to the breeze waltzing past the papaya and orange trees, their leaves waving gently around her. The skin on her plump arms roughened into goose pimples in reaction to the mild cold.

She and Mama shared a deep love for this place. Even the sun had a distinct shimmer compared to polluted cities, with enough space for families to thrive, unlike the sardined homes in Awka, where she lived.

She had seen the children play with their cousins earlier, chasing after squawking chickens and bleating goats that hurried to get out of the way. The chaotic scenes blurred into memories of the spring of her youth, when she, Adesuwa, and Uloma were free-spirited, playing with reckless abandon like the new generation.

Footsteps approaching her from inside pulled her out of her reverie. Uloma appeared, sighing as she sat on the low stool. She was a tall woman with a toned physique from years of manual labor. A mole jutted out of her chin, and her hard eyes softened when she laughed. Her long, kinky hair was braided in cornrows. Omo could not remember the last time she had seen Uloma in a different hairstyle.

The cousins observed livestock settle into their habitat for the night, content with the comfort of each other's presence.

"Uncle Donatus and the elders want to know if Adesuwa is attending," Uloma mumbled, avoiding her cousin's fierce expression. No one knew why the sisters were not on speaking terms, and Uloma suspected Omo knew more than she let on about the issue. Nonetheless, she could not accuse Omo of hiding the truth without proof.

Omo stiffened.

"They say it's unheard of that she would only send money and not come for Mama's burial," Uloma continued. "I'm not sure she would come; she hasn't been here since five or six years ago, once Aunty turned eighty."

"She cut herself off from the family, Uloma. She doesn't want to be involved in this matter," Omo hissed, her brows creasing into a frown. "How can a good daughter cut off her people and put Mama through so much stress? After everything we did for her. She even changed her name to Karen!"

"Adesuwa must have reasons because the Adesuwa I know—" Uloma beat her chest "—would never have done this without something happening." She swatted away a mosquito from her outstretched legs. "Mama asked her several times, but she said nothing. I thought Mama's death would at least move her."

"How did you manage to call her?"

"Mama saved her number on the phone." Uloma caught her breath, a tug of grief pulling at her. "Mama would have liked me to tell her."

"Yes, Mama mentioned it at times. She has forgotten we got her to be a big woman in the city." She sneered as if it would trivialize Adesuwa's success.

Uloma bobbed her head in response, her eyes focused on the fluttering leaves. After a moment, she spoke in her usual practical tone. "Mama worried about Adesuwa not speaking to you, sister Omo. No mother wants to see her children fighting, *mba*."

Omo closed her eyes and rested her head against the wall, her arms tingling from a gust of wind. Passersby greeted each other beyond the compound; Mama Godfrey's loud voice rang across the road, calling out to her son a few houses over. Her mind vividly painted Adesuwa in Lagos as a woman standing before a mansion with several cars and housekeepers.

She and Bid had searched for Adesuwa for a week after discovering the note in the living room. She sourly recalled her mother's calls to complain that she had not told Mama that Adesuwa had started her National Youth Service Corps (NYSC), a mandatory national program for a year after graduation. She had gone along with the older woman, half relieved that Adesuwa lived several miles away but resentful of their mother's garrulous concern for her younger sister. Over those weeks, her face corrugated into deep lines of worry in fear that the girl would mention things that were best left settled, afraid that Adesuwa would revive dry bones. Living in a jittery state for a few years presented the worst part for Omo. When Mama called to complain and ask to settle what happened, raw fear threatened to close her throat, so she could only mumble unintelligible words to end the call.

She could not deny that at some point in those years, she decided that her sister was better dead than alive, for the secret would remain so. Her unease at Adesuwa's silence continued to be a virulent wound in her mind—a boil that festered with pus yet was not ripe enough to burst.

"She's in Lagos, doing well for herself." The rustling leaves swayed back and forth as if in muted agreement. "But she cannot be too busy to attend Mama's funeral."

"Too busy for her mother," Omo snorted.

The conversation stalled when someone inside the house called out to the younger woman.

"I'll call her again; I don't believe she won't come to Mama's burial. It's unheard of—" Uloma's voice disappeared as she dragged her feet into the bungalow.

Omo exhaled and scratched her forehead, smoothing the uneven lines to calm herself. She did not want Adesuwa here;

she did not want her near the house, and she did not want her younger sister to see her in wretched clothes and shoes. Her gaze fell on the wrapper over her legs from four seasons ago. The fabric darkened under the blanket of the night as though offering her a reprieve from reality.

She shut her eyes and raised her head to the ether to curb the tears that had formed. It was clear that the years had been unkind to her. She studied her body under the silvery glaze of the moon, from her dust-peppered feet on the clay earth to her flabby waist. It must be laughable that a large woman like her could feel small, but so were palm nuts hidden beneath layers of fleshy, fibrous fruit. Her propensity for self-aversion was not alien. For years, she thought of herself trapped under layers of predicament. Also not alien were derisive thoughts on her appearance that segued into the issue of meager finances.

Her mother had helped her with finances to augment the modest income from the shop, and although she knew that Mama sent money from the monthly allowance Adesuwa set up, Omo could not turn it down. Her last phone call with her mother had been heated, with her shouting at Mama, who grumbled about sending money to her older child. Mama had complained that it felt unconscionable and disgraceful.

Mama must have thought she was unbothered by receiving handouts—that living off her mother's kindness must be what she wanted. Omo could no longer stomach the frustration.

Her words spilled out before she could stop them, for life had anchored itself onto her shoulders. Omo blamed her mother for her marriage and her stolen youth. She had been unrelenting in her accusations, citing Mama for favoritism, and in frustration, uttered those words they swore never to mention. Mama remained silent, a brief but heavy silence that caused Omo to feel a crushing wave of regret. In the end, Omo took money from Mama again, thanking her in shame.

Omo tilted her head up to the stars, white blots of ink in an otherwise dark sky, wishing she could take back her words from that day, but cracks on a broken calabash could not disappear, and a cracked egg could never be unbroken. She sighed. With Mama gone, she had more to worry about in finances. Her children depended on her, and Bid was a father by biology and nothing more; Nora waited to register for her first semester of university, and the money she made was barely enough for food and rent. She let out another ragged sigh and closed her eyes, humming amid the rhythmic chirps from crickets.

FIVE

Present Day, 2024, Lagos, Nigeria.

Tunde drove up to the parking lot of the apartment building in Ikoyi. He greeted the security guards at the underground carriage as they stood at attention, their expressions hopeful that he would give them a tip. He descended from the SUV and pulled a few notes from his navy kaftan. The guards accepted the token with wide grins, raising their hands and shouting, "Our president!" He waved them goodbye with little thought to their gestures, heading toward the elevator.

His eyes sparkled, and his mind raced, frivolous with anticipation as he thought of Karen. She sent him a sultry picture when he sent her a message about his journey to her house. God, he loved that woman; he should not feel so deeply, but Tunde did, hoping she might return his feelings one day. Tunde stepped into the elevator and pressed the button for the fifth floor. The elevator dinged and began its upward ascent.

The first time he saw Karen, he was dumbstruck, staring at her with a strange intensity, his body unable to move. Her skin possessed a shine that glowed to punctuate her ebony beauty. The image of her in the black pantsuit she wore that day haunted him for weeks. He found himself searching for her in crowds. Karen stood out in a way no one else did. She was striking with a lithe figure and very light brown eyes. She wore a self-assured aura that commanded attention and followership, yet he sensed a vulnerability hidden behind her eyes. Those eyes, with their caramel depths, held so many secrets. Tunde knew she lived her life numbed by the world; she possessed a hardness carved by pain. That quality of uncertainty he nursed about Karen made her enticingly mystifying. He wanted to peel back her mask and find out what rested behind all that coolness. He wanted to know her—to understand what made her smile, what made her cry, what made her love.

It had amused him to discover that he was not the only man in the office who swooned in appreciation on every occasion she came to the operations department. He kept it to himself, but he was no different, with a feverish curiosity about her more potent than any woman he had encountered.

Tunde allowed himself to continue his musings as the elevator shuddered to a stop. He stepped into a dim lobby with an impersonal painting hung on its white walls. Being a philistine, he paid it no mind and walked straight to the end of the corridor leading to her apartment door.

She had worked with his boss and started to talk to him. First, it was a caustic remark about a presentation he put together, and then she began to ignore him. He battled immediate nerves during those sparse times he caught her staring. Her beautifully carved eyebrows scrunched upward, creating fine creases on her forehead, with eyes that gave nothing away. He mulled over those old days. Replaying the moment in a continuous loop, almost fearing that he would become obsessed.

At last, he reached the black door of Karen's apartment and sent a quick text on his phone, letting her know he had arrived. Tunde swallowed, tapping his leg to quell his impatience, and his breath hitched, recalling standing in front of her hotel room in Ghana in a desperate frenzy, where he, Tijani, and Karen had gone to oversee a new office setup. That was the place where the dynamics of their relationship had changed. They had attended dinner, and she had worn a beautiful maxi dress; Tijani had declined to leave his room because of a stomach bug, so they had sat in stoic silence until he drew her into his chatter.

His friends could not call him a chatterbox, but he needed to impress the self-possessed woman across the table that night. Uncertain what to say or do with her staring down hard at him, he was fidgeting and restless, but he was rewarded later.

Vivid memories of their explorations in Ghana tightened his pants around the crotch. The sound of movement from the other side of the door brought him back to the present, and

Karen opened the door. He felt as giddy as he had that first night two years ago. Tunde entered the apartment with a wide grin at seeing the woman on his mind all day.

***

Her home smelled of sandalwood and a distinct fragrance he could not place; the flames from candles on a white rustic bookshelf cast dancing shadows in her sizable living room.

"You are so beautiful." Tunde pulled her into his arms like the short gap between them could widen into an ocean.

Karen allowed him to draw her closer. His warm hand on the small of her back seeped through the silk robe to her skin, and she shuddered, a tide of desire washing through her, entwined with the delicious timbre of his voice.

"You didn't tell me you were back until I saw you at the meeting." He mumbled, his warm breath blowing through the fabric as he nibbled on the rounded curve of her shoulder.

They tore off their clothes, stumbling over each other, over the wooden coffee table with her laptop, and onto the blue velvet couch.

"I didn't think that I was supposed to." She laughed in a breathless voice, her body thrumming with desire.

"No," Tunde pulled back, watching the shadows dance on her bare breasts. "No," he said again, more to himself.

They spoke of nothing else and allowed the magic of the night to take control. What followed was a satisfying silence.

***

The pleasurable interlude stretched into the early morning hours before either spoke again. They ate on the dining table by the balcony sliding door with plates of pasta and glasses of red wine, an unobstructed view of a crescent moon sitting atop the Ikoyi Link Bridge. A floor lamp opposite the dining furniture emitted a dull yellow hue. The pungent scent of sex lingered, mixed with faint traces of sandalwood.

Tunde said, "I've been thinking of how we started all this."

Karen paused her meal and rolled her eyes, her body sated in the afterglow of lovemaking. "Don't tell me you're about to go into that romantic mumbo-jumbo nonsense."

"How's that nonsense, *ehn*, thinking of us?" He lifted a brow as threads of laughter appeared at the corners of his eyes. "You're macho for a woman. You know that, Karen?"

"Macho because I'm not sentimental?" Her eyebrows scrunched together. Then, she gave him a mocking smile. "Isn't that why you're here? I can't imagine I would have been useful if I were a damsel in distress. Don't you love a woman who seems unattainable? It's like a challenge—I heard."

Tunde's chest rumbled with a chuckle, the sound traveling across the living room. "That's hard to imagine." After a beat, he asked, "How was Ghana?"

"Ghana was Ghana," Karen sighed and resumed her food.

"And how are you?" He watched her eat. "I know that you're troubled. A vein sticks out on your forehead when you are." He tapped his forehead.

Her hand flew to her forehead, tracing a vein that stood out like a speed bump on an otherwise smooth road, and her eyes widened in surprise.

"Tell me."

"My mother died."

"Wow," Tunde's hand covered his mouth. "I'm sorry." He reached across the table to place his hand over hers.

Her playful manner transformed into detachment as his hand clasped over hers.

"I'm sorry," he spoke with an undertone, analyzing her for signs of life in her demeanor as the living room light cast a shadowed sheen across her face. "It bothers me that you don't talk about your family, but your mother's death must have been a hard blow."

She slipped her hand from under his, leaving his hand cold.

"Karen," he whispered. "Are you okay?"

Karen drew a breath. "She lived to eighty-six; it's no surprise." She pushed the abandoned plate of food away and leaned back in her chair, her jaw ticking as she kept her eyes on the table. "You're never prepared for it, I guess." She shrugged.

"When is the burial?"

A chill gripped her, and she wrapped her arms around her body, yet it was not enough—she wanted his arms around her. "I sent money to cover the burial. I'm busy at work," she mumbled.

Karen could not justify mentioning it, as that part of her life remained hidden. Mama's death may have shaken her more than she thought, shaken her to her core, and opened the chest of painful memories to leave her vulnerable, as though years of hardness had melted upon her mother's demise. Her mind had turned against her, dulled by riotous thoughts and dreams that bogged her down, threatening to spoil everything else. But Tunde was not everything else or everyone; he was Tunde, different in an indefinable way.

Tunde gasped. "You can take a few days off; that's allowed."

"I have not taken a day off in a long time," Karen stated. "I don't intend to do that now." She caught sight of the crescent moon, and its brilliant shimmer filled her gaze. A loud vehicle hiccupped along the quiet roadway below, wherever it went, and if it did not give up.

Tunde's flummoxed gaze burned a hole through her chest.

"We are talking about your mother's burial here, not a vacation," he snapped. "That must mean something even to you. It's the last chance to say a proper goodbye."

Karen bit her bottom lip to keep it from quivering. She cursed herself for letting her guard down with him.

"Leave it alone, Tunde," she muttered as the truth became more difficult. "I'm not sure why I mentioned it."

Tunde studied his half-empty plate. "I assumed there must be some trouble with your family since you seldom mention them."

Her hands itched to be occupied, so she curled them into a tight fist under the table.

He shook his head in dismay. "What could be so horrible that you are choosing not to attend your mother's burial?"

Tunde observed her slip into a steel mask the world knew, saddened for the woman before him. He had always been curious about this part of her life. The last time Karen mentioned family, she had confided, with a dispassionate voice, that the rest of her relatives resided in the East. It seemed strange now to see her as human, as though news of Karen's mother's death made her more of a living being, more of a person.

Karen glanced at a dark clock on the wall and stood. "I've got a meeting later today. It's two in the morning. We should sleep."

Tunde nodded, observing her as she cleared the plates and headed to the kitchen, her face molded into a wooden expression. After a moment, he walked to the kitchen and saw her leaning over the sink. He hesitated, confronted by a new side of Karen who seemed pitiful, but she rearranged her features as soon as she heard movements, making him almost believe that he had imagined her expression.

Unable to indulge Karen in her game of pretend, he hugged her from behind, trapping her stiff frame between the sink and the hard wall of his body.

"Karen …" Tunde groaned.

She kept mute.

"I won't mention it again." He drew a breath. "Don't be mad at me. I don't want you to regret anything. I know you are a strong woman." He pressed his nose into her cropped hair, inhaling a waft of coconut oil. "But strong people are human too; you can't fight that."

Karen closed her eyes for a moment, melting in his touch, and turned to face her lover within the tight enclosure of his arms.

"I shouldn't have mentioned it. I forgot how emotional you can get." She gave him a rueful smile.

His breath fanned her skin, and she shivered.

"Let's go to bed." She opened her hand, and he took it.

SIX

March 2010, Awka, Nigeria.

Omo sat under the awning of her shop at the Eke Awka Main Market entrance, hoping for a new customer since the last person in the morning. The store was small, but it had enough space to display her wares on makeshift shelves, and the landlord agreed to rent to her for fifteen thousand naira. The previous tenant had painted the shop a ghastly mahogany, and one could identify the slap-dash work of a handyman. Mr. Moghalu, the real estate agent, swore it was the best deal she could find at such a busy market's entrance, making it a prime location to sell colorful George fabrics and local handmade beads. A fan hung in a stilted limp at the center of the ceiling. Mr. Moghalu had assured her in those early days that the landlord would replace it once she moved in, but after a year, she had given up on expecting much from an unseen landlord with only the agent on the line.

The sun blazed, punishing on a Wednesday afternoon. A presenter on the loud transmitter radio at her neighbor's stall assured higher temperatures for the rest of the week. She observed the comings and goings of market load carriers trailing behind buyers, on their heads piled mountainous baskets of produce they would carry until the client relieved them of it. She clucked at the load carriers with pity, watching them go by, their bodies glistening with sweat. Mama Obioma sat two stalls down from hers with smoked fish of various kinds, and Obioma—a boy with perpetually wet nostrils—rained curses at the electric companies. Hawkers paraded their wares, many of them with a sachet of cold water, while store occupants sat outside calling out to passersby. The men stripped to their vests, and the women folded the edges of their wrappers, waving the triangular ends at their faces as makeshift fans.

Omo let her mind wander, unbothered by the commonplace buzz around her.

Ever since she gave birth to her third child—a third girl—her in-laws made clear their immense disapproval of her inability to bear a son. In truth, this was the reason she had asked Adesuwa to live with them. Bid considered that his youngest sister, Nneka, would move in with them, and she knew that would be the first stage of their marriage crashing. In-laws in her part of the world were to be taken with a grain of salt—they cradled you in their hands and used those hands like a noose around your neck.

Before getting married, she had nursed the hope of returning to school someday, a trade school, at the very least, to learn fashion design. She knew that she could not be called a beautiful girl. However, she made up for it with intelligence. She told herself to make money first, and men would come before life dealt her a cruel fate in the form of her husband. Now, she sat overweight with her vitality nonexistent, beaten down and trampled on. She should have known nothing would change when Bid had been promiscuous during their courtship—she should have known that Bid would never settle down as a family man after marriage. A man like that would never be satisfied.

Perhaps she had felt obliged not to complain during their courtship since she had insisted that she would not be intimate with him until the wedding night. Yet he cared for her, and her reticent gratitude masqueraded as love. He bought her new clothes, promised to sponsor her schooling, and ensured her mother lived comfortably in the village.

Only years later did she recognize the sinister truth about Bid and the rest of his ilk. They were drawn to shiny things like moths to flame. They were lions, relentless in their hunt for prey. Men like him advocated for traditional values but chased the non-traditional as though it were a prize from their sole contest. Men like him were prize hunters, to whom a caught prey held no more appeal, its splendor tainted from damage.

Bid, her Bid, had encouraged her to eat more during her slim-figured years, saying he loved his women thick. Coupled with childbirth, she allowed herself to put on more weight. Now, there was an irony that this man, a two-faced man, chased after slimmer women but sneered at Omo's size in disapproval. His clothes brought home evidence of his lust, but she played the ostrich, perhaps approving of his behavior so she would not have to perform conjugal obligations.

The sound of footsteps approaching the shop forced her out of her sober reflection. Omo rose at the sight of her visitor, her uncle's wife, Aunty Uche, with a welcoming smile plastered on her face.

"Aunty, good afternoon."

"How are you?" Aunty Uche responded dryly in Igbo, huffing as she sat on the plastic chair Omo had stood up from. She, too, was a heavy-set woman with a plain face that lit up from a rare smile.

"Do you want something to drink, Aunty? I have Fanta." Omo entered the store to get the beverage. She set it on a stool and carried both to her aunt, who fanned herself with the edge of her wrapper.

"The weather is so hot, *eh*!" Aunty Uche ran a finger over the beads of perspiration on her forehead and flicked them to the ground. "I can't understand who we offended in this Nigeria!" She uncorked the bottle cover with the edge of her teeth, her throat bobbing as she gulped large portions of Fanta. She then put the bottle on the stool and studied Omo as though she had seen her for the first time since she arrived. "Omo, *kedu*? How are you?"

Omo glanced at the atomic splatter of sweat on dry concrete, sticking out like a sore thumb. "I'm fine *o*, Aunty."

"You don't look it." Aunty Uche scratched her scarfed head and pinned Omo with her gaze. "Is Bid giving you trouble again?"

"What day has he ever not given me any trouble?"

"Hmm, men!" her aunt released an exasperated sigh. "Eh, that is how they are! Is asking if they can sit too much at home, *ehn*, *biko*? All they know is to chase after young girls and spend money on alcohol!"

"Aunty," Omo grimaced. "I'm tired, honestly. If it's not one woman today, it's another tomorrow. How can he call himself a pastor and be like that?"

"Just because he's a pastor doesn't mean he's not a human being," her aunt responded in resignation, her shoulders hunched over the stool. "As a woman, you must be more patient. That is all you can do. The bottom line is that he comes back home, *abi*?" She smacked the back of her hands on her thighs. "*Abi*, what else can we say? How many of these pastors are good *sef*? Go and ask around. Many of them do all sorts of things behind closed doors." She gestured into thin air. "Is it because they are not saying their own? This is Africa; you better leave all this English thinking for *Oyigbo*—"

Mama Obioma caught Omo's eye from the other side of the path between shops, waving a thousand naira. Omo understood that the woman was searching for change and gestured that she had none.

She turned to Aunty Uche, who had stopped talking at the other trader's interruption, her lips pressed with little enthusiasm. It was not a shock that her aunt maintained this disheartening perspective; she had heard it often but kept mute, unwilling to face another lecture from her aunt and mother. They had always advised her to be patient in marriage; she ought to be grateful, they said, that a fine man like Bid would ask for her hand in marriage after she had not completed her education. He went further, they said, giving her money to start her business. In truth, she wished she had not married him, living with a disquieting knowledge that she would have achieved more on her own.

If the world ended and heaven fell, it would be better than this. There was a role reversal, where Omo fell into feeding the household while her husband chose to be tight-fisted. Did her mother and aunt know how she felt seeing Adesuwa attend university? Did they understand that she felt like life took it upon itself to remind her of what she could have been at every turn?

"That is how it is for a woman; you must endure," Aunty Uche continued in a sober tone, her eyebrows knit together as if pacifying a child. "Women are like glue; they hold the family together." She clasped her hands. "Do you think people could get married if every woman got angry that their husband's eyes were roaming? You must put your head down and give him what he wants. That's men for you."

"Aunty—" Omo narrowed her eyes away from Aunty Uche in mounting displeasure. She cupped her chin in her hand, resting the elbow on a crossed leg. "I'm not the one who gives sons; if I could, I would. It's not like I'm barren. For God's sake, we have three beautiful daughters!"

"Taah!" Aunty Uche rounded on Omo. "Taah! Shut up! What will a daughter do for you? Did you not change from your father's name to your husband's the moment you married? You're talking so ignorantly, you this girl!" She wagged a finger at her niece.

"We already have three daughters! I'm not the one who creates sons; things are too expensive to have many children, Aunty. Our daughters are enough, and they ought to be enough!"

"Let them be expensive! Yes, let them be expensive!" Aunty Uche crossed her ankles in front of her. "You don't know that the glory of a family rests in sons? You don't know that only one foot is planted in your husband's house until you give him an heir. A woman's place is not secured until then. That is why the man is running after anything with two legs; even his family encourages him!"

"Bid would follow women even if I give birth to ten sons! A leopard cannot change its spots." She clapped her hands in frustration, ignoring the older woman's snicker. "I'm not part of my father's family because I would be married off one day, and I'm not part of my husband's family until I give him a son— then who do I belong to?" Omo glared at the sun, gnashing her teeth and crossing her arms. "*Chei*! Are women not cursed?" She muttered loud enough for the other woman to hear.

"*Eh,* this girl." Aunt Uche sighed. "Okay, remain like that! Until they chase you out of your husband's house or he leaves with his own two legs before your eyes come down. Pride goes before a fall!"

SEVEN

Present Day, 2024, Lagos, Nigeria.

Stephanie sat among her friends as they chatted about the goings-on in their lives. The loud chatter around them in the restaurant was almost unbearable, though Dami had warned them that it got busy on weekends. They had planned the night for weeks, continuing to reschedule due to conflicting timetables. However, Stephanie thought Saturday might be a poor day to relax while sitting in a busy restaurant, but she was happy to spend time with her friends. Speakers boomed from all corners with the latest hip-hop singles, and the venue overflowed with patrons.

She listened to Trisha describe comic encounters in her office while fiddling with the straw of her Sangria. Everyone laughed, but her mind lingered on Tunde and their plans for tomorrow.

She drew her mind back to the present, making noises to show interest in the conversation.

"You've been silent," Dami declared.

Trisha and Amaka peered at Stephanie across the plates and cocktails, their dark heads cocked to the side.

"Anything new with you and your work?" She grinned and wiggled her eyebrows.

Knowing looks passed among the other women. "Your man, who you insist isn't your man."

Stephanie rolled her eyes, holding back laughter. "There is nothing new. Tunde's just a colleague."

"Come on," Amaka groaned. "We've heard this several times before, *abeg*!" She laughed as she nudged Dami.

"We all know you've been dying for him since school, Steph. You forgot we went to the same university, *abi*?"

"Amaka, I told you we're friends and nothing more," she chuckled. She picked up a cracker and a piece of cheese from the dessert on Trisha's plate as her friends fastened their eyes on her.

"And …?"

"And?" Stephanie repeated.

The music changed to Nigerian hit tracks, and a few people danced, interrupting the newcomers trying to find seats. A woman stood up, raising her large denim-clad buttocks as high as possible, and wiggled and shook with cheers from various tables. They cheered her on until the woman sat down to a round of applause.

"And?" Dami quipped, inciting a round of laughter.

"I told you he is seeing someone," she drawled, forcing a smile. "I told you guys, *naw*."

"And we agreed that you should find out who this person is," Trisha responded. "He's secretive, *sha*. Me, *o*, I don't like men like that. I'm sure he is dealing with a married woman or a crazy one."

Dami nodded vigorously, launching into a roundabout story about a married man she dated once. She ended the story and asked Stephanie why Tunde couldn't tell her if she were his friend.

Stephanie shrugged. "I don't know. I suspect he doesn't trust me enough."

"Yeah, but it's so creepy to be secretive about who you're dating, except if you're doing something wrong." Amaka pointed a limp potato fry at no one in particular. "That's why I don't trust these men, *sha*. They're always creeping around because they see you and, like, three other girls." She ate the potato. "I'm telling you, men will disgrace you! He's probably just talking to you for the sex."

"Sex *keh*?" Trisha frowned at her friend, her eyes wide in alarm behind her circular lenses. She turned to ensure the couple with a child sitting behind her did not hear and continued, "Someone she's been close to since working at the office. It's been about two or three years. They've been out to dinners and hung out.

If he wanted sex, he would've made a move; let's not act like Stephanie is ugly and he's not a man."

"Well, is he a man that likes women?" Dami lowered her voice, her hand covering the side of her mouth. "I don't think this is normal. He doesn't mention a word about who he's dating. Is he gay?"

"*Ahan*." A peeved Trisha shook her head at Dami. "So, because he didn't sleep with Stephanie, he's gay? You and your wild conclusions!"

"Okay, so what is your answer then?" Dami scowled.

"I think he's someone who keeps certain parts of himself private," Stephanie muttered to end the conversation.

"I think you should check his phone while he's not around, *sha*," Dami huffed, nodding as though the other women couldn't see the solution before them.

"Yeah, I think so too," Amaka seconded. "It's about time you face this thing, honestly. He's placing you in limbo, and you don't know if this woman is real. *Kai*, men *ehn*."

Stephanie's thoughts flew to Karen, but she scolded her friends. "I don't think that's right. It's his phone. What if I get caught? If he finds out, he'd be so mad." She shuddered.

"Why are you talking like this?" Dami snorted. "How else do you expect to find out if he's secretive? At least you'd know where you stand. This whole thing has gone on long enough."

"You could also talk to him face to face and ask where you stand," Trisha added.

"What sort of suggestion is that?" Amaka glowered at her friend, shaking her head, her penciled brows drawn together in mild annoyance. "Don't do such a thing. Don't even try it! Do you want to look desperate?" She hissed and focused on Stephanie, "*Abeg,* check his phone, dear. Don't you want to know who you're up against? He doesn't have to know, *naw.* Stephanie, you *sef,* you're too nice! Quickly check his messages, and that's it."

"CIA!" Dami gave a mock salute. "You're the one who should be the Inspector General of Police, hands down!"

Everyone laughed, and the conversation changed to more humorous topics. Stephanie chimed in, but her mind lingered on her friend's idea of how to deal with Tunde. The woman with the sizable buttocks stood up again, this time dancing to "Twe Twe" by Kizz Daniel.

EIGHT

Karen avoided all thoughts of her mother's death with increasing strain. Memories threatened to overwhelm her whenever she sat alone, infringing on her thoughts and robbing her of concentration. Karen had felt Tunde's concern at the office, which angered her for confiding in him. His naked sympathy spurred a wave of resentment within her. She avoided him on Friday and through the weekend, afraid that she wanted to hurt Tunde to feel better—that she needed an avenue to release the ball of negative energy from within her because he felt too deeply for her. She was a bundle of contradictions regarding Tunde, drawn to the earnest way he wore his emotions on his sleeve yet intimidated by the thought of him preserving those feelings solely for her.

Sometimes, Karen saw that fleeting concern in his eyes and wanted to hurt him. To make him feel a little of the pain that she carried and locked up deep in her mind, Tunde always kept silent and bore her lashing out. Karen suspected he yearned to reach within her, take her burden, and make it his own. His earnest devotion had to be what she resented the most about him, about them, how easy love came to him, and how he loved her as though she deserved it.

After dinner, she sat on the cozy red loveseat, cocooned by a blanket. The evening news played on the TV, but Karen paid no attention; her brows crinkled in concentration as she read a book. She sipped a glass of wine, her face flushed in the soft candlelight, but even wine could not lift her mood.

Karen felt her cell phone vibrate on the wooden stool beside her feet. She placed her book on her lap and peered at the phone. Mama's name hovered on the screen; her heart lurched with the futile hope of a woman adjusting to grief. Karen pressed the receiver and turned on the speaker.

"Hello."

"Good evening," Uloma answered.

She took a deep breath, embracing a wild, impulsive hope that Uloma's sonorous voice would transform into her mother's. "Yes. Have they made burial arrangements already?"

"Yes"

"I hope the money is enough."

"Yes," Uloma mumbled. "I still have some change left."

"Keep it. "Use it how you like."

"Thank you."

The call went quiet, and Karen waited because her cousin was not finished.

"Are you coming for the burial? It's this Saturday." Uloma continued without giving her a chance to respond. "Uncle Donatus, Omo, and everyone else are here. They've been asking if you're interested in coming at all. What am I to tell them?"

"I don't know yet," she let out a slow breath to untangle knots of guilt as her voice came out demure. "I have work; I'm not sure I'd be able to come. They can continue; I'll visit later."

A sigh broke the brief silence on the other end of the line.

"Why? Can I speak?"

"There's no need to ask if you're going to say it, Uloma," she massaged her throbbing temples.

"Adesuwa, you have not acted well at all. Aunty loved you so much, you know that. She always talked about you with pride. She used to say that you're big in Lagos and that you would allow her to visit more often." Uloma proceeded with advice in Igbo after another sigh. "You can't lose her like this, sister. It's not good. Remember, God himself said that we should honor our parents. If you still go to church."

Uloma's words hit close to home.

"That's enough, Uloma," Karen murmured under the weight of her cousin's statement. "I loved Mama, and you know that." She swallowed. "I just—"

"I know, sister, you have a funny way of showing it, but I believe you loved Mama. I don't know what happened to you, but this is Mama. No fight is more important than your mother right now."

"You've spoken well," Karen stared at the floor. "How are you?"

Uloma made a hum of agreement. "I'm fine, but it's hard to be happy because Auntie's death is painful."

"These are the last moments we'll have with Mama before the burial. I think you should try to come." The woman tarried on the line. "Okay, sister, I said I should call you to give you updates."

"Thank you," Karen uttered with a choked voice, staring at the mute motions on TV. "And Uloma, thank you for caring for Mama. I won't forget it."

"It's not a problem, sister; she was also my mother. Goodnight."

"Goodnight."

With that, the call disconnected, and Karen let out a ragged breath. Her mind rebelled against going home, yet it was the right thing to do for Mama and herself. Her conversation with Tunde did not help assuage her guilt. In a spell of solitude, her focus shifted to the matted cover of her book, and she pulled the blanket closer to her chest. A *Pepsi* advert jingled on TV, casting her roaring guilt into a dull thrum beneath its bubbling rhythm. She strode out of the living room and away from her clashing emotions.

NINE

Karen leaned against her bedroom window overlooking the quiet road, watching the full moon appear farther through low clouds. The world outside was grainy through the window mesh, but the distorted view and scattered clouds offered the tranquility she needed before sunrise. The distant star reflected on calm waters under the bridge, creating picturesque scenery as it sat at the structure's apex.

A horn blew afar, and cars moved from her vantage point like caricatures. Beneath her apartment, in one of many developed apartments in Ikoyi, a streetlamp flickered with its white hue. The city appeared beautiful at night, and Karen let out an anguished sigh. It dawned on her that her toiling mind, narrowed on work, had inadvertently caused her to forget her appreciation for bewitching nights like this. Now, Mama's death forced her to contend with the upheaval of her framed life.

She rested her head against the wall.

She had dreamed of Mr. Jakande, his touch, his mouth, the feeling of him between her thighs. She rubbed her tired eyes. Fleeting thoughts settled on old friends, on Ada, whom she cut off after she moved out to escape everything. The need to separate the old from the new, to sever the ties that bound Adesuwa to Karen, was overwhelming.

By then, she had convinced her ex that he would be better off without her, and Mr. Jakande had found a new woman to prey on. She had met her once at the office lobby, amused by the woman's naivete as she spoke with a colleague. It had shocked her that she had felt giddy—a twisted pleasure knowing they shared a secret, an unavoidable blemish to their characters. She knew that soon, this woman would change, become disenchanted, and lose all hope in the world.

She often thought of that woman and how she had buckled under pressure at work, lasting a year before quitting. Meanwhile, Karen stayed on, refused to cower away from responsibilities, and became the Chief Finance Officer. She had traveled to beautiful countries and lived in an apartment with the best skyline view in Ikoyi; she had made a name for herself, evident in her wealth and connections; she was part of the aristocracy.

In hindsight, it was no surprise that her pride had been wounded when Mama had grunted, unimpressed at her hard work; her mother had made it clear to her the day she shared her promotion.

"I'm happy for you."

The haphazard choruses of chickens in the background did not mask the disappointment in Mama's voice.

Karen frowned and slouched into the driver's seat of her vehicle. The car keys jangled in the ignition. She peered at the gray clouds gathering, the smell of rain becoming more poignant at each passing moment. "What is it now, Mama?" She huffed.

"No, *o*, nothing, my child."

Mama exhaled a loud, dramatic sound that displayed her displeasure. "You're doing all these things in Lagos, yet you shut your family out."

"Mama, I didn't shut you out."

"Are you sure? We've not seen you in so long, and your sister, things are tricky for her in Awka. Have you asked after her?"

Her eyes rested on the bank across the street from where she had parked in front of the office. A Nigerian flag hoisted on a tall pole fluttered in the steady breeze.

"I can't celebrate one child and worry for another when you can help your sister," Mama responded in Igbo. "I don't want to believe you'd take care of me and ignore your older sister."

"Mama, it's enough," Karen snapped, her knee hitting the car keys, which jangled again. "It's enough. I called, hoping you'd congratulate me, but instead, you're bringing up that woman and her husband. You do this every time."

"Adesuwa!" Mama gasped, "Is it Omo you are calling that woman? That's not how I raised you!" She wheezed through a dry cough. "Lagos has truly changed you. Is it wrong for me to talk about your older sister, or is it pride that makes you think that you are too big for any of us?"

Karen gulped back tears, frustrated by her mother's insistence on wedging Omo in their conversations yet worried about Mama's wheezing. "Mama, sorry, I don't want to talk about Omo. I don't, and I've said it many times."

"You and your sister are breaking my heart." The older woman sounded distraught. "I know that siblings argue; after all, I've argued with your uncle many times, but to continue keeping malice for years, *haba*? Your father wouldn't have allowed this if he were alive today."

Karen closed her eyes, unsure of how to comfort her mother. Mama often brought him up in an argument, a final weapon in an arsenal of emotional blackmail. He had died before she could imprint his face onto her mind, and her recollection of him was limited. Still, Mama had mourned him for a long time and declared how much they were in love, choosing not to remarry as her oath of devotion to her husband and focus on their children.

"I'm sorry," she stated in a wobbly voice. "But I need to go now, Mama."

"You are running away as usual."

Karen felt a sting of guilt as she choked out a lie. "No, I'm in the middle of traffic; it's getting worse."

Mama fussed over her a little before the call disconnected.

The moon disappeared and took the blanket of night with it, bringing her back to the present day. She had achieved success, yet she searched for new challenges. Like the vanishing night and the elusive, distant stars, happiness eluded her. Mama's death left another gaping hole in her life, magnifying that gnawing feeling. She trembled at the thought, succumbing to an instinctive need for maternal comfort, which she had denied herself over the years. She remained unsatisfied, not as happy as she once hoped.

With a sigh, Karen forced herself to step away from the window and prepare for work.

TEN

May 2010, Awka, Nigeria.

Bid shut the door and pulled the thin brown curtains together, coughing from a spell of dust. He grimaced, wondering for the umpteenth time whether department cleaners ever washed the curtains before letting out a long-suffering sigh. He took solace in the office's privacy, knowing they would not be disturbed. He deposited himself in the shabby executive chair, ignoring its loud protest under his weight. Anita perched close to him on the edge of a large table that occupied most of the space in the cluttered office.

The ceiling fan wobbled and squeaked, with stray papers flapping from the cold gust. A small fridge hummed in the corner behind his seat, with rows of books stacked on a shelf to his right.

He listened to Anita's endless complaints of financial woes, stifling a yawn as she spun a meandering tale of her plight in

Nigeria's economic crunch. Her voice slid into a distant drone as he thought of their first meeting, heralded by a mutual friend in Port Harcourt.

She had been with his friend until she moved to Anambra, and the rest fell into place. They met once in a blue moon, and Anita kept him satiated. Her dispassionate approach to their encounters endeared her to him. She ignored the elephant in the room, his marriage, and made no attempts to transform their arrangement into a respectable relationship.

He sent her twenty thousand naira, and she squealed in excitement, pressing her breasts on him in a tight hug, yet she swept his hands away when he slipped them down to her denim derriere. Today seemed like one of those days after work, filled with routine banter between them—a push-pull game they played where Anita needed money, and he obliged. Still, she would hold back before giving in to his advances as though delaying his reward preserved her dignity.

His lips curved into a tight-lipped smile as a ripple of sexual frustration coursed through him the moment she opened her legs to his view. His mind painted a vivid picture of another woman. He squeezed Anita's fleshy thigh, pretending that she was the woman his body longed for, as he debated on whether the other woman would be willing to give herself to him if Bid offered her money—if she would also open her legs the way Anita did on the table if he gave her money. His thoughts spiraled out of control as he slid in and out of Anita on the littered table with documents scattered about the desk and some falling on the floor at awkward angles. No, the other woman would not act like that, he decided, the thoughts quickening his pulse.

When it was over, and he leaned back in the chair, spent, Bid caught sight of the Christian calendar behind the door. Its pages flapped from the fan, and his eyes darted to the wall clock, accosted by an urgent need to have Anita out of his office, as though the image of Christ stared at him in dismay.

Long after she had gone, he reached for the leather Bible sitting precariously on the table, its edges frayed from use. Bid opened to the verse sure to absolve him of his sins and went through his prayer ritual. Yet, his mind lingered on the other woman—what she would look like on the table where he had taken Anita. He had imagined Anita morphing into this woman as he came to release. Bid sighed as his body stirred to life again, grunting with disgust.

***

Adesuwa walked with relish from her final class for the semester with her friends, Gloria and Ada. They walked in the Harmattan evening, their arms covered in long sleeves and their feet not so much. Vehicles zoomed past while pedestrians powered on. Hawkers, hoping to appeal to students with their wares, thrust baskets of goods along the sidewalks. They chatted about choir practice and school, with occasional interruptions to avoid colliding with passersby.

She was oblivious to the appreciative male glances as they threaded through traffic. The chocolate girl bloomed into her youth, her eyes a shade of liquid brown so light that strangers joked she appeared to be a mami wata, a water spirit—elders swore these celestial beings were beautiful. People first noticed the startling contrast between her eyes and skin. A beauty spot lay on the corner of her left eye, with full lips and long, crinkled hair often packed in a bun. As expected of a conservative church member, she wore free-flowing skirts and blouses that covered her body. Her innocence attracted men, and modest clothes did little to hide her rounded hips and full breasts, which were in proportion to her slim and supple build. Her beauty and lack of conceit drew people to her.

They said goodbyes, and she entered the Department of Civil Engineering building, where Uncle Bid worked as an associate professor. She walked past Ixora and various plants that added little to improve the aesthetics. The faculty building was an old white structure, now peppered with clay dust and unkempt from lack of maintenance.

She mused over her mother and their conversation earlier, mindlessly weaving through scores of students. She spoke to Mama often to renew her commitment to living with Omo, although her older sister tested her patience. Her sister had made a radical change from the promises she had made before they left for Awka. Her sister had not told her she would work like a donkey. Omo was as prickly as the skin of soursop fruit, and sometimes, Adesuwa suspected her sister harbored a particular malice toward her. Once, Omo struck her because she had burnt yams for breakfast. Mama had admonished Adesuwa when she shared her suspicions, reminding her that Omo was like a second mother, as there were about ten years between them.

Adesuwa smiled to herself, preparing to receive another plea for patience from Uncle Bid. She knew Omo experienced trouble in her marriage as Uncle Bid's relatives hollered for a son. He was the first son of the house, and it proved unacceptable that he had no heir in tow to continue his legacy. It was as though it took only a woman to make a son when they blamed Omo. It could only be her fault, they howled. They warned Bid to marry a woman from their place. For this reason, Adesuwa bore her sister's frustrating presence with endurance.

She passed busy classrooms until she reached Uncle Bid's office. She knocked on the door, announcing herself, and walked in. A small fridge hummed in the left corner behind his seat, with rows of filled bookshelves on his right. Uncle Bid shared the office with another associate professor who had relocated to the United States with his family. Her brother-in-law sat behind a large desk cluttered with documents and a window behind him. The office appeared smaller each time she visited, she thought to herself.

"How are you, Adesuwa?"

She returned his smile and sat in one of the chairs before his desk. "I'm fine, thank you, uncle."

Uncle Bid had bushy brows and a bottom lip that dominated his dark face, accompanied by a stocky frame of medium height. What he lacked in physical appearance, he made up for in character. He was a pleasant man who held an esteemed position as a pastor in the church. His keen interest in her personal life humbled her. He would take her out on their way home and soothe her with a present after Omo offended her. He called it their little secret, and she agreed with childlike excitement, as a girl would with her father. She took him as an adoptive father, her eyes shining with gratitude. If it had not been for Uncle Bid's job, which gave her access to cheaper tuition, she would not have been able to attend university.

"Classes?" He placed a piece of paper on his desk.

"Very well, sir. I had three today. We had a test too, Mrs. Anyawu's class."

"You know your sister's angry with you, right?"

"Uncle, sister Omo's always angry with me," she replied. "I explained to her yesterday that I also have choir practice on Wednesday, and she flared up. We're preparing for worship night this Sunday."

"That's very good," Uncle Bid said, smiling. "Our God shall reward you as you praise his name."

"Amen, sir," her tone was reverent. "Thank you, sir."

"But you still have to apologize to your sister," he continued, coming around the desk and leaning on its wooden edge beside where she sat.

He took her hands in his with a slight smile.

Adesuwa's mind raced, and she fought to maintain composure. The larger hands covering hers seeped warmth into her skin like a cold, damp cloth.

Uncle Bid tightened his hold. "Your sister and I are like your second parents, and we want what's best for you," Uncle Bid stated in a low tone. "You know she cares for the children alone; she is often tired."

She swallowed, locked in an uncomfortable stare. "I'll apologize once we get home."

"That's good, that's good," Uncle Bid said, putting his hands in his pockets.

She did not notice how he surveyed her crossed legs beside the desk.

"Very good," he repeated, smiling.

ELEVEN

Present Day, 2024, Arondizuogu, Nigeria.

Karen arrived in Arondizuogu Town early Saturday morning. The town buzzed with life; Oliver De Coque played on a loop from nearby shops that placed their speakers outside their doors to attract people. Commercial activities outside the hotel commenced; many traders put their wares opposite the hotel, ready to approach guests entering or leaving the premises. Their children found it exciting, chasing after glossy cars with trays of smoked fish and mangoes, prepared to sprint away as soon as they sighted the police. None of these amused her. Karen did not care that the children carried their wares on shaved heads and the beggars in tattered garments pressed their noses to the car's windowpane while it stopped in traffic.

She had called Tunde in the car to distract herself from her haunted surroundings; as expected, he sounded pleased that she had traveled, giving her minimal respite.

Her thoughts prevented her from demanding to change rooms, but her lips curled in distaste when she entered the hideous king's suite. Karen sat on the edge of the bed, studying the yellow walls. An old television set with an antenna sat on a wooden desk. The door to the bathroom stood ajar, and from where she sat, she could see an old water closet and a poorly tiled cubicle. Karen sighed. Her bed was passable, although the faded red flowery bedding clashed with the walls. A wooden wardrobe, a bedside lamp, and the Holy Bible sat on the desk. Thankfully, the room had an air conditioner. It did not meet the standards of her choice of lodgings, but the hotel was near where she needed to be. It took all her willpower not to ask her driver to turn back.

Sitting alone in the hotel room heightened her anguish. The thought of being around her relatives left her lightheaded, as though her guilt over Mama had taken a different form. She could call the driver now and tell him they had to return to Lagos. A hand squeezed her head, squeezing while she gasped and gulped in the air. Wincing, she reached for the painkillers and bottle of water in her bag, believing that her body opposed the idea of coming back home.

Karen cradled her head in her hands, focusing on slowing the hammering in her chest; she could almost taste a metallic fear. She may have changed her name and told herself that a part of her being lay dead, but it could not possibly be dead if she reacted this way to visiting—the years only tucked in shame. Yes, shame was a living, breathing thing, a leech attached to her person. Its stench drifted around her during the day and took shape in the shadows, lurking behind her eyes until nighttime, when she lay in bed, apprehensive to peer into that darkness.

She let out a strangled breath with some determination to attend the burial. She would leave once the funeral ended. Being among her family members would be too much to bear. Her stomach churned as she suffered from rambunctious thoughts, but she could not stop them, not here, close to her mother's home. There could be frayed nerves and fights; Mama did not need that on her big day.

She leaned back against a pillow and checked her phone, staring at a message from Uloma sharing that everyone was excited to see her again.

This sacrifice she made coming to Arondizuogu would have to be enough. She had come here as a last resort to rid herself of her culpability in causing Mama pain, eating up her insides all these years. The guilt of holding secrets was a cancer that spread across one's life, causing sorrow. For Mama's sake, she had never mentioned those things. She wondered if she had been selfish, afraid of the heartache it would evoke if she had told Mama. She knew that Omo would keep quiet, no matter how much her sister heaped the blame on her, and she could not imagine a world where Omo would admit her part in their estrangement.

***

June 2011, Awka, Nigeria.

The room had a trace of talcum powder. Omo moved around the cramped room as she tidied up after herself, hanging her towel on the rack in the adjoining bathroom and putting on the nightie she had laid aside. The room suffered from heat with no electricity, and the rechargeable fan had run out of batteries. Omo glanced at the bags of forgotten luggage stacked behind the bed, which spilled out on the sides, and her husband reading the Bible on the bed before he turned in for the night. What did they say about removing the wood log in your eye before seeing that of your neighbor? Her lips quivered at the irony; for a man with so many vices, it seemed comical that he would be so religious.

She had spent days racking her brain on how to ask him for money. They had argued the last time she had asked, and she had augmented the funds by taking from the diminutive sales in her shop. For a man who loved to be generous outside, he had to be the most miserly man toward his wife and children. Omo sat on the bed, sighing, preparing for the inevitable war that would erupt.

"Bid," his name came out in a steady, low tone.

"*Kedu?*" her husband grunted, his eyes on the Bible.

"I want to talk to you about the upkeep money," she stated as his expression closed off. "There's not much food in the house, and—"

"Did I not give you money for the house two weeks ago?" he pressed his lips together.

Omo took a deep breath. "You gave me ten thousand. That amount is insufficient to feed six people and cover our expenses." She pushed her annoyance down as her husband maintained a plastic facade, threatening to fill her with doubt as though she were crazy to demand more respect. "I don't have any profit from the shop."

"How come?"

She shrugged.

Bid snickered. "You're funny *o*, Omo, hilarious. What does the Bible say about a good wife?" he waved the book. "It says a virtuous woman looks good to the ways of her household and eats not the bread of idleness. If we want to live by example, as church leaders—"

"This has nothing to do with the church! What are you going on about? This is the upkeep for the house. Would you rather we all starve?" She clapped her hands, then crossed her arms, shaking her legs. "You have a Bible passage for everything you want to avoid, or are we not reading the same Bible?"

"Watch it! Omo, watch it!" he bolted upright. "I've warned you about how you talk; your uncle warned you, and you're still very disrespectful!" Bid scoffed, a vein throbbing in his neck. "I don't have money. What exactly do you think I should do, for God's sake?"

"If you gathered the money you give those skinny girls, I wouldn't have to be—"

Bid slammed the Bible shut and tossed it on the bed.

Omo flinched.

"Thunder, fire you!" he screamed, his eyes flashing with fury.

"Me?" she shrieked.

"Yes, you Omo, thunder fire you! You don't like peace at all! You saw me reading and charged at me, hurling insults!" Bid rasped as he jerkily rose from the bed and gestured at his wife, whose mouth hung open.

"Bid, won't I ask you for money to feed your children, or which one is all this preaching?"

"The skinny girls you've mentioned, how many of them have you seen, or did they tell you they're eating my money?"

"Okay, don't be angry, sir," she screwed her lips to the side as her words dripped with sarcasm. "Please, I need money for our children."

"I don't have any money," he hissed, clutching the Bible and leaving the room.

"You don't have or don't want to give your wife money for your children's upkeep?" Omo shouted after him. "Shameless man!"

TWELVE

Present Day, 2024, Arondizuogu, Nigeria.

Karen stepped into her mother's homestead, enveloped in an air of self-consciousness, her skin flushing under the scrutiny of others. The women from the various sects whispered as she passed, shaking their heads and clucking among themselves, unsettling her as she stepped deeper into the compound. Even the trees taunted her. She had meditated on the way to Mama's house, played, and replayed all scenarios in rising disquiet. Yet, she was incapable of curbing her anxiety upon stepping into the compound. Eyes followed her, emphasizing the distance between her and her family, that she was a stranger in the luscious compound she grew up in. The stark reality lodged itself in her mind. She stepped into the old, mudded, unpainted bungalow, ignoring the activities outside as thick smoke and chattering filled the air. The women cooked and sang mournful songs in their traditional mourning uniforms, and well-wishers, family friends, and strangers trooped in and out of the house.

She passed a woman wailing in the clay sand while others consoled her. She did not recognize this person, but in villages, it was a foregone conclusion that strangers, distant relations from an uncertain part of the family tree, joined in mourning, weeping as though they were competing to outdo each other in wailing.

Karen's eyes narrowed on her sister when she entered the sitting room. It was Omo in the flesh, holding her gaze with an unreadable expression; Omo who was not also Omo, at least not in the way she remembered. Omo's hair had not been so gray, her mouth had not been severely pinched, and her eyes had not been so bleak. Her chest tightened and slid into her stomach. She squeezed her hands together, unable to keep them still, conscious of the sweat forming in her palms. She gave her greetings to everyone in the house and avoided her sister and Uncle Donatus. They recognized her as well, but stayed away from her. The women hugged her, and the elders admonished her for not visiting often.

The weight of Karen's environment crowded in on her. Standing in her childhood home, thinking of her mother and Omo, Karen gritted her teeth to stop her eyes from smarting. She allowed Uloma to guide her to the old-fashioned loveseat by the window, apart from everyone else.

She gathered herself behind dark, oversized sunglasses. Her night had been plagued with fits of despair, with memories taunting her dreams and disdain for herself at her weakness;

she had been unable to hold back tears as they came in the dead of night.

Karen surveyed the gray walls of her mother's home. The house no longer smelled of Mama's incense, diffused in the sea of various scents. She experienced a new wave of grief that her mother's gradual erasure had begun even as they gathered to mourn her. Large photographs from her childhood and a photo of Papa hung on the wall. Karen recoiled at an old picture of her and Omo smiling at the camera; she sat by Omo on the bare earth under a mango tree behind the house, placing an arm around her. Omo smiled at her, trusting in that picture. A lump caught in her throat, and she pushed the glasses higher up the bridge of her nose.

Uloma hovered beside her chair. The woman, younger than her by a year, remained the same as when they had met five years ago, except that her eyes were dull with grief. Karen discreetly observed the sunlight settle on Uloma's profile, highlighting her strong features as she broke into watery smiles at anecdotes about Mama.

***

In the later part of the Afternoon, when the sun's intensity had subsided, the family and guests congregated at the gravesite marked by a plain slab behind the bungalow. The earth, relieved of some of its content, gaped open, waiting to swallow. Karen wondered if they shared the same bleak thoughts as pallbearers lowered the coffin into the ground; the air had turned grim under rolling gray clouds.

The service passed in a blur as she threw a handful of brown earth into the ground, staring at the wooden casket that contained Mama. At that moment, tears slipped toward her mother. Someone whose name she could not recall passed her a tissue, and she dabbed at it from beneath the sunglasses; her encumbrances had been replaced by a glib acceptance that she would never hear her mother's voice again. People wailed around her, and others who put on brave fronts comforted the bereaved. She let herself shed silent tears, crying for her mother, for herself, faced with the finality of death, an end that would never restart.

Karen moved closer to her cousin as Uloma whimpered, tempted to stretch her arms around Uloma yet needing comfort. The divide between her and the rest of the family seemed magnified again, and she thought about the coffin and how solitary it appeared in the grave, highlighting her separation from the rest of her kin. It occurred to Karen that she had not given her love to the woman who had brought her into this world as she ought to because of the incidents that had shaped her life. She had unwittingly punished her mother because Mama might have been the last link to a past she sought to bury.

That was why she never wanted to come back. What had her mother done to deserve that? Nothing. The woman had loved her; she had been proud of her.

Her life philosophy weighed on her as the day dragged on. By evening, she was exhausted from the tirade of emotions and sat in a plastic chair on the veranda, watching men finish covering up the grave. She dabbed at another tear that had escaped the corner of her eye.

"Adesuwa."

She turned, and Uncle Donatus came into sight.

"You seem well."

"You too, uncle," Karen replied, observing the working men, their sweaty backs glistening in the sun. She did not want to see her uncle's weathered face. He seemed slimmer than a decade ago, with a slight limp on his left leg.

He stepped in front of her, blocking her view of the men and her escape.

"How have you been?"

Karen grunted in response.

Uncle Donatus cleared his throat, a guttural sound filling the tension between them. "I'm happy you are here, although your mother would have loved that you came while she was alive."

"I tried my best." Karen stood up, ready to leave the house and the town.

"No, we don't celebrate the living after death. Of what use is it to them, *biko*?" He shook his bad leg. "Anyway, we must talk before everyone goes home by the end of today or tomorrow. There's a lot we must settle in your mother's account since she died without a will."

Karen flinched. "Uncle, my mother is barely cold in the ground, and you want to start on her will?"

Uncle Donatus squinted at her. "How do you mean?"

The faint thumping of shovels digging loose soil from a mound of earth at Mama's grave interrupted their conversation.

"That we buried your sister less than four hours ago, and you're talking to me about property!"

"Adesuwa, is it not you that I'm talking to? What is wrong with you?" Her uncle puffed his chest, his protruding belly almost touching her. "We won't see you forever now that your mother is no longer alive. Have you greeted your sister today since you got here?"

Karen raised her hands to stop him. "Uncle, please. I came here for the burial and nothing else! Let's not pretend that all is well. Let's not start what we can't finish! Please, and please, let's not pretend like we are okay."

Uncle Donatus's scabby lips were agape as he scanned the area around him, turning left and right as if she had vanished. "Adesuwa! I cannot admonish you again. Are you now too big to talk to?"

"Uncle, please," she responded, raising her hands to silence him again.

His mouth opened and closed in shock.

The men working on the grave had stopped to watch, baffled by Uncle Donatus's raised voice, his Igbo accent thick with rage. "See what Lagos did to this small girl of yesterday."

Uloma, Omo, and the other guests rushed out of the house, alerted by Uncle Donatus's shouts.

"*Ndo*." Uncle Donatus's wife moved beside him, placing a hand on his shoulder and directing venom at Karen. "*Ndo*. Now is not the time for this."

The woman nodded in agreement, moving closer to her uncle in solidarity. Karen's eyes flew to her sister and Uloma, who avoided her gaze. They stood behind Uncle Donatus in apparent discomfort. Her lips curled in a scowl, her body shaking with trepidation. The time had come to leave home again.

Karen stormed off to the car parked beside the compound, and the children, peering into the glossy vehicle, ran off. They were the least of her worries. She had to leave; she had to. Her uncle bellowed from the veranda, surrounded by the women placating him like the chickens they fed, rallying around him as though he were to be revered and had never been a foolish man.

Fury crashed into her like a raging sea, halting Karen.

Her cousin, who had run after her, doubled over, panting.

"This!" She pointed toward the homestead. "This is why I didn't want to be here!"

"Adesuwa!" Uloma's eyes were wild with distress. "Tell me what happened. What's so wrong, Adesuwa?"

She glared at the woman.

"Adesuwa, talk to me. What happened?"

Karen's mind raced, shaking her head to shut out tumbling feelings—painful, betraying feelings. She was thirty-four, for Christ's sake. It shouldn't hurt her this much. She counted down from one thousand in multiples of seven, taking slow breaths.

"Adesuwa, please." Uloma cried, struggling to appeal to the woman in front of her and the girl who her older cousin once was. The years they were close with no thought for tomorrow.

Karen glanced at their environment, thankful for the closed windows, discouraging the driver from listening. "Don't call me that," she spoke under her breath. More controlled, she wrapped her arms around herself. "You should ask Omo."

"Why? Ask her what? Answer me, please."

A gentle breeze Karen may have enjoyed, whipped by, fluttering the trees lined along the concrete fence beside them. She blinked away tears.

The conversation turned reticent, and the lull stretched for an eternity.

"I won't be coming back here. I'm leaving tonight," Karen stated in a brusque tone.

"Why?"

"Why? How can you ask me why?"

Uloma shook her head in despondency, helpless to stop her cousin from leaving and strained by heightened emotions. "You need to throw up this worm that is eating you inside."

Karen glared at the foreboding compound one last time; the women gathered around Uncle Donatus, and the smell of dying firewood embers mingled in the wind. She sniffed back tears and entered the waiting vehicle, bidding her mother a silent goodbye.

THIRTEEN

Present Day, 2024, Arondizuogu, Nigeria.

The household settled into bed except for Omo, who sat on the veranda. A kerosene lantern burned by the door; soot formed behind the glass, hiding a bulb of fire within it, providing a circle of quivering light. She moved away from the lamp and heat, preferring the night breeze.

Adesuwa's presence disturbed the house; the trace of her lavender perfume lingered even with the windows open. Adesuwa was different—more beautiful and distant. Omo had thought that if she ever saw Adesuwa again, she would pound Adesuwa with her scarred fists and curse her. Yet, she felt ashamed when she saw her sister, as though her dress became more tattered and her plumpness became more apparent. Her mouth clammed shut, refusing to obey her command. Adesuwa's open contempt made her want to cower and hide; those eyes that had looked up to her a decade ago now turned against her, loaded with accusations.

Omo had spent the day mulling over her childhood with Adesuwa. There was no grand memory but a lackluster recollection of Adesuwa's small, trusting hand in hers on an ordinary sunny day. She was not sure why she had thought of that day, but it stayed with her during the burial, magnifying as the pallbearers lowered Mama's coffin into the earth. She had wept a little, comforted others, smiled as people mentioned Mama, and struggled to keep her spite under control when Adesuwa entered her field of vision.

Uncle Donatus came to the veranda, chewing on a piece of bitter kola. His temples creased as he ground the sour fruit in his mouth until he swallowed, followed by a loud belch. Omo murmured a greeting, watching him amble to a plastic chair dressed in the Ankara print the family had chosen for the burial, dragging his feet encased in white flip-flops.

Uncle Donatus made a guttural noise, stretching his bad leg before him. "*Ehen*, how're you, Omo? We haven't had time to discuss things."

"I'm well, uncle, thank you." She offered a bow.

"I have something to discuss with you." He glanced across the dark compound. "Your mother mentioned some things to me before she died. Yes." He craned his neck toward the house. "Uloma! Uloma!"

Her cousin answered in a muffled voice from inside.

"Bring the beer for me from the fridge!"

They fell quiet as Uloma joined them with a bottle of beer and a glass, the side of a stool pressed between her arm and body. She set the stool on the ground, placed the items on it, and opened the beer before disappearing inside.

"That girl. She's still as slow as ever." Uncle Donatus griped, pouring beer into the glass. The light from the lantern illuminated a prominent scar on his upper lip. He resumed the conversation after taking a swig of beer. "*Ehen.* She told me of your wish to move to Lagos." He gave her a keen look. "You want to find work and all that. Now that your useless sister has shown her hand, how will you do it?"

"Hmm. I don't know, Uncle," she smacked her hands in resignation. "Lagos can be tough, but I can get better work there. My children are getting older, and I need to cover rising expenses at home. Thank God Nora got admission to the university," she continued, referring to her first daughter. "She didn't get in last year, but now that she has, we must sort out her registration. That's why I want the family to help me, Uncle."

"Help you? Help you, you said?" Uncle Donatus's shoulders shook with laughter. "Why do you think the family would help you, Aiferiaomo?"

Omo was appalled. "Uncle, I have no other family to turn to. You know how tough things have been for the past few years."

"Things have been tough for all of us. *No be the same Nigeria we dey?*" Her uncle shook his head. "You say things are hard, but you want to leave for Lagos. Ha! *Biko*, is that place not expensive? You want to stress everybody, or is it me with my bricklayer work that would help you?"

"But, uncle," Omo's voice fell off, and she swallowed her indignation, her eyes misting. "Uncle, this money isn't for me; it's for my children!"

Uncle Donatus took another long sip of his drink.

Omo straightened her back as she put her hands on her head, her bosom thrust forward in her blouse by her actions. "After everything my husband did for the family, who do I turn to now?"

"Omo, you remember I told you not to leave Bid," he responded in an even voice, leaning forward and squinting at the shadowed profile of his niece against the flickering orange flare of the lantern. He wagged his finger at her and launched a proverb. "What a child cannot see standing, an elder can see crouching down. I warned you, didn't I?" he leered, unaffected by her crumpled appearance.

"But, Uncle, you were there. You know what happened wasn't my fault," Omo's voice shook. "How can you blame me for my husband walking out on me, on our children? Are girls not also made by God?"

"A boy is the heritage of our culture. You know this all too well. Just because your father was an Edo man does not mean your mother didn't teach you the Igbo tradition." He drank the remaining beer in his glass. "Even this house—if not for your father, who built it, and my sister's wish to leave it for the two of you—it should be reverted to me," Uncle Donatus wore a solemn expression. "Your mother helped the family with finances, and now that she's gone, we're all in the same boat. Now I'm moving back to the village to spend my old age with your Aunty in peace," he continued. "I suggest you do the same."

"Uncle," she folded her arms against a sudden chill, staring at the older man with tear-stained cheeks, her lips trembling from crying. "You know I can't do that; I have children to think of, *naw*. You have children, too; you know how expensive it is. It's not my fault their irresponsible father left us penniless. You were close to Bid; you should've cautioned him whenever he came to you to complain."

Uncle Donatus snickered. "Isn't it time for Nora to marry? Marry her off so that she can help with the household. There are eligible men around here looking for a wife, Aiferiomo; isn't that so? Didn't you marry around her age?" He belched, expelling the odor of alcohol. "I wonder whose fault it is. If not for my respect for Bid, I should have told the family what you did by now."

Omo recoiled. "What I did, Uncle?" She clapped, streaks of drying tears glistening as she shifted into the light. "You and I know that the fault lies with Adesuwa; it's not just me that you'd disgrace if people know. Isn't that what you and Aunty Uche said at that time?"

"Hmm," her uncle nodded, leaning in the chair, "but it's a woman's job to secure her home. Men are promiscuous by nature." After a pause, he asked, "Where's the girl now? She only came here once after your mother begged her—mistreated my sister! Now she has the effrontery to show up." He shook his head. "*Nawa*! This is what all this Lagos journey does; we're losing our daughters to Western life." Uncle Donatus coughed up phlegm and spat in the sand beside the concrete floor. "I'm not surprised anyway. It's because she's now big in the city, an ungrateful child."

A tense silence fell between them.

"Uloma said Adesuwa went back to Lagos immediately. She didn't wait for her mother's body to turn cold in the ground, *tufia*!"

"She knows she's not welcome here," Omo croaked.

Her uncle's eyes flashed angrily. "If that girl wants to come here, you can do nothing because I won't send her away! Or you don't know this burial happened because of how much she contributed?" He pinned her with scorn as though blaming Omo for her poverty. "She may assist with your issue; your mother said she has a big house in the city."

"And you think she would help? We have not heard a peep from her for about ten years, Uncle. Me *o*, I won't accept a dime from that girl."

"Okay, don't collect, don't collect, be waiting for me. You better humble yourself; if not, the end is always a failure!"

"That's not my concern, Uncle." Omo got up, her abrupt movement toppling the stool she had been sitting on. "I should collect money from that—" she stammered, "that small girl! *Chineke* over my dead body!" She snapped her fingers over her head as people would when they warded off premonitions.

"Okay, I've warned you, Aiferiaomo! Think of your children. Pride won't get you anywhere," Uncle Donatus pontificated. "I warned you to be patient with your husband, but you didn't listen. Is it today that a man has affairs? We're in Africa; men are men. If you had stayed, we wouldn't be having this issue."

"Uncle, you have not spoken well, *o*!"

"Taah!" her uncle countered, spittle flying out of his mouth. "You better watch it! Adesuwa is the only person who can assist all of us; that's why it's suitable for a woman to remain in her husband's house!"

But Adesuwa lived unmarried, she wanted to say. The fire flared in its containment, rising and falling as swiftly as her anger, leaving her spent from their sparring. Uncle Donatus made an elaborate show of ignoring her, whistling and shaking his leg, and she studied him with a curious mixture of spite and despair. The uncle, whose loyalty could be bought, turned against her after Bid left. She must have been foolish then; she ought to have known better. She deplored the strange blindness that fell on a man when another man stepped out of line—an unquestioning loyalty. She shook her head and sniffled, frustrated at talking to her uncle; the ears on either side of his head turned deaf to topics unrelated to money. Every time she tried, he reminded her of why she begrudged him, yet she had no one to share her thoughts with.

FOURTEEN

Present Day, 2024, Lagos, Nigeria.

Karen woke up with a start. Her dreams had been troubled since she returned from the burial two weeks ago. This time, the nightmare evolved from a dark lump lurking beside her bed to a snake coiling around her; the more she struggled, the tighter it coiled. Her heart, hammering from a troubled sleep, mellowed into a steady rhythm as the bedroom shifted into focus. A beam of sunlight lined the room in unequal halves. It cast a yellow column on the bed.

She reached for her phone, remnants of sleep weighing on her eyelids like an anchor as she glanced at the time, stifling a yawn. Karen heaved her sluggish body out of bed. The ground seemed to move beneath her feet as her head reeled. She slumped on the edge of the bed, pressing a hand over her eyes to repress the sudden attack on her senses.

At length, Karen got up slowly, not trusting her legs to support her weight. She ambled toward the bathroom, breaking as a tide of nausea washed over her as though she had never rested.

Mama had a small parcel of farmland that Omo put up for sale since she had firstborn rights to the property. Karen had balked at that, but her memories of the events during Mama's burial quieted her. As some consolation, Uloma had the grace to concede that Mama would never want them to sell her legacy. But Omo needed money, Uloma stated; the shop in Awka was in crisis, the funds would be used to relocate to Lagos, and Omo's children needed to return to school.

No part of Mama's possessions came to Karen, and no thought was apportioned to her. In her mind, Omo had expunged the last trace of Mama as though their mother had never existed. Mama had been a traditional Igbo woman and would not have wished for someone else to have control of her property besides her children. It saddened Karen that she did not have the strength to fight for Mama and more so that she had nothing of Mama to remember her by.

A warm shower later melted her anguish, and she focused on reviewing the early afternoon appointment she had scheduled with Mr. Charles to celebrate the successful end of her consulting services for a business he and Majekodunmi had started. Majekodunmi had asked her to offer her expertise, as she had done for him on various projects. At the same time,

Majekodunmi mentored her in taking over his position as the Regional Manager for Western Nigeria when he retired from Wemco. The thought of a new position within her grasp brought a smile as she got ready, calm at last, although Karen suspected it was brief.

***

"It was lovely doing business with you, Mr. Charles," Karen smiled.

"Yes, of course," the older man's oval face lit up. "Please call me Charles. Ayo is a brother to me, and you and I have worked together for almost a year. I should invite you to our church soon. It's full of young ones like you, my dear; there are fine brothers there!" He grinned, his eyes crinkling in the corners, emphasizing the freckles scattered across his nose.

"Thank you." Karen raised her chin, feigning a smile.

"Of course, of course." Mr. Charles chirped, "I told Majekodunmi that an intelligent girl like you should be married; a big shame, eh!"

She echoed an assent, and her smile waned as she let her mind wander while he continued his unsolicited advice on singlehood. Mr. Charles was an old gentleman and a self-proclaimed devout Christian. Her vague rhetoric as a Christian put him at ease; in return, she was barraged with invitations to his church and sympathetic remarks about her marital status. Karen, who had not entered a church since her early twenties, wondered what he would do if he found out. She could not help her condescension toward people who put faith in others because of religion, and to her, Mr. Charles exhibited a certain naivete in not recognizing that people wore various masks: the church, the house, the office, and the different faces of one person.

She observed the restaurant with the Purple Orchid insignia at her discretion. White plush seats with golden legs melded with gold and black silk tones on the wall. The oval room spread across the ground floor of a building with a boutique above it, with a few tables filled and people talking in hushed tones. A bartender worked behind a paneled bar lined with various drinks. Karen smiled at the man again through the rim of her glass of juice, watching him have his glass of beer. The bespoke decor and expensive menu attracted corporate clientele, and Mr. Charles had let slip that he often came here with his family. She had hoped to impress him, so he knew she paid careful attention to what he liked.

Two men in black blazers entered the establishment, pulling Tunde forward from the back of her mind. Karen bit her bottom lip to stop a fresh smile from forming.

"I would mention it to Ayo as well."

Karen remarked, slipping into the conversation with ease. "I appreciate that. I look forward to hearing what Mr. Majekodunmi says."

"Ah, yes. After all, he referred you. He gave glowing recommendations, and he was right."

"Yes, thank you." Her smile was more relaxed, and her eyes sparkled.

A waiter came to their table for dessert. They declined, and she asked for the check. She insisted on covering the bill, though she knew he could afford it because it was wiser for her to foster future business projects. Mr. Charles relented with gratitude.

"I'm surprised you're not eyeing his position once he retires."

Karen's ears perked up, and she gave him a sharp look. She tapped on her side of the table, bridling a tug of impatience. "Well, what do you think about my chances for the position? I hope I've impressed you with my expertise."

"I trust the board won't consider someone unqualified for the position. You have competent people in Wemco, and I think it'd be a tough choice."

"Pardon?"

"The other people are being considered for the position. It'd be super tough—between you and me. You should apply to it as well. At first, I thought you'd be the next in line, seeing how close you are to Ayo." Mr. Charles wore a shuttered expression, studying her with a foreign glint.

"And who are these other people?" Karen's tone was abrupt.

He hesitated, tapping the table with a finger. "I shouldn't be telling, but I think Tunde Awoniyi. We've worked together a few times, and he's a gem in the making."

Karen froze, her eyes widening, fingers suspended in the air—Tunde, her Tunde? Her face drained of color, and she cleared her throat, resting her fingers on the table as though controlled by a puppeteer. "You mean Tunde, Tunde Awoniyi in the supply team?"

"Oh," Mr. Charles pursed his lips, perhaps afraid that he had divulged too much information. "Do you know him?" he asked in a low pitch.

Her lips quivered into a tense smile, and she shook her head. "We worked together a few times, but nothing close, just colleagues."

An uncomfortable hush settled upon them, and Karen took the time to control herself, rearranging her features to be amenable, though her insides screamed out in disbelief.

The waiter appeared with a black check presenter, and she handed him a credit card.

"I heard his father is an ally in the industry, so there's an incentive to hire him; of course, he is also qualified."

Not as much as I am, Karen retorted in silence. "So, it's going to be a decision influenced by nepotism?" she voiced.

"No, no," he stammered, staring at everything except Karen, "but several factors go into this. I'm quite surprised you're not interested; that's all. I brought it up for no reason. It's no big deal. I'm sure you have greater plans, yes. With these large corporations, there are many opportunities, you know?"

The waiter returned, this time with the receipts. They left the building and headed down the lonely street. Mr. Charles's stride held a trace of impatience, his shoulders uptight as though he wanted nothing more than to teleport. She followed behind with less enthusiasm, befuddled by their conversation and Tunde.

It had rained while they were in the restaurant. Karen gazed at the gray sky and the vehicles dotted with water droplets, breathing in the odor of wet concrete. She remarked on the weather, skillfully steering the conversation away from work. Mr. Charles brightened and slowed his brisk walk as she stepped beside him, and he carried on an idle chat until they shared an awkward goodbye.

Her mind worked like clockwork on the way home, reviewing Mr. Charles's comments about Tunde. Karen chewed on her bottom lip as she steered her car through traffic and followed a line of cars at the toll gate. She had thought the position had been hers, and Tunde—well, Tunde stayed where she placed him—to find out that he had tossed his hat in the ring was unsettling. Did he consider leaving and moving to another state, as the job entailed? Did he think of how it would affect them, whatever vague relationship they had?

They kept work separate from their private lives, but she could not fathom this news not interfering with their activities outside of work. She left the traffic behind at the toll gate, speeding up on the paved highway. Karen wished that things could be as simple as the open road, pushing down a spurt of resentment. She had worked up the ladder through blood and sweat, and to have things turn out any other way was unfair.

Worse, she learned from Mr. Charles, not Tunde or Majekodunmi. Why did Majekodunmi make those remarks about her being a good fit and tell her his succession plans if they were not to be? Majekodunmi had mentioned that the recruitment process would be discreet, and he had never reneged on his word. No, her mind raced as she pressed down on the accelerator, lost in a world of her making. There was no way Tunde would try to overtake her. Not Tunde, who ran after her, Tunde, who assigned himself as hers.

A horn blared from behind, startling her into consciousness. Karen gasped, swerving back into her lane and releasing the pedal. The vehicle slowed to a reasonable speed, numbing the painful thump in her chest. A sore throb shot through her hands, making her wince. She relaxed her grip on the steering wheel and let out a broken exhale. Karen cursed, blaming herself for not catching wind of this information. Mama's death must have distracted her more than she assumed. She straightened, gathering her wits after concluding she would confirm with Rita and then confront Majekodunmi and Tunde.

FIFTEEN

The following Monday brought a flurry of activities, with a new project taking off. It rained all morning, water belting down from somber clouds like spears from raging warriors. The steady drum of rain outside mirrored Stephanie's turmoil over the past few weeks. She sat behind her boss, Majekodunmi, in the meeting room, half listening to the conversation around the conference table. Her ears pricked each time Tunde spoke, their tips flushing in helpless silence, yet Tunde could not allay her discomfort.

She observed Karen at the end of the table, studying the woman's precise motions and firm tone that commanded respect. Yet on such a dreary day, Karen stood out—everything that Stephanie was not. Lightning preceded sporadic thunderclaps, shaking her from runaway thoughts that chipped at her concentration. Something tugged at her, watching them sit on opposite sides of the desk while he concentrated on a laptop. She hoped that her intuition was wrong because Karen did not strike her as a woman who would jeopardize her career for a fling, especially with Majekodunmi's retirement around the corner.

The meeting ended, and the other managers left except Karen; she stood with her hands in the pockets of her pantsuit, staring at Majekodunmi.

Stephanie peeked at Tunde's wavering stance before he left the room.

"Leave us, Stephanie."

Her boss sent her a dismissive nod, and the room fell silent as Karen's gaze followed her until she opened the door.

Majekodunmi broke into a smile the moment the door clicked shut, but his eyes maintained their hardness in contrast to his broad smile. "Karen, how are you?"

"Not so great."

The tall man nodded. His rugged face showed no emotion as he digested her comment. He shifted his weight, turning slightly away from her and observing an angry lightning slash.

She shifted from foot to foot, suppressing a flicker of impatience. "I heard that the board is also considering Tunde for the position. You never mentioned anything about that."

"Tunde, who?"

"Awoniyi," she supplemented, "Tunde Awoniyi."

"Ah, yes, yes," he rubbed the bridge of his nose beneath a pair of glasses. His broad shoulders slacked, and his hands slipped into his pants pockets as he assumed a wider stance. "I knew it would be a matter of time before word got out."

"You weren't planning on keeping it from me, right?" Karen crossed her arms. "I've collaborated with you for years; you know I've wanted this for as long as we can remember."

"It wasn't my decision; you know that, Karen. You know how these things go," he rasped, mirroring her actions. "It's the decision of the board."

"Which I'm sure you didn't oppose."

"It was five against one; I stood no chance." Majekodunmi exhaled and approached her, patting her shoulder before walking away. "You know how these things work. His father's a big shot with whom we are affiliated. The least we could do is to consider his son for the position."

Karen leaned on the table; her shoulder warmed from his touch. "Are you considering Tunde because of his father or because he is good at his job?"

"No," he fiddled with a pen lying beside him on the table, his expression shifting to concentration as his lips pressed together. He peered at Karen from above his glasses, his expression set to discourage an argument. "We both know he's fantastic at his job and deserves a promotion soon. His expertise is very competitive, Karen." He broke into a brief smile, exposing white rows of teeth. "Look, I have the final say on who I pick, and you know you have my vote. There's nothing to worry about. Let's go through the motions, hmm? And you get the promotion. Do you think that I won't have your back? When have I ever disappointed you?"

She studied him at length before giving him a dense smile. "Okay, I'll trust you and go through the motions like you've suggested."

"That's a good girl!" Majekodunmi grinned. "Now, let's get this project sorted out. I have much riding on this, and you did well with Charles. I know it'll win the rest of the board over if you can bring in a major investor before your promotion. I suggest you start working on your contacts."

"Sure," Karen replied, this time with a more genuine smile.

***

July 2011, Awka, Nigeria.

Adesuwa dashed from the university chapel premises onto the street, her feet sinking into the mud from an afternoon shower as she headed to the bus stop. The air felt slightly cold, and she rubbed her arms to warm up. Scores of students moved en masse through the street, some camped by the bus stop ahead. Adesuwa hummed a song as she waded through people, clutching the bag over her shoulder. She had promised her sister she would be home before eight so Omo could attend the women's prayer vigil at Uncle Bid's church.

She glanced at the leather watch around her slim wrist and grimaced. It was almost seven, and she had hoped she would arrive home earlier, considering the reasonable traffic heading back to the professor's quarters at the other end of the university. Chuka, the lead organist in the church, stopped her for a brief chat. She smiled at herself, remembering the pleasant colleague, as she quickened her pace, mulling over their conversation until a familiar car honked and slowed beside her. Her lips broke into a tentative smile as she peered into the car and found Uncle Bid studying her from the driver's seat of the old Honda Civic.

"Get in," he stated firmly, his lips set in a grim line.

Adesuwa slid into the passenger's seat, breathing a sigh of relief. "Good evening, uncle. I didn't know you came for the service."

Uncle Bid grunted and kept his eyes on the road, his jaw ground in frigid silence.

She swallowed, her gaze fixed on the cars lined up in front. She folded and refolded the strap of her bag resting on her lap.

"Who was that boy with you?" Uncle Bid's gruff voice broke the silence, and his Igbo accent became more noticeable because of his displeasure.

Adesuwa gaped at her brother-in-law.

"Who?" he threw her a scathing glance as a horn blasted from the car behind them. He peered at the rearview mirror and clicked his teeth.

"He's in my choir. He's our choirmaster," Adesuwa spewed, fidgeting with the safety belt across her chest. "I'm sorry he took up my time. I promised Sister I would be home by seven."

"Is he your boyfriend? So, you've started following these small boys."

Uncle Bid cleared his throat and lowered his voice after a pause. "I thought you had more sense than this, Adesuwa. Be very careful with men, especially boys your age. They all want one thing," he lifted a finger. "They're like vultures, always on the hunt, searching for food."

Startled by his sudden attack, she blinked back tears. "Uncle, I'm not following anyone. He's someone in the choir," her face crumpled in fright. "I didn't know that time had gone."

In the blink of an eye, Uncle Bid veered off the road into a quiet side street and turned to focus on her. Her mind raced, yet she returned his gaze with a pinched expression, her face flushed from unreleased tears.

A hand went to the back of her seat, dangling beside her shoulder. She shifted toward the door, pulled backward by an unknown force.

"You know I'm your uncle; I'm saying these things out of concern," he said. "I see that you'll become someone in life, and

I don't want you to turn out like your sister. You're close to final exams now, so focus on that and leave these small boys alone."

Adesuwa dropped her eyes to her hands, which were clammy from her tight clasp. The shift from anger to gentleness unsettled her, evident in the stilted words that escaped through pursed lips: "What do you mean, 'like my sister,' Uncle?"

A calloused finger brushed her right shoulder, leaving it cold. Adesuwa felt trapped under a spell of unease, compelled to remain frozen to avoid offending Uncle Bid. She shifted her feet, battling a mounting confusion at his inscrutable expression and the nervous energy present in the car. "Uncle, we need to get going." Her voice was spasmodic. "Sister is waiting for me."

Uncle Bid said nothing. Her tense shoulders slumped a fraction at the sound of the engine coming to life. The awkward energy dragged on as Adesuwa focused on the retreating buildings, blurring out of sight as the car plodded through a patch of potholes. She craned her neck to the window, aware of the man's presence beside her. Her heart thumped in an erratic sequence, and Adesuwa picked at her nails as a foreign sense of guilt washed over her, convinced she had seen a part of her brother-in-law that ought to be for her sister. She chewed on her bottom lip, searching for a rational explanation of the situation, arriving at her father's absence as an answer.

She sighed under her breath as the car parked in front of the familiar block of flats, and her hand went straight for the door.

A strange weight lifted from her shoulders at the prospect of near escape.

His hand fastened on her arm before she could leave, and she turned to him with one foot outside the door, torment written all over her posture.

Uncle Bid leaned back, wrinkles forming between his eyebrows as he observed her with an unreadable expression. "Adesuwa. You know you're a beautiful young lady. You remind me of my sister, and I don't want you falling prey to these small boys," he continued, a smile parting his dark face. "Don't be angry, ehn, *biko*; I'm looking out for you."

Adesuwa nodded. Unsure of what to say, she observed a woman's receding stature at the end of the street with a balanced tray of tomatoes on her head. She repressed a wave of panic and mumbled her thanks, dashing out of the vehicle, out of his sight.

Bid watched Adesuwa's body sway as she disappeared into the building. His lips parted slightly for a moment, and he banged the steering wheel in a sudden burst of anger at how he had let his guard down. He shouldn't have charged at her like that.

Images of Adesuwa with the boy in church bombarded him like a kaleidoscope of colors. He balled his fists, his face twisting into a sour expression.

He released a deflating sigh in the confines of his car as the force of emotions wore off. Under a cloud of serenity, he fretted, tapping on the wheel as he reflected on Adesuwa's panicked frame and the intensity of his feelings. If Adesuwa were older than Omo, he would have turned his efforts into wooing the former. He loved how much Adesuwa trusted him. Her innocence intrigued him whenever he saw her, the way her eyes lit up with pleasure as she talked about something she liked, or he took her somewhere on their way home, especially after she argued with her sister. Bid let out a deep breath, assessing the endearing qualities of his wife's younger sister and cursing his luck that he wound up with the older one, Leah, as Jacob did.

Adesuwa had to be his test of faith, like watching an apple dangle from the serpent's hand; this time, the apple was too close to home. Bid rubbed his face with a shaking hand and closed his eyes. He murmured a short prayer as he felt his desires stir to life and pushed himself out of his car, concerned about a girl almost twenty years younger.

SIXTEEN

Present Day, 2024, Lagos, Nigeria.

The end of the week could not come soon enough, and Karen deflated with relief by Friday. She lit a row of scented candles on the bookshelf, watching yellow flames spring to life and inhaling the intertwined scents of apples, cedarwood, and soy wax. She settled into the loveseat, the silk of her kimono caressing her skin, a glass of bourbon in hand.

Karen kneaded her shoulders, moving her head in gentle circles. Much to her chagrin, she tapped her feet in anticipation, ready to leap when Tunde knocked on the door. She rested her head on the chair, her eyes transfixed on a brown blot on an otherwise spotless ceiling, acutely aware of a well of impatience at the thought of basking in her lover's arms.

A cavernous emotion made her turn to him each time, and it frightened her to think about how she gave in to it with little resistance—or what would happen if he walked away from them, from her. Her spirits fell, and she took a swig of her drink, flinching at the pungent taste of alcohol, yet it was not enough to shock her out of introspection. She stayed longer with Tunde than with any man, even Michael.

Michael and his boyish interest in stargazing, with whom she had learned to appreciate the elusive peace stars symbolized. She had cared for Michael but had sunk too deep into herself to enjoy his solemn declarations of love, and his feelings were wasted on her.

Michael had observed her one day as they lay in his bed, spent from a morning of sex.

"Why can't you be normal like everyone else, Karen?" His brows furrowed. "You hate it when I show you how I feel. You're so damn hard on yourself. It's like you refuse to let me in."

Karen stared at the fan rotating in an endless sequence.

"Don't you love me too? At least, something?"

She turned to him and smiled as she did whenever he complained about her cold response to his desire for intimacy. He blew a huff and gathered her into his arms, loving her with renewed vigor.

But Michael could not change her mind, Karen thought, as a rumbling sound brought her back to the present. She stared at the door and waited, the room radiating orange in the candlelight, but the phantom noise disappeared, leaving behind fluttering cackles from the combusting wicks.

Karen took another sip of bourbon, grimacing at the taste. The smooth texture burned through her throat, carrying her into the past. She had concluded that Michael's cries of undying love were like those of a dreamer, not because he understood what it meant to love but because the word had quantified their shared passion.

In a way, she was grateful to her ex-lover because it was under Michael's influence that she had gotten a job at Wemco Oil. The day Michael told her, they sat in his living room, watching a movie, and cuddled under a blanket.

"Hey," Michael whispered, his breath warm on her ear. "I got you an interview."

Karen's eyes widened as she whipped around to him. "What do you mean, Michael?"

"I got you an interview?" His eyes were glued to the TV screen, though his lips had curved into a smile.

"I heard you the first time," she giggled, then laughed, her eyes sparkling in the glow of the TV. "Where?"

"Wemco Oil. You've heard of it? The large oil—"

"Oh my God!" She squealed and hugged him, "Oh my goodness! Michael, you didn't have to. No, I mean, I'm so grateful! It's so hard to get in there!"

"Yeah, yeah," Michael joined her laughter, "My godfather is a boss at Wemco. Akinyomi Jakande, Mr. Jakande."

"Wow, Michael!"

"You deserve it, babe."

His eyes twinkled in pride, and she hugged him again—the closest she had come to loving him.

Before him, her ambitions had come with the humbling enlightenment that all her efforts combined were not enough to make her debut into elitism. Her first job in Lagos was as a receptionist at a small law firm for a paltry sum of sixty thousand naira monthly. Her chest inflated in adulation, reveling in the knowledge of money in the bank, a first step into adulthood in her mind's eye, the emancipation of oneself from the mercy of others. The bubble of importance did not last long; her cocoon of success shattered when she stepped onto Victoria Island. It became apparent that poverty colored her measure of accomplishments, and her job was equivalent to an average life in Lagos. The island was a symptom of true success. The cars and houses took her breath away; the groomed women smelled of expensive perfumes, wealth, and confidence. The Ikoyi axis boasted of material success. Ikoyi was her new dream, and Lagos was the city of dreams.

With renewed ambition, she resumed job hunting, but Lagos carried a dark truth woven into threads of promise. It was an almost physical barrier separating wheat from chaff. The world of her dreams remained out of reach without an existing upper-class member to provide entry into the city's circle of aristocrats. The masses called it *long leg*, the elite few who could make things happen with just a phone call.

Michael had marked the beginning of her various forays into riches to secure her place in a cruel world. She did not have the privilege of being born with a silver spoon. Karen had tasted poverty, dined with poverty, and slept beside poverty. She had been alone with no earthly advantage that set her apart from the hungry population. Average, with no uniqueness, homogeneous as the rest, as though mass-produced. She was a woman with a little more than a penny to her name, nothing to give except her beauty, and beauty would take her far. Her beauty, for which she had felt disdain, was also a tool. It had seemed a logical conclusion to make lemonade from the lemons thrust upon her; after all, there were no favors in Lagos, only transactions.

The smell of Mr. Jakande's office overpowered her senses—the odor of damp paper. The memory, like bile, made her gag as it forced its way into her throat, pushing her into the present. Karen shuddered and downed the rest of her drink, her eyes narrowing at her disturbing memories.

***

They snuggled together, naked under the blanket. Tunde pressed a kiss to her forehead, and Karen closed her eyes for a moment, swayed by the tide of desire his lips evoked. She forced her lethargic body out of bed, throwing on the kimono strewn on the chair by her bed. His eyes followed her fluid movements as she walked to the window, determined to put some distance between them.

"Tunde …"

He watched her, waiting, his lower half covered by a blanket as he propped his head on a pillow.

"Why didn't you tell me you applied for the regional position?"

Tunde sighed and glanced at the white ceiling. "I knew we were going to have this conversation sooner or later. I hoped it wouldn't be today since we've been busy over the last few weeks."

She sent him a pointed look. "We must; we're both vying for the position, Tunde. We've managed to keep out of each other's way in the office, which is why this," she pointed at herself then at him, "has survived as long as it has."

He turned to her with pleading eyes, the sheets crinkling from his jerky movements. "Do we have to discuss this now? I don't know what you want me to say." He paused. "I applied for it, but I don't think I stand a chance since most of these things are by recommendation."

"But you applied, and your family's connection puts other candidates at risk of a fair chance." She leaned back against the window and crossed her arms and legs, her visage masked by the pale evening, casting a silhouette from her bust to head.

"You mean it puts you at risk," Tunde corrected, his brows drawn together. He sat up, exposing the chiseled expanse of his chest. "There's nothing I can do about who my father is, Karen, and you know that, but it doesn't mean I should deny myself opportunities because of that."

"But you knew I would try for the position."

"How would I know? We hardly talk about you. Heck! I get you to open up to me on this bed and nowhere else."

She had the grace to color at his accusation.

"Karen, I don't think this should come between us. I won't let it, and I hope you won't either."

Her pulse quickened at the sound of her name from his lips, smooth and sweet like honey. She averted her gaze. "I've wanted this position for the longest time; I have no rich father somewhere or an extravagant connection. It's all been by my hard work, Tunde." Karen stepped away from the window, dithering to join him in bed. The fading gleam of sunset fell over her eyes, hiding her skepticism from him. "You must understand that I feel a little resentful of that fact."

Tunde sat on the edge of the bed, drawing the sheet against his crotch, his feet planted on the carpeted floor as he massaged his temples. He dropped his hands to his knees and gave her a dead look.

Karen matched him with an icy one of hers, retreating to the shadowed cloak of the sky outside, her body in rigid command.

A stoic silence fell over the room, trapping them in a battle of wills.

"You've always been ambitious, and that's one of the things I like about you," Tunde made a half smile. "I would never dream of standing in the way of your achievement. I don't believe they would consider me for this role, Karen; besides, it's time for me to branch out and try other aspects of the field. If it means trying in-house or considering other offers outside the organization, I would." The sheets fell away as he stood up, revealing the beauty of his tall height. "But I don't understand what drives you, to be honest; it's like you're constantly searching for something."

Karen took in every inch of his body, from the toned muscles to the confidence in his stride as he walked to her. Her body hummed as he closed the gap between them, her back arching toward him. She turned to face the window, her flushed face exposed to the world, her mind racing as he pulled her by her waist away from the light and into his arms.

"What do you mean?" Karen asked, breathless.

"I worry about you. You're so career-driven that it's like you block out everything else. It's as though you're blocking out everyone."

Tunde's breath fanned her skin like a feather.

"You know how I feel about you. Even though you like to pretend that what we have is casual, you know how I feel, and I won't let you use work drama to spoil this." He mumbled.

"Tunde—" She turned around to face him, but he kissed her, smothering whatever she started to say.

"It's okay," he released a ragged breath onto her lips. "You don't have to respond to that."

Karen complied, her body sizzling with desire. She responded to his kisses with hunger, giving up her armor to the wonderous security of his arms. That evening, for the first time, she let herself be loved, cherishing the time they spent relearning the secrets of their bodies.

***

Uloma walked to the row of benches. She moved, tired and stunned at the turn of events, unaware of everything happening around her. Her body seemed pulled toward the seats; her legs wobbled, and she slumped on the bench, propelled by a collage of events from the past few hours. She watched the ebbing shivers in her hands, drawing long breaths in and out until she reclaimed her control. What tragedy, she thought, what unfortunate timing.

The reception area of the inpatient ward reeked of bleach and sweat from the heat outside, though a standing fan whirred by the nurse's station. Uloma closed her eyes to the murmuring, the slamming doors, and the scraping metal on the concrete floor. The horror on her older cousin's face as an impassive doctor shared the diagnosis dug its tentacles into the recesses of her mind, causing her to shudder awake.

The diabetes grew worse, and surgery was recommended because Omo had developed gallstones. For now, she could go home with medications by evening so that they could free up bed space. However, she needed surgery as soon as possible, the doctor had stated, digging his hands into the pockets of his lab coat, his gaze flickering over the rows of occupied hospital beds that spanned the ward. Uloma heard a roaring in her ears, drowning out the doctor's following statements and the loud noises outside the louvered windows. Her eyes followed the wall charts as though she had been thrown into a mirage— the COVID-19 prevention charts, the measles and smallpox vaccination adverts.

"How do I get the money for this treatment?" Omo remarked under her breath, low enough that her words could float away undetected. "I can't afford this admission; I have the children to see to, and now I pay for surgery."

Uloma did not respond. Omo was speaking not to her cousin but to herself, as one would in a moment of defeat.

"I'm fed up, Uloma." Omo's shoulders quaked with the beginning of tears. I'm tired of everything."

Uloma squeezed Omo's hand, clinging to the remains of her control and unable to look at the woman. She had never heard her cousin cry in their adulthood; her sniffling was like a sorrowful tune, rich in history and pain. Uloma stole a glance at the woman's crumpled face, glistening with streams of tears, and her endurance broke at once, her cheeks becoming wet with grief. Comforting words crowded into her mouth, but she could not bring herself to speak, wrapped in misery as Omo broke down—a woman who never cried. What could she say to be of use? Would she lie to her cousin and promise it would be all right? Life had shown its hand, dealing blow after blow, and her hope shriveled up today.

Uloma conceded that they had not understood what relocating to Lagos would entail. It crossed her mind that Omo might have become overconfident in her chances for success after seeing Adesuwa at the funeral. They had moved after the land was sold, but in no time, the reality of unemployment dashed the hopes and dreams they had nurtured about the city. Omo had tried to get a job, but with no degree and failing health, it proved difficult in a town overflowing with migrants like them. Even the children grumbled about sitting at home, but there was no income for school. Most of the money from the land had paid for Nora's start at university—money for food, registration, and accommodation. There was always something that needed money. They both opted for cleaning positions in a neighborhood church. The meager wages kept hunger away from the door, and they were able to provide Omo's medication with the goodwill of the congregants. With this latest development in Omo's health, they were back to square one, worse than before.

Long after Omo's cries had tired the ailing woman to sleep, Uloma drew a troubled breath, her eyes downcast as she observed a lone ant scramble away from her feet on the concrete. They could ask the church for help, and they would assist them—at least, she hoped they would. They were good people, she hoped. Her mind drifted to Adesuwa; she could ask for her help. Indeed, Adesuwa would not wish her sister dead. No matter what had happened, she would not wish it on Omo. Uloma crossed her arms over her bosom, resting her chin on her chest as her heavy exhale fanned the edge of the frail bedsheet wrapped around her cousin. She frowned at the sleeping woman in thought. Omo would never agree, but things had come to a point where pride was a useless emotion. For what good were plans and dreams after death?

SEVENTEEN

"Guy, hurry up, *make we dey go,*" Boma fumed, stamping his foot as if the person at the other end of the call could see him.

Tunde assessed the flat, casually surveying the bare living room. His friend lived in a bachelor pad with two other housemates, managing a budding computer parts business as his friends cum housemates went to work. A rectangular glass dining table stood at the end of the living room and closer to the kitchen. On the other end, they sat on two leather couches borrowed from Boma's parents before a large TV placed on the floor with a PlayStation attached.

He suspected the PlayStation belonged to Boma. As far back as university, his friend had been a game addict and often skipped classes to stay in the hostel with his games. Boma's grades had suffered. Boma dropped out of school in the third year, declaring that education must be a scam and that he would open his own business. Tunde recalled with some chagrin how people called Boma a dullard behind his friend's back.

At last, his friend terminated the call with a hiss.

"Can you imagine these people?" His pimpled face folded in annoyance. "I've been waiting for them so that we can go out. Since! *Na them invite me, na me dey wait.*"

Tunde chuckled and glanced at his wristwatch. "I'm leaving soon. Stephanie's coming around two. She wants us to go for an art thing."

"*Ahan!* Stephanie, Stephanie!" Boma slapped his thighs as he howled with laughter, echoing throughout the living room. "That babe hasn't given up since undergrad!"

"It's not like that," his lips parted into a sheepish grin. "We're just friends, guy. I told you, *naw.*"

"*Abeg!*" Boma held up a hand. "Don't start that one here," he postured on the leather couch, his growing belly straining from his fitted tee shirt. "Is it me you want to lie to? I've told you to finesse that girl several times, but you're playing romance with your madam." He squinted at Tunde and laughed again. "It's all good, *sha*; I don't blame you. Better to enjoy with a madam than a secretary."

"*Haba* guy, why are you talking like this? Guy, I've told you that it's not like that. I love Karen, and I want to marry that woman."

"Because of sex?" Boma turned up his nose, his mouth arched in annoyance. "Tunde, don't start that talk today. Do your parents know this Karen, *Kedu*, or *wetin be her name? Kai,*

Tunde, you scare me when you take these things seriously. Enjoy yourself, and move on! Do you think the woman is looking for a husband? Someone who is thirty-six, she's run through already."

He crossed his arms, lifting an eyebrow. "Karen is thirty-four, not thirty-six."

"Okay, *no vex*, Jesus Christ. Savior of humanity, continue. I've told you this romance will get you in trouble one day. You're a man, Tunde! These bitches aren't loyal, guy. Wake up!"

His friend was bent on villainizing a woman he did not know, and Tunde wondered how they remained close when, where Boma was loud, he was quiet. Although they made a strange pair with a few diverging philosophies on life, his friend sometimes gave insightful advice, and he appreciated Boma's candor at those times. Tunde sighed and leaned back on the couch as the other man ranted about women's atrocities against men. Nonetheless, he was curious to know what Boma thought of his and Karen's discussion about the job promotion. His friend wound down from an overbeaten speech about women being the closest family to the snake species, and Tunde shared his thoughts.

"So," the dent in his chin became more prominent in a thoughtful frown as he drummed his stubby fingers on the leather upholstery. "What do you want to do?"

"I don't know, to be honest. I'm thinking of applying to other places. I think I've been at Wemco long enough."

Boma stayed quiet, and Tunde thought the man had not heard him until Boma clapped his hands and clicked his tongue.

"Tunde, I'm very disappointed in you. *Kai!*" he boomed. "If *to say* you weren't my friend, I'd tell you to leave my house. True!" Boma touched his tongue with the tip of a finger and raised the finger to the ceiling.

"*Ahan*, guy, why are you talking like this?"

"Tunde, look around you. These bitches ain't loyal!" Boma sneered in his most Americanized voice, jumping to his feet, his short frame stiff with anger. "Wake up, Tunde. You said you want to leave your job because of a 'woman.' Woman, *o!*" he gesticulated. "Woman!"

"I want our relationship to work, guy."

"Forget that one! Are you the first to sleep with your boss? Why do you always talk like this, guy?" Boma sighed. "I don't know why you like *wahala*. Leave the woman and focus on your career; she already has success! Don't let pussy bring you down!"

He scowled at his friend's crude statement.

"Why do you like to follow women who behave like men? She has enough; she still wants to continue taking as though she has mouths to feed at home. Women like that are stubborn and not concerned with being decent," Boma gnashed his teeth. "All this feminist nonsense women *sef*, I don't understand what this world is coming to—" His phone rang as he postulated, and he picked it up.

Tunde waited for his friend to end his phone conversation, Boma's words stinging at the back of his mind. He ground his teeth at a spurt of regret. He had believed he could sacrifice Wemco for Karen, but his mind wavered. Perhaps it was not bad not to excuse himself from being considered for the promotion; he may not get it at the end of the day.

Boma ended the call and motioned to leave, patting his pockets to ensure he had all his personal effects. "Guy," he said. "Don't let a woman dictate your life. If she loves you, she should sacrifice this promotion for you."

He stopped and admired his brash friend before they left the house, the statement resonating with him. The topic changed, which Tunde welcomed, still smarting from Boma's onslaught of words.

***

They walked to the SUV by the gated fence of Tunde's apartment building, discussing unimportant details about work as they slid into the vehicle. The shrill tone of his cell phone ended the conversation, and Tunde picked up the phone and greeted his mother.

Stephanie looked out the window, uninterested in the quiet street, as Tunde mumbled into the phone beside her. The blistering sun radiated heat on the dashboard, which evaporated in the air-conditioned vehicle. His musk cologne permeated everything around her, as though his scent had imprinted on the property like an animal would when christening an object. The scent shrouded her senses, and she struggled not to lean into him, her mind swirling into a heady daze at his nearness.

Her companion chuckled, and she glanced at him beneath her lashes. His mother's husky laughter in the background reminded her of Amaka's giggles and the sobering memory of the evening with her friends. She shifted in her seat from sudden restlessness as she pored over Tunde's phone in her mind's eye. Stephanie gritted her teeth, her heart pounding at disregarding his privacy for her selfish interests.

"Damn," Tunde muttered once the call ended. "I forgot the documents my mother asked for." He stretched behind his seat, sorting through items in the back. "I meant to go to my parents after I dropped you off."

"Do you want me to check your apartment? I can run upstairs."

He turned forward and unbuckled the safety belt. "I don't think you'd find it. Give me a minute, and I'll pick them up. I'll be quick, I promise."

He climbed out of the car, letting in a rush of hot air before shutting the door.

Stephanie watched him head down the side of the road and disappear into the premises, taking her heightened senses along with him. A kiosk stood on the other side of the road, a few feet away from where they were parked, and a mallam knelt praying on a mat toward the north. The sunshine shone a dazzling light onto the driver's seat, and a glint caught the corner of her eye.

It was his phone.

Her heart somersaulted. The car engine purred, and the blast of the air conditioner made a steady thrum. What luck, she thought; it had to be fate. She took the phone and peered toward the vertical expanse of his building. The stray beat of her heart had ramped up, pounding in her ears as she slid the screen up. Her rationale was in a state of suspension, with the fear of getting caught warring against a consuming need to find the answers to her endless questions.

The lock screen wobbled and returned to its original state. She tilted the phone forward, hoping to see thumbprints on the screen, and followed the pattern she found. The device unlocked, and Stephanie smirked. Dami's investigative skills had come in handy. Her anxiety soared as she glanced out the window to ensure Tunde remained out of sight. She went straight to his messages.

Stephanie's eyes grew wide as she gasped. Her eyes were glued to the phone screen, teleported to a world where time and space were suspended until a car driving past snapped her out of her trance. She darted her eyes up just in time to see Tunde approaching, a brown envelope in his hand, and hastily placed the phone in its original position with moist, trembling hands. Her face had heated up somewhere in time from holding pricks of unshed tears, and she flexed her jaw in furious ticks, determined not to cry with him around.

With some strength, she passed through the journey to the venue in limbo; her words spilled out of her mouth before she could speak, like water, unable to take form. Standing next to Tunde became more suffocating as the day wore on—her heart was torn to shreds, patched up, and torn again. She knew that the drastic change in her countenance perturbed him, but he grew tired of asking, and the vehicle became a tomb of silence on the way home.

At the end of the evening, when he stopped the vehicle in front of her house, Stephanie got out of the car, exhausted, surrounded by a dense fog of confusion from a riotous spectrum of emotions—anger, betrayal, and despair. She stood still, watching the car travel out of sight, her head aching from repressed feelings and her heart breaking into a million pieces.

EIGHTEEN

February 2011, Awka, Nigeria.

The visitors swallowed every word out of Bid's mouth, clinging to them like thirsty men in the desert. Omo sat beside him on the double settee, close enough to show a united front, far enough that their hands would not touch. Her head balanced on its side, cupped in a hand resting on the arm of the chair, half listening, half watching, like a stranger looking in from the outside.

They discussed the happenings in church with deliberate sighs at a congregant's misfortune, like Pharisees in their religious concern. They clamored for gossip, impatient to launch smear campaigns over another member's misfortune like vultures circling rotten meat. Her smile waned as the conversation continued, a side faltering from its pinned curve. Omo regarded Bid with a hooded gaze, her flesh prickling with his pontificating and charismatic smile churning out Bible verses and sermons, and she wondered when her husband would face retribution.

The chatter grew quiet, and Omo slid out of herself to find Adesuwa clearing the dishes at their tables. The male visitor threw Adesuwa an appreciative glance, his eyes following her movements, and she folded her lips to curb a scathing remark. Omo turned to Bid, who wore a blank expression. His eyes met hers, and an abrupt fear twisted in her gut, for she could not read what lay behind their brown depths. Omo watched Adesuwa, her heart ramming into her chest.

"Leave it," she snapped.

Eight pairs of eyes turned to her, stunned at her sudden outburst.

She cleared her throat with a forced smile at the man and two women, Bid's glower heating her side. "Leave it, I'll do that." She rose and picked up Bid's plates, exiting the sitting room to the safety of the kitchen.

Adesuwa entered the kitchen, shattering Omo's bubble of solitude, and a ripple of irritation hovered beneath her skin. She stood over the sink, staring at the dirty plates piled into a mound as high as her burden of keeping her feelings in check, exhausted from the strain of worries, regret, and malice.

"Don't ever come to the living room while we have guests," she stated at length, Adesuwa's eyes boring into her back as she washed the dishes, a chore to keep her hands busy until she was strong enough to reenter the world. "Do you hear me?" she asked after she was met with silence.

"But sister—" Adesuwa began to protest.

"Do you hear me?" Omo's voice pitched higher. She plunked the last plate in the rack and turned to the younger woman.

Adesuwa pouted, staring at her with glossy eyes. "Yes, sister."

Omo dried her hands with a napkin and ran her eyes over Adesuwa. Her sister was beautiful, with a line of pain etched between her eyebrows. Omo clenched her jaw from a slam of envy as Adesuwa stood amid the drab kitchen, holding a mirror to Omo's face. She had grown to resent Adesuwa for embodying the beauty and possibilities for a future she would never have.

"We need to get you new clothes. Your clothes are too tight."

She migrated into her daughter's bedroom, blinking at the sudden intrusion of light from the fluorescent bulb, her sister's forlorn countenance lingering in her mind. Her fair skin flushed with a shimmer of guilt as she settled on the edge of the bed in her children's room, assaulted by the stale stench of urine from Nmesoma's bedwetting.

Bid used to treat her like an angel fallen from the sky, and she was reminded of it for an obscure reason today, with the visitor staring at Adesuwa as though she were the only woman in the room. But Bid's eyes scared her for a reason she could not fathom. She grimaced as another wave of urine odor swung at her.

Omo exhaled, slouching over her knees as her back ached, yet she did not want to join Bid and the others. She felt alone, but sitting in the living room had been lonelier. Omo sat up after the spasm of pain subsided, staring at a point on the faded blue wall, peering into spiraling thoughts of her husband, of Adesuwa, of how she felt cheated and alone, of how her marriage loomed over her as though a mountain, tall and imposing before her had obstructed her path. The outside's laughter filtered through the thin walls, tightening her chest as though it jeered at her, reminding her that she could not escape them or Bid. Her husband's voice shouted for her younger sister, and Omo squeezed her eyes shut, desperate to block out the images and the sounds outside evoked.

The door swung open, and she sputtered a cough from the intrusion. Adesuwa entered the room.

"Sister, are you okay?"

"Yes." Her voice cracked, and she cleared her throat. "Yes," she stated again, unwilling to regard her sister.

A hand came on her shoulder. She flinched and slapped Adesuwa's hand away. "Why would you touch me?" She stood from the bed, her nostrils flaring with anger.

"I'm sorry," Adesuwa backed away, her eyes glittering under the fluorescent bulb. "You seemed worried, sister. I wanted to make sure you're okay."

"Mind your business!" Omo spat, glancing at her sister at the boarded hole in the wall constructed for an air conditioner. "What is it?"

"Uncle Bid asked me to call you," Adesuwa replied after a quivering breath.

Omo nodded, turning to Adesuwa. A rush of malice swept over her, and she peered into the mirror that was Adesuwa, propelling her to share at least a fraction of her pain.

"I don't want you leaving the room or kitchen when my husband is around," she sneered. Her robust frame appeared menacing as she lifted her chin, casting a shadow underneath.

Adesuwa's lower lip quivered. "Sister, did I offend you?"

"You don't know how much I—" Omo took a sharp breath and walked to the door. "I don't think you know how you'd ever get it."

"Sister—"

"I mean it. I'll oversee everything once Papa Nora gets home. Go to church and focus on your studies. That's why you are here. I saw how that man in the living room leered at you." She continued, shoving an image of Bid's expression aside, her voice shaking in trepidation. "You might as well have been naked! What's all the church for if you're jumping around and misbehaving? You're a lady; act like one!"

***

Present Day, 2024, Lagos, Nigeria.

The deserted swimming pool appeared darker turquoise under pale clouds, and the serene and clear water reflected a dreary image to her as she sat on the pool's edge with her feet submerged. The water lapped over her skin, stroking her calves in soothing waves.

Karen leaned back on her hands, her face heavenward as she closed her eyes, letting go of the stress from previous weeks into the water. Her nightmares had become a black sea of sinister voices that she attributed to exertion from the impending promotion and the search for new investors. On bad days, the shame she feared at night mutated into her waking hours, its weight almost crushing her lungs so that she struggled for air. She had been surprised when Majekodunmi's approving pat on her shoulder and the chorus of praise he relayed from the board did nothing to ease her anxiety.

The most coveted position had become paltry, and Karen wondered if her mother's death had taken something from her.

The hunger for success, her fierce need to come out on top, had been replaced by lonesome nostalgia for her childhood, the days when sisters sat under the mango tree, trading stories and eating roasted ube—Omo, whom she shut out of her life. Karen opened her eyes to a helicopter flying overhead. She watched the blades cut through the sky, hauling the rest of the aircraft out of sight, her lips curled in a wistful smile. She sniffed, staring at the water as though her feelings had spilled into the pool.

Her arms wobbled as they supported her weight, and she hauled her sluggish frame out of the pool. She stifled a yawn, beads of water plopping onto the floor as the pool swished from calm. A few minutes later, too sluggish to go home, Karen lay on a damp sun bed under a towel, welcoming a lull of sleep. She shuddered awake from the piercing ring of her cell phone. She groaned, reaching for the device, and Uloma's name appeared.

"Hello?" Her eyelids sagged, burdened with sleep.

"Sister, good evening. How are you?"

A young couple entered with a girl, and the girl jumped into the pool's shallow end.

"I'm fine."

"Were you sleeping? Your voice—"

"No, no," she cleared her throat and sat up, staring at the couple watching the girl from a sunbed near the pool. "I'm fine."

"Sister, we need help. It's Sister Omo. Her diabetes has gotten worse. She needs surgery."

Karen's heart slammed in her chest.

"Sister? Did you hear me? I said Aunty Omo has gallstones."

"I heard," Karen's eyes dropped to a bead of water on her black swimsuit.

"We need money. I wouldn't call you if it weren't urgent," Uloma burst into tears. "The hospital wants nine hundred thousand. We've been begging, but they only removed forty thousand. Where will we see that kind of money?"

Karen observed the empty sky ahead, her mind bare yet calming, a sizzle of anguish rising.

"Hello?"

"Uloma, I don't know what to say. You know I've removed myself from anything that concerns that family."

"What do you mean by you have removed yourself? Ehn, Adesuwa?" her cousin barked. "We're talking about life and death. Even if you're angry, you can't turn your back on your sibling, for God's sake, sister." Uloma's voice rose to a screech. "If she dies, who will care for Nora and her sisters? Is it me? There's only so much I can do! We've begged everywhere, even Uncle Donatus, but he will never have money in this life."

Karen placed her head between her knees, the phone still propped by one hand against her ear. Her head throbbed. "I can't," her voice shook as her forehead creased with unease. "I can't," Karen repeated, a tear plopping on her thigh, then turning into waterworks. She wiped her eyes, taking a long breath to calm herself.

"They said Lagos changed you! So they were right? Adesuwa, they were right!"

Karen pressed her wet eyes together, shutting out the image of her sister, of Mama at Uloma's words. Those words had taken root on a day when her mind and body were too exhausted to hold up her defenses, and she crumpled into tears.

"Will you fold your hands and watch your sister die?" Uloma continued. "*Ehn?*"

Uloma's gasp echoed through the call, and she sputtered apologies, surprised at Karen's intense reaction to her scolding.

"It's fine," she snuffled, wiping her nose with her free hand. "I must go now."

"Adesuwa. Adesuwa, you weren't like this before. Remember, you weren't like this before."

"Don't call me that," she uttered with a waver, ending the call with fresh tears. Her skin prickled as a calm wind wrapped around her. She curled into a fetal position, uncaring of the attention she might have drawn from the couple.

NINETEEN

May 2011, Awka, Nigeria.

Adesuwa sat with her friends in the corner of the crowded library, books splayed on the graffiti-covered table as they studied for the finals. She sighed for the third time within an hour, her thoughts entrenched in her strained relationship with her sister.

Omo became colder as the weeks rolled by, and Adesuwa suspected that Uncle Bid was the source of Omo's unhappiness or the strain of caring for her daughters. It was baffling because Uncle Bid appeared to be a good man and a respectable pastor in the church. She knew they often argued, but Mama once mentioned that Omo was stubborn. Adesuwa frowned at her book, the words dancing away from the pages as she slipped further into her thoughts. She and Omo were never very close, as they had a significant age gap, but their relationship had never deteriorated to this stage.

Adesuwa sighed and snapped her books shut. She signaled to her friends that she was leaving and left the library. The sun hid behind white clouds, which cooled the radiating heat from the orange blur of fire; she squinted, adjusting to the shift in brightness from the fluorescent-lit library to the light outside. She strode down the street, wrapped in a world of her own making, until a familiar voice broke into her thoughts. Adesuwa turned at the sound of her name, her face parting into a smile as Segun approached.

"Adesuwa." He doubled over, his face contorting into lines of laughter as he wheezed.

"Segun," Adesuwa's eyes twinkled, her heart tingling at his nearness as he straightened. "Were you also reading in the library?"

"Yes, yes. Where're you heading to?"

"I'm walking back to staff quarters."

"Do you mind if I escort you?"

"No, please do," She responded in haste, flushing at how enthusiastic she may have come across.

They fell into stride along the side of the road in companionable silence, avoiding vehicles and pedestrians. Wedged on the sidewalk between passersby and a shallow gutter, her mind tangled in loops with each step beside the tall man.

"How have you been?"

"I'm good," She answered. "I've been busy with my thesis and exams. Are you done with yours?"

"Yeah," his arm brushed against hers, "I've been busy with the student union, but I can help you with yours."

"Shouldn't you have finished the handover by now?"

They stopped under a tree at the junction of her street.

"Did you think about that thing we discussed?"

His eyes bored into hers, and her face heated in a low flush as she bent her head.

"Segun, you know how things are at home. I don't know if a relationship now is a good idea."

"You're a big girl now." He kicked a pebble in the sand beneath his feet. "Your family is ready to welcome someone for your hand."

Segun's face broke into a lopsided grin. A breeze ruffled around them, carrying the scent of his cologne. She smiled at him, oblivious to the world around them.

"Let me think about it some more, hmm?"

She flinched as he leaned in to tuck a stray strand of hair behind her ear, her skin tingling with awareness. She tucked in the beginning of a smile, glancing at the unsuspecting pedestrians across the road.

"You know how much I like you."

A car zoomed past them, and Segun peered ahead of her with a start. "I think your uncle's car just passed!"

"My uncle?" Adesuwa's eyes widened, and she stepped away from him. "He comes home at this time," she replied in a small voice. "I should hurry home."

Segun nodded. "Let me walk you."

"There's no need!" She interjected. "It's a few houses away now." In her fluster, she turned toward her street. "I'll be fine."

"No problem." He gave her a tight smile. "Can I text you to make sure you're home safe?"

She nodded. Her eyes lit with pleasure, and her uncle was forgotten at the sight of Segun's smile. She heard him chuckle as she scurried away.

***

Bid was seething with anger. He opened the car door, intending to leave, but anger pressed against him like an anchor, and he slammed the door shut. Adesuwa appeared ahead, hurrying toward the building; she slowed and peered toward the vehicle before continuing.

His knuckles whitened from clenching the steering wheel, and he let go, his breathing steadying to its normal rhythm. A picture of the two at the junction replayed in his mind, and he breathed. Was Adesuwa so clueless about her effect on males? Her innocence was charming, but it had transformed into a source of annoyance, like a rose with thorns. He got out of the vehicle with more haste than needed and stalked toward his sister-in-law until he caught up with her as she climbed the stairs leading to the flat.

Her movements were tense as his presence hovered a few steps behind. Bid made no move to call her. His eyes followed the sway of her hips, and he felt himself stir in contrast to the anger that had driven him to run after her. Their footsteps pattered on the concrete as the woman's unease drifted toward him like perfume. He berated himself for lashing out at her the last time they were alone; it was not her fault that she did not know the wiles of men.

He loitered at the foot of the last flight of stairs, giving her headway to go out of sight, cursing himself for being aggressive with her, for Adesuwa was a delicate flower that blossomed under care. She had grown into the most beautiful woman he had ever met in recent years, reducing him to a humbling mess. Her sister's beauty paled beside hers, filling him with regret that he had not waited for Adesuwa since they met when she was a teenager. But one thing was sure, Bid decided: he was tired of fantasizing.

***

A week had passed before she found herself alone with Uncle Bid. The air around them was dense with strain, and the thought of being alone with him made her squeamish. After church, she headed to the car with the children, navigating the sea of congregants swarming out of the chapel.

When she arrived with the children, Uncle Bid was chatting with a few people standing by the driver's side. Her heart plummeted as the passenger's seat beside him sat empty. She ushered the children into the backseats and hesitated, tempted to squeeze in with them, but the people who had taken her brother-in-law's attention waved them goodbye, and she found herself in the front.

Adesuwa shuddered at the dread spreading like ice within her; in disarray, she picked at the cuticle beside her nail, fixing her gaze outside as they traipsed through traffic. Guilt, like a lump of coal, sank in her stomach, and she felt these foreign emotions toward Uncle Bid.

"How was the service?" Uncle Bid asked after the children's squeals subsided.

"It was good, Daddy," Nora revealed her gapped teeth with a grin.

"That is good," Uncle Bid nodded as he moved the car. "What did you learn?" He glanced at the girl through the rearview mirror.

"We learned not to steal or tell lies!" Chidiogo chirped before her older sister could speak.

"Yes, Daddy, and they shared Fanta!" Nora piped up. "And Mummy took Nmesoma because she was crying."

The children giggled and jumped into another conversation between themselves. Adesuwa, half-listening, felt a nudge on her arm. She turned to see Uncle Bid staring at her as the car stood in traffic.

"I asked how church went," he smiled. His bottom lip jutted forward, making his lips appear to dominate his face.

Her eyes remained fixed outside the window. A plantain hawker walked away from a car in front, pocketing money from a sale.

"It went well, Uncle," she mumbled.

"So," Uncle Bid sighed, "can you tell me why you've been acting strange? Did you fight with Omo?"

She studied the clasped hands on her lap, unsure of what her sister had said to him.

"You can tell me."

Adesuwa glanced at him as he gave her a half smile, his plump bottom lip appearing wider, and she averted her eyes, taking a deep breath. "No problem, Uncle. I've been busy with finals, and Sister is always angry." She gave him a plastic smile.

Uncle Bid glanced at his sister-in-law, noting the change in her disposition toward him that was evident in her answer. However, he told her he understood.

Adesuwa released a jagged breath as she battled the urge to run out of the vehicle. As the car inched toward their street, they passed the junction where she had been with Segun. Her shoulders sagged as warmth flooded her mind, dislodging the tension she had carried into the car.

She was young, and her youth betrayed her, exposing her sentimental expression to Uncle Bid. He frowned, clenching his jaw as he parked the car in front of their home. She ran out of the car, oblivious to the change in his demeanor, but neither noticed the woman watching from the veranda.

TWENTY

Present Day, 2024, Lagos, Nigeria.

Stephanie avoided Tunde, nursing her heartache and rising apprehension as she saw him and Karen in the office. He had caught on faster than she had imagined, frowning each time she declined his invitations to meet outside work. Her words had not yet formed; she had nothing to say. The love she carried for him persisted, but it was laced with a grudge from watching them interact. She had told her friends, who rallied around her in pity, but it still hurt, and their pitying glances exacerbated her bruised pride.

Stephanie exhaled as she drove into the Lekki Phase One estate's gates toward Tunde's house. Light showers spluttered on the car, and she turned on the wipers as the world ahead appeared watery. She tightened her grip on the wheels, her brows arched together, as her heart sank to her stomach in anguish.

The bits of courage she had gathered threatened to scatter around her as she arrived at his apartment complex. She parked outside, listening to the engine wind down as she allowed the brief purring to give her respite. Stephanie reviewed her convictions, placing a hand on her chest to strengthen her confidence. Tunde could not be a willing participant; he could not be with Karen of his own free will. The woman had turned thirty-four earlier in the year, six years older than him and his boss. Karen had taken advantage of her position and lured him into an affair with her.

Yes, those were plausible explanations, she thought, heading into the building with purposeful strides. She would not let this happen; the office had strict policies against sexual harassment. It would wreck Tunde's career if the word got out.

Tunde opened the door at the third knock with a look of surprise. "Stephanie." He stepped aside and closed the door after she entered.

Stephanie walked into the furnished living room, rubbing clammy palms on her jeans and swallowing her fear, which had risen in crippling anxiety. They stood facing each other—he in slacks and a large T-shirt—and her chest tightened as tears formed in her eyes. She watched him stroll to the TV and turn it off, and the tears she had held back the last time they met fell in seconds. He had been lounging while she suffered in an emotional mess, and Stephanie was filled with malice.

Tunde put his hands in his pockets, wearing a grim mask. "Stephanie, what's wrong?" he frowned at her. "You didn't inform me that you'd be coming."

Stephanie walked to the large windows, turning halfway from him as she wrapped her arms around her waist. Her eyes rested on the parking lot that separated his block from the others.

"What's wrong? You've been acting strange for a while."

She took time to gather her strength.

"Stephanie."

"What's going on between you and Karen?"

"What?"

"What's going on with you both?" Her voice rose as she swung around in time to see the shock register on his face. "Tunde, what's going on between you and Karen?"

"Steph—" He started toward her and stopped.

"I know you're having an affair, Tunde." Her voice quivered, and she tapped her foot, riding through a fresh wave of pain that flooded over her. "Don't bother denying it."

"An affair?" He scoffed, clenching his fists to his sides. "I wasn't going to deny anything. How did you find out?" He followed her eyes as she glanced at his phone on an ottoman, his eyes widening as understanding dawned on him. "Oh!" he thundered. "Did you check my phone? You checked my phone the day we went to the art event, right? How dare you, Stephanie?"

Stephanie gulped, glaring at Tunde's hardened posture.

"You had no right," he growled.

"I admit I did, and I'm sorry, but don't you see that you have a bigger issue here?" she countered. "Do you know what this could mean for her, for you both, if people found out, or are you doing all this because of the promotion?"

"And are you going to be the one to tell them?" he sneered. "You checked my phone, Stephanie. You had no right, no bloody right."

"I'm your friend, Tunde; I was worried about you! Tell me it's because of the promotion!" she rushed to grab his hands. "Tell me it's because of the promotion, say it, and I'll forgive you!" She pressed his knuckles to her lips, her eyes wide in a silent plea. "Your affair with Karen cannot continue, please!"

"No, no, no." Tunde yanked his hands out of her grasp, the force knocking her off balance so that she held onto a nearby table. "How dare you? What do you mean by forgive? You have nothing to do with this!"

His chest heaved as he paced by the entrance door.

Stephanie rushed on, her face flushed and wet with snot running from her nose. "You think I didn't notice how you peeked at each other when you thought no one was watching?" She threw her hands in the air. "Anyone with half a brain would figure it out if they paid attention." Stephanie paused, taken aback by the contempt in his eyes. "I know you are angry,

Tunde," she trembled. "That woman is manipulating you. She's what? Six years older than you? Do you think people would give you a pat on the back for this?"

"I love her," he hit his chest with a hand. "I love her, and that's none of your business."

She gasped, her heart breaking again at those words she longed to hear were ascribed to Karen.

"I love her," he repeated in a hoarse tone. "I'd leave the company tomorrow to save Karen from any scandals. I'll gladly do it. That's how much she means to me."

"Tunde," Stephanie cried, inching forward toward him. "You're confused; you don't know what you're saying." She cleared the catch in her throat, her forehead crinkling into grooves. "You have your life ahead of you; why would you want to taint your image for someone like her? Have you thought of what your parents would say?"

She walked away, shaking her head. "Do you have any idea what they say about her?" Her eyes glistened with fresh tears. "Do you think you're the only man in her life, and what? You're the one for her?"

Tunde's jaw ticked with anger.

"It's not her first rodeo mixing business with pleasure, you know? And this won't be her last," she sniffed. "I'll be damned if I watch you throw your life away. I won't stand by and watch you put yourself in a situation far above your head. Tunde, you're young; you deserve someone better; you deserve someone more your age, someone who's loving, who's not an ice queen!"

"Like you?"

Her mind rattled from the pang of pain and embarrassment his snide remark evoked, and she choked back a fresh batch of tears, determined to protect her salvaged pride. "Yes, is it a crime that I've always cared for you? Tunde, you can hate me all you want," she rasped, pointing at him. "But that wasn't fair to mock my feelings for you. You led me along, even while you were with her. I should have realized it sooner."

"I did no such thing!" he threw back at her. "I made my stance with you clear from the first day, and I've never gone past that. I'm sorry if you got the wrong impression, but I never gave you hope of anything else happening between us."

Stephanie snickered, crossing her arms to stop herself from sobbing. "You're right. I did it all to myself, but say what you will. This thing between you and that woman must stop. I won't let you throw your life away like this."

Tunde exhaled, gripping the edge of the sofa beside him. He closed his eyes, massaging his temples. "Stephanie, you should leave if you can't get it through your head that you can't police my life."

"I won't let you throw your life away!" she screeched, standing at the door to the apartment, unwilling to leave without a resolution. "You might hate me now, Tunde, but you know I'm right," she implored as the fight drained out of her.

"I can't," he retreated further into the living room with a scowl. "I love Karen."

Tunde's words landed the final blow, and Stephanie closed her eyes as they pierced her heart like daggers. She walked out of the apartment in sorrow, knowing that it would be the last time she would be there.

TWENTY-ONE

Uloma burst into the quiet flat with news from the church. The girls were on their way back from school, thanks to the church's sponsorship of enrolling the children in a public school, which would provide some relief if sister Omo's health issues did not loom over the household. A grim atmosphere had settled over the flat, seeping into everything—in the bedrooms, kitchen, and bathroom—hanging over her, Omo, and the children like a wet blanket.

She entered the kitchen, puffing from her arduous journey up flights of stairs to the second floor where they lived. The kitchen was empty and smelled of food, as though the vapor from cooking had permeated the walls. She lit a lantern, the flame turning the dark kitchen into an orange hue. Uloma strode out of the kitchen, carrying the lantern to sister Omo's bedroom. She knocked and entered at the muffled answer from the room.

Omo heaved her aching body to an upright position on the bed as Uloma entered. "Uloma, welcome."

"Thank you. Good evening, sister."

"How was work? I managed to cook some rice and stew for you and the children."

"Thank you," Uloma said, placing the lantern on the wooden table by the door. Then she sat at the foot of the bed, away from the shards of sunset on the tattered Formica wardrobe. "I have news from the church."

Omo grunted, plagued by the disillusion she harbored toward religion since Bid left a decade ago. She bit her tongue as a disparaging remark bubbled up her throat, swayed by Uloma's face brightening up in excitement. After all, she had clung to a church for many years until the satisfaction from fellowshipping withered at Bid's betrayal.

"Yes, sister. The vicar said they'd raise another twenty thousand. It's not much, but it's a start." She grinned, "And he sends his prayers."

"I suppose I should be grateful," Omo replied, caught between gratitude and disillusionment.

"Yes, sister." Uloma's hand sank into the mattress as she rested her weight on it. "It's not easy for strangers to cough up money for people who have just started working. At least we know things are getting settled."

"Until when? We're delaying the inevitable. I still need eight-forty thousand for the surgery; we need to eat. Nmesoma and Chidiogo need textbooks and clothes."

"Sister!" she harrumphed. "Anyway, I spoke to Adesuwa," Uloma muttered, glaring at a basket of clothes on the floor beside the wardrobe.

The air seemed to freeze in the cramped room, and Uloma's skin prickled under Omo's shriveling look.

"Why?" Omo seethed with a quaking voice. "Why would you do that?"

"Sister!" Uloma jumped to her feet. "We don't have any other options! Where will we find the money? It's been over a month, and the medication is expensive. You listed the things we need money for. Well, this is the solution." She opened her palms, eyes glinting from the reflection of the dying sun.

"Somehow, we'll figure things out as we've always done without her help," she countered, her lips puckered as she ground her teeth. She folded her arms.

"Not after we pay for the treatment, medication, school fees, and feeding from the ten thousand I'm making as a cleaner?" Uloma retorted, her chest rising and falling with anger. "This thing must stop. It's enough. I'm tired, sister Omo. What happened? What did you do?"

Omo's jaw dropped. "What do you mean by *what I did*?" A sharp pain seared through her, and she winced, unsure of whether it emanated from her ailment or the abrupt hammering in her chest. "Uloma!" Omo chided.

Uloma glowered at the blue wall before her, her hands on her hips. She locked her gaze with Omo's and sighed, her shoulders dropping. "I heard your discussion with Uncle Donatus after the burial," she said as she sat on the bed.

Uloma leaned forward and studied her with keen eyes.

"Sister Omo, please tell me what happened. This has gone on long enough. You know I'm right, and I can't take this suffering anymore."

Omo let out a deep breath, drifting to the past for the umpteenth time since her visit to the hospital. "What did you hear, Uloma?" Her voice grew so small that it sounded unnatural to a large woman like herself.

"Sister, it's not about what I heard. Whatever secret you are hiding is eating you both alive. You know that whatever you hide in the dark is exposed later. There's nothing new under the sun," she gestured upward. "We need Adesuwa's support, now more than ever, whether it's acceptable or not. You can't be in this condition when your sister is a few kilometers away. It's enough, *biko*."

Omo stared at the younger woman, but she could not see beyond what had happened that terrible day a decade ago, the day the end began. Omo cleared the phlegm in her throat, her heart on a steady rise, victorious in quenching a violent urge to scream, thrash about, and give way for her frustrations to manifest. The truth loitered in her mouth, yet she was unprepared to divulge the virulent tale after all these years. Uloma would never understand—no one would.

Omo clutched her stomach as it turned, bending over to brave the unease. People would gnash their teeth and steer clear of them as though misfortune were contagious. The devouring human desire to protect herself, innate and as old as time, availed, and her antipathy toward wagging tongues won over conscience. She turned to face the wall, squeezing her eyes shut, ignoring Uloma's frantic calls. Her memories jeered at her; they were painful—the betrayal and loss of a life that could have been, knowing that things would never be the same.

The door slammed shut at last, indicating Uloma had left after what seemed to be a while. Was it all her fault? Omo thought. Was she that unattractive, or was she too stubborn, refusing to be intimate with him after the second time he gave her gonorrhea? Their union had suffocated her, but Omo had done what she had to do for the sake of her children. She did not know where her fault began and ended, but amid her malice toward Adesuwa, she knew she had not protected her sister well enough.

Adesuwa—Adesuwa did not come from their mother, but Mama loved the girl more than her daughter, Omo, who had Mama's blood in her veins.

The lines of Omo's face deformed into irregular contours in the depth of her reminiscing, barring the vindictive side of her that held some contentment when Adesuwa had been sullied—a wicked yet satisfying emotion. In those days, she blamed her vindictiveness on Adesuwa's transgression, but time, a resource that brought forth wisdom, revealed that her grievance with Adesuwa began when they were younger.

Perhaps Adesuwa bore her penance wherever she was, but Omo knew the time would come when submerged things would resurface. She grieved for her mother, but it comforted her that Mama did not live to see it unfold.

She wheezed as she hoisted her heavy frame out of bed, resting against the wall to peer into the blue blanket of the night. Roaring generators rumbled from various buildings, and she flinched at the first whiff of smoke from their exhausts, choking her as life had. Her life felt unfair; life felt too cruel. Her anger at the carefree life Adesuwa lived—the life she had helped create so her sister would have better opportunities— and the trace of resentment she had surrounding Adesuwa's birth, not recognized until adulthood, had hardened into hatred over the decade. Indeed, Uloma's determination to ask Adesuwa for money while her own life remained in an endless loop of hardship was the final straw for Omo.

***

June 2011, Awka, Nigeria.

The mother's guild meeting lasted longer than Omo would have liked, and her strained smile faltered among the chattering women. She had become an expert in lying and pretending. Watching her husband preach, enduring his pontifications and indignation at evildoers while she sat staring at him across the podium in disappointment as he strengthened her reservations about their religion. Who would want this religion, seeing all this, seeing all she endured? Omo studied the women in their colorful George wrappers and the scarves on their heads. She went through the motions, laughing when they laughed, clapping when they clapped, and nodding when expected—her visage blank, masking the pain behind her eyes. Her face had grown tired of smiling and pretending; she had grown weary of it.

Omo grew more impatient as the meeting neared its end; the cream walls of the church had become suffocating. She was the first to leave after the meeting, standing at the bus stop within ten minutes. A few women greeted her, and Omo raised a hand in greeting, her face set in a frown under the punishing sun. A *danfo* arrived, a yellow bus with black horizontal stripes, and she got in, flanked by two women at the bus stop. The *danfo* bounced along the untarred road, jostling the passengers around each row of five people. She was pressed on each side to make space for the fifth grumbling passenger in their row, tucking one foot behind the other. The ride was solemn—except for the occasional shouts from passengers who wanted to alight and the conductor's routine cries at bus stops for new passengers—perhaps due to the stench of crayfish from a trader who had entered with her produce basket, lamenting to the conductor hanging on the door of the moving bus, about the lack of space at the rear end.

Bid had called her uncle and aunt, and she was going to their house after church to listen to their scolding and more praises of her husband. Then she would go home and lie flat on the bed until he plunged his seed into her, grunting and groping.

The two women from the bus stop chatted over her head. Omo shifted forward, irritated, and ended their conversation. Their glares bounced off her back as she fixated on the clay earth beneath the rust-perforated floor of the *danfo*.

Omo exhaled. Life was tiring, and she was tired. Her mother depended on her for emotional support after her father died, adding to her helping at the little shop and taking care of her sister, a toddler at the time. The force of her mother's dependence increased over time and extended to financial support. It turned suffocating, like a brick resting on her shoulders, yet her sister never had to take responsibility for anything. Constantly praised and pampered, Adesuwa never lacked anything, though they had to scrape what little profits they made to save for something Adesuwa wanted.

They merged on a highway, and the wind howled through the windows. Omo rested her chin on her chest, drawn into a reverie as the road blurred into a hypnotic streak.

A tight fist crushed her heart, and she sighed. She had always thought she seemed so pale and pitiful beside Adesuwa. But what did Adesuwa know about suffering? They shielded Adesuwa from the harsh realities of life. It had always been that way.

On the other hand, in recent years, Omo had to admit that she married to escape the poverty looming over her family. Looking back, she fancied herself in love at the time; it became clear she had made a rash decision. Now, drowning, Omo had no one to help. A piercing shard of loneliness sliced through her, and she tucked her lips inside, extending another breath. No one asked her how she felt; it came with her position as the first child. There was an excruciating acceptance that she must be willing to accede to the expectations of others, and she was unraveling under the burden of her birthright.

The *danfo* pulled up at her designated stop, and the people in her row got down to make room for her to leave. She pushed through the narrow space, panting as she stepped out of the vehicle. Her face heated up in embarrassment as she glanced at the four disgruntled faces under the sun. Now, battling with guilt that she had failed herself, she walked away.

TWENTY-TWO

Present Day, 2024, Lagos, Nigeria.

Karen's eyes darted across the sea of heads in the conference room. Her brows creased together as she twisted the plain ring around her finger under the table. Majekodunmi was not here. He had promised he would be here. She swallowed her disappointment but held on to a flicker of hope that he would show up. Mrs. Ogunbiyi sat beside her—a lanky woman with permanent frown lines around her mouth—their conversation had tapered off after a few pleasantries.

The rain poured outside as gray clouds spat up water from the blue yonder, and the patter of water wetting the earth droned beneath the chatter in the room. Karen cleared her throat, thinking of Rita's surprise when she had asked her assistant to schedule an appointment at the doctor's next week. Her skin prickled from Tunde's gaze burrowing through her clothes, but she forced her eyes to her notepad rather than meet his questioning glances. She had blown him off for two weeks, battling with deteriorating health and the news about her sister.

The news twisted her dreams more; some nights, she would wake up in cold sweats, rushing to vomit in the toilet.

The room fell quiet when a loud cough rang across the table, and the occupants' faces wore different masks under the harsh beam of white, fluorescent lights—brows dipped in concentration, glinting eyes behind pursed lips hiding a buzz of excitement, poker faces contrasting with shifting feet beneath the table. A preamble of recent developments across the organization ensued, the updates dragging on and magnifying the tension in the office. The human resources director, Mr. Francis, came to deliver the news, and there was a collective sigh of relief in the office, as though the taut rope that bound everyone together had been pulled free.

"Good afternoon, everyone. I'm sure we're all ready for the big event." Mr. Francis's chuckle transformed into a sputter after meeting an audience of unimpressed faces. "Right, Mr. Majekodunmi and the CEO would have loved to be here, but they have another meeting. However, they send their congratulations."

Karen's heart plummeted. She swallowed the niggle of apprehension forming in her throat. She had a stellar record; she did everything right—Karen thought—she had always been promoted, and Majekodunmi said the board was impressed with her performance on their last project.

The staff sat taut with bated breath as Mr. Francis continued at the top of his voice, "We, upper management and HR, want to congratulate Mr. Tunde Awoniyi on his promotion to the official head of regional operations in Western Nigeria!"

Thunderous applause rang across the table, drowning the rain outside as a timid Tunde got on his feet, his head bent under the weight of others' congratulations. Karen's heart pounded, and she gasped for air, her eyes wide in shock as they swarmed around Tunde like flies, slapping his shoulders and shaking his hands. Mrs. Ogunbiyi hesitated, unable to meet her eyes as she muttered a stilted "sorry" before joining the festivities. She met Tunde's pleading eyes across the table before leaving the conference room. Karen did not congratulate him.

She staggered to her office. The pounding in her chest became more excruciating as a new reality dawned on her that impaled the shock of losing the promotion. The rain drummed harder outside, and a bleakness settled over her office; her trophies that gleamed in the sun became shadowed effigies of mockery. She held her head as her mind reeled in disarray. The nagging feeling of what could be wrong with her became transparent as a wall partitioned the truth. She was pregnant. There could be no other explanation for the changes happening in her body.

Karen laughed, an unnatural shrill from a woman who had been put together moments before. She slammed her body against the wall, trying to control her rasping breath through an aching chest. Her sweaty hands wrapped around her stomach, and tears streamed down her face.

The door opened wide, and Tunde rushed in, but Karen paid no attention, her eyes blinded by tears.

"Karen." He gasped at her hysterical state. "Karen, talk to me! What's happening? I've been calling your name since you walked out."

She squeezed her arms tighter on her stomach as her breathing slowed to gasps.

"Karen. Answer me, dammit!" Tunde slammed his hand on her table. The items on the table rattled, and a pen rolled to the floor with a clink. "Is it because of the promotion? Is that why you're like this?" He ran over her appearance with frenzied eyes.

She winced and sniffled. "Oh, Tunde," she choked.

"I'm sorry, okay? I didn't know. I swear I didn't know until a few days ago, and I didn't know how to tell you!" he sputtered. "I …"

Karen drew herself up, her eyelids rimmed red, as she stumbled to the other side of the desk. She pulled out a face tissue from the box on her desk and dabbed at her face. "Now is not the time, Tunde," she replied in a hoarse voice, giving him an impassive look.

"Karen."

"What is it you want me to say?" She snarled. "Tunde, congratulations. Now leave me alone; I need to think."

"Karen, stop."

"Tunde, please leave!" She stormed across the office, yanking the door wider, unperturbed by Rita, who hovered outside.

Tunde hesitated. His eyes gleamed from a stroke of lightning outside as his mouth curled downward.

She turned her face away, her grip on the doorknob slacking as the burst of negative energy dispelled into agony.

"We're not finished." He walked out of her office.

Karen slammed the door.

TWENTY-THREE

July 2011, Awka, Nigeria.

Trigger Warning: Sexual Assault

The children were asleep in their bedroom, and the house settled into peace. Adesuwa dragged her exhausted body along, a big yawn escaping her. She bathed from the pail of water she had fetched from a communal well downstairs. Welcoming the rare silence, she changed into her cotton nightgown, shrouded by a sense of serenity in being alone, bar the children. Their parents left for a church night vigil the night before that would last until five a.m., giving her enough time to relax from her older sister's suffocating presence in the house, and Uncle Bid, although kind, gave her an uncomfortable feeling over the past months that caused her to become more aware of him.

Adesuwa walked around the modest living room, inspecting the appliances to ensure the sockets were turned off. Chidiogo often forgot to do so, as her mind ran in many directions, fleeting and jumbled together like any child's—earning a whooping from Uncle Bid as he gave her a stern lecture on electricity bills. *The electricity bill*, Adesuwa scoffed in amusement, checking a socket behind the old television set. Electricity was unreliable in the professors' quarters. They had to re-boil the meat stored in the old white deep freezer until it tasted bland. The freezer had become furniture for sitting, as the children sometimes did. Its white plastic coating chipped off in various corners, revealing rusting metal underneath.

The clock showed almost midnight before she entered her room, which doubled as a storage space for tubers of yam, bags of staple foods, and items from Omo's shop—stacked high up a corner and blocking half the small window.

She must have dozed off because she opened her eyes to the sound of movement outside her door. Adesuwa dragged herself off the mattress with great difficulty and opened the door, expecting to see Nmesoma, who sometimes wet herself. She stifled a gasp of surprise when Uncle Bid stood by the entrance to the kitchen, muttering to himself a few feet from her room. Adesuwa closed the door quietly and lay on the mattress, spreading the Ankara print wrapper over herself, drifting into tendrils of sleep.

A knock rapped on the door.

"You're still up?" Uncle Bid's words were muffled outside the room.

Adesuwa sat up, her eyes laden with sleep. She tied the wrapper across her chest and left the room. She greeted Uncle Bid in the living room, squinting as her eyes adjusted to the beam from a rechargeable lamp in his hand.

The living room stayed reticent for a moment. Adesuwa scratched lightly at her thigh, suppressing the temptation to return to bed.

"Prepare some tea and bread with butter for me," he instructed with his voice an octave lower so as not to wake the children. His brows knit together. "Bring them to my room. I need to return to church before they notice I'm gone."

"What of the night vigil, Uncle?"

"*Ehen*, what about it?" Uncle Bid frowned. "I'll go back later. I have a stomachache, so I came to rest a little." He put a hand on his stomach.

"Sorry, Uncle. I'll bring some medicine," she sympathized, heading to the kitchen.

"Thank you," he turned toward his room. "Omo is in the women's wing for their vigil; I still have to pick her up so we can come back together."

Adesuwa found the medicine and felt her way through the kitchen with a sliver of moonlight peering through the narrow window. She walked to the master bedroom, holding the tray in both hands.

"Uncle, I'm coming inside," she knocked, balancing the tray on one hand.

A gruff response filtered through the door, and it opened with Uncle Bid standing behind the wooden frame.

"Put the tray on the stool beside the bed." Uncle Bid closed the door. "And arrange those clothes beside the stool. Push them back into the bag behind it."

She glanced in her brother-in-law's direction as he melted into the darker half of the room, pushing down her irritation.

"Hurry up," Uncle Bid hissed.

She scowled at the clothes piled on the side of the bed as she tended to her task. It did not occur to her that something had changed, that an oppressive stillness had settled in the room. Her sister's husband wore a different, unfamiliar mask. This was not the mask that smiled at her or the mask that preached on the pulpit in the church. The man who crept behind her wore the mask of the devil, poised to pounce, his 214 pounds of weight waiting.

It happened in a split second. That was all it took. The impact of Uncle Bid's weight landing on Adesuwa left her dazed on the unmade bed. Terror sprang from her throat like scalding hot water at his face from above her, veins throbbing on the sides of his neck.

"Uncle Bid! What are you doing?"

"Shh!" Uncle Bid pressed his hand over her mouth. "Be quiet," he pinned her with the bottom half of his heavy frame, and his arms went on either side of her head.

Her eyes grew to bulging disks in their sockets as his intent dawned on her. She thrashed about and wept. She bit down hard on his palm, her teeth stinging from the deep immersion as she tasted the salt on his skin.

He struck her stomach, the force knocking her out of breath, then another one—blows that seemed they would never end— as he avoided her face, careful not to leave bruises.

Adesuwa struggled, her heart thrumming to dangerous levels as she yelled at the top of her lungs for help.

The devil stuffed a sheet into her mouth, muffling her pleas in the cloth until she choked and sputtered for breath in the limp fabric drenched in her saliva.

How could he do this? How could he do this on a bed he shared with her sister?

She squirmed, charged with a flare of adrenaline, begging the minute a hand found her thighs and forced them apart. She closed her eyes, too distraught to see Uncle Bid's expression above her, to see what he did. She heard him moan from far away; his touch on her skin was cold and damp, as though separate from the places he had not groped. Adesuwa wept when the searing pain came, stealing her innocence and taking her with it. She fainted.

***

He touched her after, his fingers delicate on her bruised skin. He begged her as she wept. He had snatched her innocence, her life. She flung his hand away, her stomach churning at his touch. She moved, somehow, stumbling out of hell, her head ringing and her throat hoarse. She dragged her battered body along the walls of the corridor leading to the bathroom. The wall felt cold and unwelcoming, and she entered the bathroom to wash off what had happened, the feeling of unwelcome intrusion as her body throbbed.

Adesuwa stumbled in the dark with the moonlight as her guide. She sat on the floor for a long time until she gathered the strength to pull the offending dress off her frame, and Adesuwa caught sight of her body in the mirror. The splinter of moonlight that had lit her path shone on her skin with disgust. For the first time, she saw herself; she saw the youthful body flushed from its first induction to sex, however unwanted. She saw herself for the first time, the way her hips curved and the rounded swell of her breasts, and she knew this offending body lured the man to her.

Bile rose to her throat, and she rushed to the toilet, collapsing over the bowl. She expelled the bile that had risen in her throat—some splashing over her chest, running under her chin—flinching at the stench of her vomit. More tears flowed in shame—in revulsion. Her head throbbed some more, but she remained on the cold floor for ages before collecting her battered remains. There was rustling at the front door, and a loud slam pulled her off the ground and into the shower, washing off every trace of him.

She floundered in darkness, for her life had changed. Her skin no longer fit snugly over her bones; they prickled, cooled, and prickled again as if she had bathed with swine—her body felt foreign, as though the act had forced her into another skin.

She would never forget this horrible night. She would never forget.

TWENTY-FOUR

Present Day, 2024, Lagos, Nigeria.

"You told, didn't you? You're fucking—"

Stephanie turned to see Tunde storm toward her. The other secretaries gave her sharp looks like she had taken center stage in a disreputable show. She shuddered as he stood before the group of five, his eyes blazing with anger directed at her. Her coworkers backed away.

"Tunde!" she muttered through tightened lips, her face burning at the rapt audience. Stephanie turned to them, muttering "Please excuse me" with a faltering smile, and walked out of earshot to a corner in the lobby.

Tunde's heavy footsteps followed.

Neither spoke for a minute; his heaving filled the space between them.

"I know you told your boss, so don't deny it. I saw you after Mr. Francis announced the promotion!" Tunde accused.

"I did it for you, Tunde," she raised her chin. "It was a matter of time before people found out, and it would have cost you both your jobs."

"Remind me again how you thought this was helpful. We differed on this issue, but it wasn't your place to do this. You are not my mother. How dare you? I can't believe you could be spiteful."

"Spiteful?" Stephanie scoffed. "Majekodunmi promised that you wouldn't come to harm," she responded in a level tone as her insides quaked. The naked contempt in his eyes frightened her. She had not thought things through, blinded by anger, seeking to hurt as she had been hurt.

"At the cost of Karen's job?"

"You and I know that she won't lose her job. Besides, Majekodunmi wanted to kick her out. Her influence over management is strong, and you know how these old men think."

Tunde ran a hand across his face. "Look at you," he sneered as though he were staring at a piece of trash. "Look at you trying to justify what you've done."

"Tunde," Stephanie answered in a gentle voice. "You know I never want to hurt you. Telling Majekodunmi was the only way."

"The only way for you and me to be together? Because that's not happening after this."

He waved his hand toward the office as she took a sharp breath.

"It's the only way to be free of what you're doing."

"Be free of what I'm doing—" he broke off when they heard footsteps. The sounds faded, and he continued, "Be free of what I'm doing," Tunde repeated as if tasting her remark to determine whether it was palatable. He scoffed. "I don't want you around me anymore."

"Tunde!" Stephanie gasped, her eyes growing wide like saucers. "Tunde. It's me you're talking to!"

"I don't want you near me, near my house, my friends." His eyes were full of venom. "Stay away from me. I mean it." He turned and walked away.

"Tunde!" Stephanie called after him, uncaring that a few heads turned from the other side of the lobby. "Tunde. Tunde, wait, let's talk it out!" She burst into tears as a bleak future stretched ahead of her.

***

Karen managed to calm herself as the rain abated after an hour. She shelved her discovery for later. Rita asked if she was okay after the debacle with Tunde in her office. Karen ignored her and walked purposefully to the other side of the building. People scrutinized her, whispering, and the air around her fizzled, shrouded with anger, shock, and fear.

She had hinged all her emotions on this promotion. She had pushed her demons aside over the past months and worked herself to the bone. She thought this promotion would give her respite from memories threatening to consume her. Karen did not blame Tunde, though he should have told her when he found out he had been promoted; she was too exhausted to blame him. Karen had examined him standing in her office as though she had seen him for the first time. He was a man desperate to love her but on his terms. Yet that was how she was. She had also set her terms for love in one way or another.

She had to admit what she always knew: that he lived under her skin. She loved him, and it took a pregnancy and dashed hopes of a promotion to come to terms with it.

Now, she stood in Majekodunmi's office, incensed by his betrayal.

"I know how you got yourself into this position. I know how you whored yourself to the highest bidder. I didn't care, and I still don't if you kept that out of the office." He swung away from the tall glass windows to face her. "But this is low, even for you, Karen. Sleeping with a boy years younger than you."

Karen glowered at the man across from her and gave a short, maniacal laugh. "You? Coming from you?" she gibed. "That's rich coming from you, who's anything but a saint!"

"That's the problem with you women," Majekodunmi returned, his mellow tone contradicting a muscle twitching in his jaw. "The problem with you females is that you deflect when it's time to take accountability. You forget that you're not a man. It's a man's world, Karen. Always was and always will be."

He strolled to his chair and sat down, clasping his hands on the desk and staring at her with lazy amusement.

"My love life has nothing to do with this, Ayo." She growled, calling him by his first name with a last attempt to reason with him. Her confidence waned the longer their argument ensued. She had known the risk of getting involved with Tunde, and she begrudged her weakness in yielding to the attraction. "This isn't right," she said, pacing. "You know this isn't right. I worked hard for this."

"What's not right is a relationship with your subordinate," he responded with a roguish expression. "What do you think people would say if they found out, or do you think they would ignore it like I've done for so long?" Majekodunmi shook his head, his mouth curving in disappointment. "I thought you had the sense to keep all your business out of the office. A junior at work, for that matter."

"You didn't complain while these men brought in investments for this company," Karen retorted, glancing away from her boss, her face smarting with hurt.

Majekodunmi sighed. "Look, I'm sorry this didn't work out. You've received many promotions in the past few years. One lost promotion shouldn't be this hard on you; you're still one of the best we've ever had since I've been here."

"Is it because of his father, though?"

Majekodunmi sighed again.

"Now, I still have much love for you. I admire your work and your—er …" He walked around his table to stand beside her. "—commitment to the job. I'd hate to lose a brilliant mind like yours over this, so I suggest you return to your office and continue as usual, and I won't report this to HR." The man touched her shoulder, giving it a brief squeeze. "I was told that you've been looking under the weather. How about you take the day off? Better still, I'll place you on administrative leave starting now. I'll inform the office that you have an urgent matter."

Karen gave him a sidelong glance, shrugged his hand off, and left the office. There was nothing more to say.

TWENTY-FIVE

August 2011, Awka, Nigeria.

For the next month, Adesuwa was a zombie.

A numb, cold indifference shrouded her; her movements lacked their usual cheer, and her animated voice lost its spiritedness. A sanguine woman withdrew into a carapace of melancholy. Omo asked what happened—the tortoise did not retreat into its shell except for danger—but Adesuwa did not respond, uncaring that her older sister had given her an evil eye. Her friends voiced their concerns, and she gave noncommittal responses. The more they prodded her, the more Adesuwa retreated into herself.

There was no energy to pretend, and her insides were emptied of vitality; she became a void. Her presence became so scarce that she stopped attending choir practice and often retired to her bedroom. She could only grapple with silence to maintain an element of control over the wreck of her life. The air in the flat carried a new strangeness, an unpleasant cage narrowing daily. The flat became living and breathing, its walls soaked in her repulsion. She had begged to return to Arondizuogu, but her mother refused, saying Omo needed help. Mama grew worried, asking why she was so adamant about coming home, but Adesuwa insisted without explanation until her mother yelled at her to stop whining.

Segun called often, but most calls went unanswered. Her mouth had clamped shut, for how could she say what her sister's husband had done to her? The sparse days she picked up the call were with stilted conversations filled with monosyllables, so much so that he stopped calling altogether. But his estrangement did not move her, not when all she could think about was dying—of getting rid of her body, of removing her skin—but to whom would she speak? Who would listen to her, believe her?

***

Omo studied Adesuwa as she moved around the house, subdued. She was puzzled, and a sense of disquiet burrowed in her mind. Her sister, who glowed and bubbled, seemed worn out and dour over the past few weeks, creeping with an aura Omo could not describe. Yes, something had to be wrong. She stifled an urge to sit Adesuwa down and ask about the problem. She waved it away. Omo placed second best, even as the first child. She had never been able to draw people in as Adesuwa did. Was this not what she had wanted? For Adesuwa's blinding vibrance to be muffled?

Still, she loved her sister; a modest part of herself admitted that. Just life, the unfairness of life, created resentment. She had made sacrifices for herself, leaving school when things got desperate at home, so she married Bid to escape. Omo never loved him—maybe, once, she thought she did—but she had respected him and hoped it would be enough. Alas, she jumped from the frying pan into the fire. He presented a worse fate than her life at home. At least her parents loved her; they just loved Adesuwa more. She had to make sacrifices like the dutiful first daughter and child, and they praised her for it, but she wondered if the same would be required of her younger sister if the tables were turned.

Omo looked at the younger lady creeping back into her room after completing her chores. She left Adesuwa alone. After all, it was what she wanted: Adesuwa to be mellow and live quietly at home.

The thought of home sent her mind to her husband. He became more attentive over the past few weeks, not raising his voice and giving her whatever she asked. He came home earlier and spent more time with the children. At first, she had been suspicious of the roundabout turn in his behavior. Omo sighed. She would not complain since she wanted this from him: to be a better husband and father. Some celestial being must have answered her prayers. Perhaps, in time, her desire for him would be revived.

She smiled to herself, getting up to make dinner. She would continue to pray more in the next vigil for God to keep him this way now that he had answered her prayers.

***

Present Day, 2024, Lagos, Nigeria.

Omo had always imagined the hour of truth to be an oppressive moment that would define the rest of one's life. She was right and knew when her moment had come to unwrap the truth. It had been a gradual process to arrive at it, like little drops of water—time—welling into an ocean, so she decided that they could not continue like this, spurred on a close shave with death two days ago from the pain in her abdomen—so excruciating that Uloma and Nmesoma had rushed her to the nearest hospital. They spent the rest of their savings on the hospital bills, and now, they had no food except for the small bag of *garri*, dry cassava grains that swelled when mixed with water, which would last until the end of the week.

Omo tied and loosened the wrapper around her chest in the heat. She was unsure how often she repeated the process or how many times she hoped there would be electricity at night. She shifted her weight to a more comfortable position, hovering on the verge of changing her mind; the unease threatened larger than life, but she called Uloma into her room with a heart that threatened to tear out of her chest. Her hands trembled as though her body rejected the decision, evoking a sense of vertigo. Omo closed her eyes, forcing saliva into her dry mouth.

Uloma entered the room. "Sister." Her hand went over her mouth as she yawned.

"Sit down, Uloma." Omo peered at Uloma beneath her eyelashes. She stood up, leaning on the wall, and sat down again, fidgeting with her chipped fingernails.

Uloma sat on the bed, sensing the atmosphere condensed with glibness. "Have you taken your medicine?"

Omo nodded. She took a deep breath, closing her eyes and opening them again as they watered. "Uloma," she started to kneel, sliding her sore body to the floor. "Uloma."

"Aha!" Uloma reached for her, clamping her arms. "Sister Omo! What is the meaning of this?" She pulled her cousin off the floor, both women grunting at the physical exertion.

"Uloma, you won't understand. Let me kneel, *ewoo!*" she whimpered, her body vibrating in fear.

"Sister, you're scaring me." Uloma's voice quavered.

Omo let out a rueful noise. "I wish it were that easy to scare like this," she sighed. "I want to tell you what happened with Adesuwa." She took a sharp breath, her eyes darting from the younger woman to her feet as sweat trailed down her temple. "Uloma."

"Yes, sister."

"Uloma?"

"Yes, sister. What is it?"

"Truly, blood is thicker than water. This thing I'm going to tell you must stay between us. I kept it for so long. Only the grave can bear witness to what I say tonight." A shadow fell over her face. "Nobody else."

Uloma nodded, staring at the splintered linoleum floor, and Omo began her story. She started as a hopeful spinster, her words growing heavier as the story progressed. Omo glowered at the stripped bedsheet, the edges frayed from age, unable to look at her cousin. She could feel Uloma's growing horror, who had begun wailing, her tremors traveling across the bed as if under a terrible fever.

Yet, she was relieved by the weight being freed from her shoulders. All the same, honesty was a double-edged sword. The hand that squeezed around her heart melted into a puddle of humiliation. Her skin crawled under Uloma's contemptuous gaze as she shared her account of the terrible day with tears sliding down the corner of her eye. Then, Omo found her buxom body distorted in loud wails, recalling everything—the anger, the day that hand of hate first held her heart.

TWENTY-SIX

October 2011, Awka, Nigeria.

"Chimooo! Chai. This girl has killed me!" Omo's arms flailed as she threw her body on the floor.

"Aiferiomo, calm down." Aunty Uche begged.

Uncle Donatus crossed his arms, staring at the floor and shaking his head.

"Aunty, leave me! Leave me, let me kill this girl! She has killed me; we will die today!" Omo pushed the woman aside, her blood pumping, and charged at her sister on the floor. She hit and thrashed, deaf to the ugly sounds of flesh hitting flesh, punching anywhere she could.

"Omo—" Aunty Uche pulled her off Adesuwa.

The women panted, their chests heaving in adrenaline. Aunty Uche glowered at Adesuwa as her niece's sobs reached her ears. Adesuwa's arms were naked and bruised, an imprint of a hand mapped across her cheek, and Aunty Uche hissed at her, snapping her finger forward over her head toward the woman heaped on the floor.

"*Tufia*!" She coughed up sputum and spat at Adesuwa. The white blob landed on her victim's arm, leaving a mucus trail as it slid to the ground. "*Anuofia*! See what you've done. See what you've caused!"

"Omo, calm down! You too, Uche!" Uncle Donatus bellowed. "Sit down! Shouting and beating this girl won't solve anything. What has it done since?" He showed his palms as if they would confirm that the answer to his question was not written there.

"*Eh! Chimo*." Omo moaned, drawing herself to the settee, far from her husband. Tears streaked down her face as she recalled weeks before. She should have known; she ought to have known that an evil skulked in the corners.

How could Bid do this to her? He was a man, not a wild animal, for God's sake, and of all people, Adesuwa. Bid knelt before her and held her wrapper yesterday, weeping and swearing that he did not know what had come over him. He complained of the pressure from his family and had turned to Adesuwa, one drunk night—Bid, who never drank. The devil pushed him into it, the same devil they prayed against in many vigils, the same devil he preached against.

She glanced at Bid's dark head bent in shame. He was as still as death, unwilling to see what he had done. Contempt sprang in her so malevolent and consuming that she held on to her shivering body, rocking herself to calm.

What was she to do? She was married to the man sitting on the other end of the living room, with whom she had three children. Where would she go, and what would she tell people? That her husband had impregnated her sister. Should she be grateful that Adesuwa had a miscarriage? She closed her eyes as she sat on the couch, her legs slapping together, wiping off snot with the sleeve of her dress.

"*Efufulefu!*" Aunty Uche clapped her hands at Adesuwa. "*Ashawo!*" she continued beside her husband. "See how you've wasted your life. You want to destroy your sister's marriage. It's water spirits that behave this way. *Tufia!*"

"Mama Chinonso, it's enough," Uncle Donatus snapped.

Aunty Uche scowled at her husband and folded her arms with a heavy sigh before she kept quiet. A terse silence ensued amid sniffles from the woman on the floor.

"Bid," Uncle Donatus called out to the man at the far end of the couch. "Bid."

"Uncle," Bid answered in a subdued voice, his eyes fixed on Uncle Donatus's feet.

"Bid, this matter is serious. This is an abomination."

"Uncle, it was the devil," he chorused for the third time that day. "Help me beg Mama Nora," he turned to his wife, his eyes glistening in unshed tears. "I've offended her *chi*." The word referred to her spirit. "Nothing I say will take me back in time to change it. I'm asking for forgiveness. I swear it will never,

never happen again." He pressed the tip of his finger to his tongue and raised it heavenward. "I swear to God, I swear on everything. *Biko.*"

Omo glowered at him, hunched in the faded blue chair, and swung her gaze to the Catholic calendar on the wall. "It's a useless man who would behave this way. A good-for-nothing!" She paused for air. "I said it! I said you cannot zip your pants, and they told me that men are like this. Men are like this; men are like that. You see now? A whole pastor! If your church members hear—"

"*Kpuchie ọnụ!*" Uncle Donatus barked. "Shut up! Don't say something you can't take back out of anger!"

Omo cackled. "Uncle, are you telling me to respect someone who didn't respect himself?" She held her earlobe, turning her head to the side as though she did not hear him. "Is that what you mean, Uncle Donatus? Because I know you're not—"

"Aiferiomo, calm down!" Her uncle wagged a finger at her. He turned to Uncle Bid and chuckled like he had just finished scolding a child. "Your wife is angry, Bid, rightfully so." Uncle Donatus got up. "There is no woman who wouldn't be. They are very emotional, and this is not the time for that. Let's go out and talk as men. We must resolve this issue today."

Bid followed the older man out of the house, fidgeting with the hem of his calico shirt.

The women in the living room were mute for a while, with the occasional moaning, clapping, and hissing. Aunty Uche spoke first, moving closer to Omo. "Omo, you know that you're like my daughter. I won't lead you down the wrong path, but you see this," she scanned the parlor. "It would be best if you kept it in your belly." She smacked her stomach three times with one hand, beating it like a drum, each hollow sound resonating with her older niece. "Nobody else must know. This matter is not something foreign ears should hear. Not even your Mama, *ehn*?"

"Aunty, I'm finished," Omo sobbed with her hands on her head. "Which kind of devil did I marry? What kind of thing is this? Have I not suffered enough?"

"Omo, pull yourself together!" Aunty Uche hissed. "You see, this is the time you must be strong. What do you want to do now? Do you want to take your children back to Mama's house in the village?" She breathed, her brows dipped in a scowl. "What will Mama say? Who would help you take care of Nora, Chidiogo, and Nmesoma? As bad as it is now, it is worse in the village."

Omo quieted down; her shoulders shook with the last embers of weeping as she listened to her aunt's ministrations.

"What will you do about this?" Aunty Uche snapped her fingers rapidly, squinting into thin air in search of a demeaning word. "This—"

Adesuwa whimpered on the floor, spent from crying and despondent. From the time the truth came out, her sister turned on her as though she had seduced her husband. Omo had called their uncle and aunt, and the three of them piled on her, refusing to believe her story of rape. However, what did they know about her pain? Where were they when she would lie on the bare floor and close her eyes, thinking of Mama while he groped and grunted? Did they know that she cried like a baby when he finished? They were sure that she brought this on herself, at least in some convoluted way, and Uncle Bid kept quiet, staring into space with a vacuous expression like he had willed his mind away from the present. When he spoke, the words that came out of his mouth were endless utterances of blame piled on the devil and everyone else except himself.

"This witch!" Aunty Uche found the word at long last.

Adesuwa's skin bristled under their loathsome sneer, but she welcomed it. They could not hate her more than she hated herself. She did not want a baby growing in her, not for this man. He came to her room many nights, and she would fight, feign sleep, and spit at him, but in the end, she was weak and afraid. It must have been strange that relief flooded into her, watching blood trickle down her leg the morning that Omo found out. Her sister had screamed, sighting the offending liquid pooling at her feet. While Omo rushed her to the local clinic in hysteria, throwing questions at her, Adesuwa kept silent, lost in a trance.

"Whether you like it or not, divorce is not an option. You know it is not done here. Do you want the world to see what is under your clothes? The shame?" Aunty Uche counseled Omo.

"What should I do, Aunty?"

"You must find it in your heart to forgive. It's part of the trials of marriage; prayers and patience will change Bid, but this girl shouldn't stay here anymore." She pointed at Adesuwa, her lips curling with disgust. "Let's thank God that the pregnancy didn't stay." Aunty Uche then snapped her fingers backward over her head, warding off evil spirits as people did when speaking of abominable things. She continued, "Once NYSC comes in December, just bundle her to Lagos. If not, this girl will destroy your marriage. Oh! This is a bad omen." Aunty Uche placed her hands between the folds of her wrapper. "Bid could find a hotel for now, but know, you can't keep him out of his home forever. He is your husband, at the end of the day."

Omo nodded; her eyes clouded in thought. "Can't I take her to Mama? I don't want her in this house."

"Taah! Did you not hear anything I said? Your mother, you mean Mama in the village? What will you say happened? Or do you want this girl to speak to the wrong people?"

Omo shook her head.

"It's not ideal, but we must choose the lesser evil. Thank God she has finished school. She can go for NYSC service once it's time," Aunty Uche continued. "Her mates are married with two children. She's no longer your headache after she leaves this house. Do you hear? This one is a bad omen."

The woman clicked her teeth as Omo delved into another session of wailing, and Adesuwa wept afresh, this time for her mother.

***

Present Day, 2024, Lagos, Nigeria.

Karen woke up with a slight ache in her body. Her dream, this time, resurrected from a long-lost memory. She dreamed and felt his mass pressed on top of her, his grubby hands forcing her thighs apart. She gasped for air, wildly scanning her domain to assure herself she was safe. The administrative leave had almost run its course, but many things weighed on her mind, and she was no closer to resolving them. She wondered if paranoia had set in. Ghosts of the past grew bolder in taunting than her strength could handle.

Tunde called often, but she was not ready to face him; she needed time to think and time to herself. Rita called a few times, but no amount of work would pull her out of her slump. Uloma called as well and left messages that remained unopened.

Karen got up to fill her bathtub with water; a nice soak would do her good.

She recalled, with anguish, her visit to the doctor and let out a breath. The doctor's empathy was like cold water on a hot day, refreshing because the woman had sensed her dismay at the pregnancy test results. Karen burst into tears in her pristine office as she held the light papers as though they weighed a ton. A feat she had not accomplished since her youth, but it felt relieving to share her burden with someone.

She watched the water gush out of the tap, pooling in the tub in an uproarious sequence, and exhaled. Drawn into the swirling pool of water as chaotic as her memories, she found it all the same mollifying as the middle-aged doctor's grasp over her quivering hands. It had been so long since someone had held her hands in comfort.

They discussed other options at length, such as placing the baby up for adoption or a discreet abortion, as she thought of nothing else than to rid herself of it. Dr. Laura sighed and explained that she would not jeopardize her license because abortions were illegal in the country. Karen wanted to scream. This pregnancy did not fit into the plan for her life; she did not want to be pregnant, and she did not want to have someone dependent on her. In truth, Karen did not believe that she could love a child as a mother ought to, and what about the father? She had not mentioned any of this to Tunde.

The doctor implored her to think about it and, in the interim, recommended a psychiatrist to Karen.

"It would help you." Dr. Laura smiled. "I can tell a lot is going on, and I want you to get the professional support you need." She picked out a brown business card. "It's a private practice; it's a bit expensive, but they are excellent and have a support group. Promise me that you'd at least try them."

She had agreed with gratitude. However, Karen placed the card on her dining table and stared at it every time she passed. Fright clawed at her, anxious for secrets the psychiatrist would uncover.

The water filled the tub, and as she took off her clothes, her eyes rested on her flat stomach. She could not believe that another life was forming in her, and she had not decided how she felt about it or whether she would keep it. A long time ago, she had decided she did not want children; Karen's stance had not changed over the years, and she did not think she had the maternal instincts to be selfless enough for another human being who depended on her.

She slipped into the bathtub, and the water lapped around her body, drawing out her anguish and invigorating her. She flicked the water in idle motions, watching the rings of water form and dissolve each time until Karen closed her eyes and drifted off to sleep.

TWENTY-SEVEN

Uloma had never fought with her cousins, not with Sister Omo. She had respected her quiet strength as the other woman navigated life. She had no qualms with Omo asking her to follow them to Lagos; her heart swelled, and she joined in moving. She felt content while they struggled to eat in Lagos, living in a dilapidated building. That is, until Sister Omo shared all that happened with Adesuwa.

Sister Omo shamed her—oh, she shamed her; a woman who cast pearls before swine. At first, Uloma sat speechless, locked in suspended animation until tears ran down her face, grieving for the sisters. Then it turned into rage at how Adesuwa suffered great injustice and how they had kept this terrible secret with them for so many years, watching the family collapse to preserve their ego so as not to fall into disrepute. Sister Omo tried to defend the decisions made years ago. Yes, she hid her shame, and she hid it well, but at what cost? Uloma asked her cousin, and she received no answer.

Was it Uncle Bid she tried protecting, a man who was so promiscuous that he would rape her sister, and what did she do to ensure that Adesuwa got her justice? That Sister Omo would leave her children around that kind of person boggled her mind. Sister Omo stayed uncommunicative as Uloma ranted and raved; her eyes were red and swollen from crying, her voice raspy, but the older woman listened. Her jaw had twitched while Uloma castigated her wickedness. The proud woman cowered under the scrutiny of her actions. Sister Omo begged her to understand and asked what she would do in her shoes. Still, Uloma remained unmoved, appalled that Sister Omo expected her to know that a young woman had been raped and treated with disdain because of the shame Sister Omo feared. She was outraged and betrayed on Adesuwa's behalf. "*Chimooo*," Uloma had wailed in tears, her hands on her head as she slid to the floor. "*Kai*! Adesuwa!"

It took Adesuwa running away for the rubbish to stop. Sister Omo ought to have taken her back to the village. Yes, at least her younger sister would have been safe if Sister Omo had chosen to remain with that man. How could she have sat by and watched, after everything, when Uncle Bid tried to enter her sister's room? A proverb commemorated sister Omo's story. Indeed, trouble was a snake; it slithered into homes and bided its time until it struck. Trouble was a parasite, growing and deriving nutrients at its host's expense.

"Are you not a witch?" Uloma's angry breath was hot as her lips drew back in a snarl. "Has the shame you desperately hid under your skirt not festered into this?"

"Age has made me wiser, Uloma. I know now that I traded one sorrow for another, but I was between a rock and a hard place." She fiddled with the bedsheet, her eyes downcast. "I should have left Bid; I kept saying one day, tomorrow, tomorrow—at least until our children got older." She sniffled.

"Your tomorrow should have been today; it should have been that instant."

Uloma scowled at her in disdain, but sister Omo avoided her gaze. The younger woman wanted to wrap her hands around sister Omo's neck; Uloma wished she would choke and die as she spoke—she wanted to hurt this woman who sat so frail and defeated before her. Uloma got up from the floor with a new conviction, and they must rectify this.

"I'm here because of Chidiogo and Nmesoma. If not, I would have walked out at this moment."

The older woman nodded as strength left her body; the avalanche of truth had taken a toll.

It did not matter that an apology may be years too late, but Mama's spirit would not rest until they did so. Uloma was sure of that; she, Uloma, would not rest until they did so. Sister Omo grew silent, knowing that her sins had been laid bare, and she could do nothing. The younger woman gave her a last look of contempt and left the room.

***

November 2011, Awka, Nigeria.

Omo got down from the cramped *danfo*, grunting as her weight settled on her legs from the high floor as she descended. She cringed, wondering if the other passengers heaved a sigh of relief after being sardined in a three-seat bus to make room for a fourth person, a large woman.

She regarded her surroundings, orienting herself with John Ikemba Street, before she headed toward Uncle Donatus's house, a short distance from the bus stop. She ambled, sweat rolling down her back in the sun, navigating the cavitied road with craters of different shapes and sizes in the once-tarred concrete. A car trotted along. A motorcyclist carried a woman and two children, one child in the front sitting on the fuel tank and a minor child sandwiched between the woman and the rider. They all appeared uncomfortable as the motorcyclist climbed and swayed on the road. She noted that the houses were crammed together, run-down buildings with moss growing on the walls and clothes strewn on rope from one pole to another in front of some homes. Children ran about in faded clothes, some in browned underwear, playing hide-and-seek beside an older woman sitting at a green gate, selling woven fruit baskets.

Omo crossed to the other side of the street where her uncle lived, trudged along, and turned into a small compound. The lines of stress etched on her face turned into a scowl as the familiar thoughts of the past weeks settled in her mind, the debilitating news of Adesuwa and Bid. She shrugged off her thoughts, assessing that the compound was more cramped than the last time she visited. An incomplete structure stood at the front, where teens sat talking. They chorused greetings, and she nodded. A man sitting on a stool glanced up at her with a basin of wet clothes at his feet. He sat in front of a molded building with bathroom and toilet stalls and sheets of corrugated iron for privacy.

She walked into the corridor of a face-me-I-face-you structure at the end of the compound, which housed rows of bedrooms facing each other. Omo blanched at the putrid smell of urine and food mingled in the air. She held her breath, knocking on the first wooden door with rapt attention. A voice shouted to enter.

The moment Omo entered, the man she did not want to see, Bid, prostrated flat on the floor and held her ankles.

"Omo, please!" Bid implored, peering up at her from the carpeted floor.

Omo gaped at the room's occupants. Her relatives sat on the brown settee, their narrowed gazes fixed on the floor as if embarrassed to face her. They ought to be. They did not tell her that Bid would be here.

Aside from the settee, the room had a bunk bed with one jammed against the blue wall and a large bed in the left corner. The ceiling fan rotated close to an old television set. In between the furniture, a small closet sectioned off the wall with its door ajar and a center table pushed in a failed attempt to shut it. New provisions littered the small table: cartons of fruit juice, spaghetti and soaps, and bags of rice and beans.

Seeing that Bid had brought gifts for them, she curled her lips with anger. Omo shook her feet out of his grasp, but Bid tightened his hold, pleading again.

"Uncle, what is the meaning of this?" she shrieked, her face glistening with sweat. "Uncle, what is this? Why is he here?"

Uncle Donatus got up in his white vest and a wrapper tied around his waist. "Aiferiomo," he replied authoritatively, "sit down."

Omo glanced at her aunt, who turned her face to the wall.

"Sit down, Omo," Uncle Donatus repeated with an edge.

Bid relinquished his hold but remained on the ground in his white kaftan and trousers. Embittered, Omo put her hands on her hip, her legs spread wide. "Uncle, this man cannot enter my house."

"Ah!" Uncle turned to his wife, then to her. "I say sit down! Are you the one who rented your house? She says *my house* as if it's your money."

Omo hesitated and sat on the edge of the bed. Her hands tightening into fists, she watched Bid get up and sit at its far end, staring at her in remorse.

"Omo," her uncle said in a placating tone, "I know you're angry." He saw her mouth poised to speak and waved his hand. "I know you're angry. Are we not angry, too?" Uncle Donatus glanced at Aunty Uche, who nodded.

She caught Bid's nod from the corner of her eye and snorted.

"But Bid is your husband," Uncle Donatus continued. "He has learned his lesson, and he must go back home. He's sorry."

Omo did a double-take, her eyes widening at her uncle as though he had gone mad. "Sorry?" she stuttered. "Sorry? As in, sorry for me or sorry for who?"

Uncle Donatus grunted. "Omo, I'm talking to you as your father."

"You're not my father, *mba*. My father would never have suggested this if he were alive. Uncle, I respect you, but this is not okay."

"Is it me you're talking to?" Uncle Donatus roared, his eyes bulging and his protruding stomach contracting as he harrumphed in his seat. "Aiferiomo! I say, is it me you're talking to?"

"Papa Chinonso, calm down," Aunty Uche said as she placed her hands on her husband's shoulder. "Calm down. Do you want the neighbors to hear?"

"What do you want to do now? How long will you keep this man from his house?" Uncle Donatus continued in a lower tone as he shrugged off his wife's hand. "You don't know that you have children for him? You want to pretend like he's dead?"

"God forbid," Aunty Uche interjected and snapped her fingers backward.

Bid kept quiet, staring at the floor.

Omo's eyes tingled with tears. "Uncle, he has been away for a few weeks. It's not even a month!"

"And so?" Uncle Donatus bellowed. "And so?" He lowered his voice, his face set in a grim mask. "Omo, I know you're angry; we are too. Bid can't stay in a hotel forever, *naw, mba*! Not if he has a home."

"How can you forgive such a thing? If Adesuwa didn't miscarry, would we marry the same husband?"

"Let's thank God she did, Omo," Uncle Donatus nodded. "Thank God she did. See, you are no longer a part of your father's house once your husband pays your bride price. You now belong to him. You know this." Uncle Donatus leaned forward in the chair. "Ehn, think of your mother; what will she say? Do you know what will happen to the family? Your sister is the problem, Aiferiomo. Did Bid tell you that he saw her with boys many times?"

She scowled at Uncle Donatus, his lips set in a grim line. "No, Adesuwa is not like that. She said he forced himself on her. Even if he didn't, how can I look past such a thing?"

"What do you expect her to say?" Aunty Uche opposed. "You don't know these girls nowadays. Can't you see how tall she is, like an Iroko tree? See her breasts like pounded yam. Do you think no man has climbed her before? Especially with what Bid told us."

"Is that a reason to sleep with her then? Her sister's husband! This man is almost twenty years her senior!"

"Worse things have happened, Omo." Aunty Uche returned, with her husband nodding. "Worse things have happened. I'm not saying it's right, but the punishment is okay. I'm a woman, too, *ahan.* I understand you, but I won't lie or tell you the wrong thing to do. We've spoken to Bid, and we've warned him. He has changed. No human being is above sin, no one."

Omo scoffed. "Changed?" She did not bother to regard the man, who had shifted closer to her. "Aunty, you say *changed*? How do you change from that?"

"Omo, please, it's enough, *biko.* These are things we face in marriage. What will you say if your mother finds out? What will you say if your children ask why your husband is not home? How long will you say he traveled, or do you want the family to return the bride price? If that's what you want, we have no choice but to do so." Aunty Uche cupped her bosom in her hands.

Uncle Donatus shook his legs, and his mouth turned downward.

"Or do you think we don't know how you denied your husband for a long time?" Aunty Uche uttered, giving her a sly look. "*Shey*, I warned you that time."

Omo kept quiet at this, her neck flushing in embarrassment. She did not want Bid in that house or near her. Omo swallowed, her brows crimped in thought, visualizing answering people's questions anytime they asked of her husband. Omo had not been to church since Bid left the house. Though he sent texts apologizing, she did not think she would see him this soon. Who would care for her children if she walked away from this marriage? Their firstborn, Nora, was still a child. She observed her hands, now folded across her ample bosom.

"What of Adesuwa?" She cleared her throat, wiping her damp eyes. "They can't stay together in that house. I know how hard it is to stay in the flat with her. I see her every day, and I want to vomit. This is too much, Aunty." Her eyes watered anew.

"I know, my daughter," Aunty Uche commented. "If we had space here, we would have allowed her to come. Chinonso and his younger brother would be home soon from boarding school. You know the holidays are around the corner." She pursed her lips. "There's no space. *Ehn* … look at what Bid has done for us. If not for him, would my children go to school? Mama is enjoying the village because of your husband. He's a good man."

Uncle Donatus made a guttural sound in acknowledgment.

"Please, my daughter. Maybe Adesuwa can stay at a friend's place?"

"Which friend?" Uncle Donatus's face darkened. "So that she would open her mouth, or worse, tell the wrong people?"

"Hmm, you're right, Papa Chinonso." Aunty Uche put a finger over her mouth, gazing at the ceiling. "*Ehen!*" she turned to them, "Let her manage in your house for now. You said that she's going to NYSC next month?"

Omo opened her mouth to protest but could not find the words. It seemed to be what they wanted. If she took Adesuwa back to the village, Mama would pester her for the truth, and who knows what Adesuwa would tell their mother?

"Buy a padlock and lock the door every night. Let her follow you to the shop so you can watch her," Uncle Donatus suggested.

"*Ehen*, that's a good idea, Papa Chinonso." Aunty Uche clapped. "It's until December before she leaves; that's the best thing. December is no longer far, Omo. You know I won't lie to you, or should I kneel and beg?" She shifted to the edge of the settee, reaching for the carpet.

Uncle Donatus made noises and held his wife's shoulders with a lavish ceremony as Aunty Uche proceeded to the floor.

"See what you're doing," he glowered at Omo. "It's unheard of for an elder to kneel before a child, *ehn*, Mama Chinonso, please."

"Aunty, it's enough," Omo mumbled. "Please, don't kneel. I've heard you."

"Bid, you too, beg your wife!" Uncle Donatus hoisted his relieved wife back onto the settee.

Her husband went flat on the floor, and she sensed she was caught in a lifelong trap.

TWENTY-EIGHT

Present Day, 2024, Lagos, Nigeria.

Uloma asked to meet, which left Karen puzzled, but she suggested they meet at a restaurant halfway between their areas. It had crossed her mind to offer her home, but desecrating her safe space did not appeal to her.

She walked to the corner booth in the boutique restaurant, her mind adjusting to being outside since she had not left the apartment since visiting the doctor. She had tried calling the number on the business card but could not bring herself to go through with it each time. Once, the phone rang, and a woman picked up; Karen's courage boomeranged, and she disconnected the call, her mind racing in fear.

She got to the booth, and Uloma stood to greet her.

After stilted pleasantries, they placed orders using the code on the glass table. Karen ordered a samosa but encouraged Uloma to eat what she liked, who settled for a bottle of Malt.

"So, Uloma," Karen began, "it seemed urgent the last time we spoke."

Uloma cradled the bottle of Malt. She had practiced what she would say, imagining they would talk at length and hug, knowing all would be well. However, the reality was a different kettle of fish. Her mouth would not move. Uloma took jagged breaths, reeling her mind back to calm. "Karen," she started, watching pearls of water trickle down the Malt bottle.

Karen drew back.

Uloma's eyes welled up. "Sister Omo told me everything."

She gaped at the younger woman as her heart sank. "What?" she squeaked. "Omo told you everything? You mean *everything*?"

Uloma nodded, scrutinizing the woman gaping at her across the table.

Karen pushed the plate of samosas away from her, shaking. She blinked back tears, blowing out her inner turmoil.

Tears streaked down Uloma's face, and she covered her mouth, smothering the wail that formed in her throat. They were silent for a while, holding hands across the table, drawing strength from each other.

Sadness shrouded her features as their hands tangled together, and Karen choked back sobs. "You see why I left and didn't look back? And Mama … I couldn't bring myself to tell her everything. I feared what it would do to her, to the family."

"I know," Uloma sniveled. "It was too much of a burden for you to carry, and horrible what you went through." She squeezed Karen's hand. "You're so strong for that, and I want you to know that none of it would ever be your fault. None."

"I blamed myself, Uloma." Tears tracked through her body as closed memories burst through the surface. "I blamed myself for a long time. I tried and tried to figure out what I did wrong or if it would end when she locked me in that room. She kept me locked in that room every night as if that would stop him from trying." Karen blew her nose into a napkin.

Uloma glanced across the airy room. The panel doors stood open, revealing a vast compound with fruit trees. She was thankful that other patrons paid them no mind and the staff left them undisturbed. "There's nothing I can say to excuse what happened." She sobbed, "I said the same thing to sister Omo. She should have brought you back to Mama; even with the embarrassment, the right thing to do can sometimes be tough."

Omo had convinced herself that she would tell people what happened, as though Karen did not have her fears. People would point at her and whisper, make snide remarks, or treat her with pity.

"She let him come back home after everything," Karen whispered through tears. "I can't forgive that."

Her cousin made a noise of assent.

"I'd be making a great mistake if I asked you to forgive such a thing, but Karen, you've suffered enough." Uloma's voice was staccato. "He's gone now; he can't hurt you anymore. I think that we've all suffered long enough." She shook her head. "Sister Omo looked like a shriveled version of herself as she told me this story, and I could see relief in her eyes; this thing ate her up for years."

Karen sniffed, tired of crying, tired of feeling, tired of those memories. She had much to think of, and this meeting thrust her deeper into misery. Mama's leaving this world had released something locked up in everyone for over a decade. She had a baby growing in her womb; she was hesitant to put a child into all this, knowing that she could not be well, not healed. How could Karen protect another person, given that she did not understand what it meant to be protected? Karen thought of the pregnancy from years ago and how she wanted to tear herself open—rip the offending thing out of her and still be aggrieved with a different type of pain, knowing that she would never love that baby the way a woman was meant to love an offspring.

Uloma pulled her out of her train of thought; she had no idea how long she had been silent, thinking.

"Karen." Uloma's eyes carried a haunted look. "I know this is too much to ask right now, but even with all this, Omo is sick. She needs surgery."

Karen cringed and stared at the triangular pastry on the table.

"Karen, listen to me. I know it's a lot, but we can't let her die. She has no money; it's almost a million, and I'm not begging for her. I'm begging for Nora, Nmesoma, and Chidiogo. Who will they turn to if she dies? Their father is useless, and Uncle Donatus is uninterested."

Karen exhaled. Her head throbbed from sobbing. "I don't want to have anything to do with Omo. It's too painful. I can't; please don't ask me to do this."

Uloma gave her a forlorn look. "I would never have asked you if we had other options. Who do we turn to?" she cried. "I'm asking for her children's sake. Let them not bear the sins of their mother, *biko*. We still can't watch her wither away."

Karen got up, drained from the conversation. Uloma joined her, dabbing her cheeks with her napkin. "Uloma," Karen beheld her cousin with newfound respect. "Thank you."

The other woman gave her a tearful smile.

"I've heard you, but I need time to think; I need time to myself. There are things that I'm dealing with now. I must process things. What you're asking is difficult for me."

Uloma nodded; her desolate expression spoke volumes. She was desperate for Karen to know she understood and would give her the time to digest their conversation. She watched Karen pay the bill, and they shared a tearful goodbye.

Karen drove out of the premises and parked on a side street. Her hands trembled, and she breathed in short, ragged gasps. A bubble of panic rose in her chest, and she screamed within the confines of her car. The car windows were wound up, bouncing her distress back to her. She screamed again, banging on the steering wheel, and stopped at the abrupt sound of the horn, which shocked her out of her delirium. Her eyes caught sight of the business card she had kept on the passenger seat, and she picked up her phone.

***

November 2011, Awka, Nigeria.

"He won't come in here." Omo scrutinized the narrow window, taking in the quiet street below. The room seemed smaller; the air was dense with apprehension. She was grateful that the children were still in school so that she could address Adesuwa. They had asked questions, wondering why their Aunty refused to leave her room.

"We must manage. Once you leave for NYSC, please don't come back here. We must manage for a few weeks until you leave."

"Sister, are you letting that man come back here?" Adesuwa put her hands on her head as she wept. Her plate of untouched breakfast tilted into the dent in the bed where her hand had been, and some of the bean porridge slid onto the bare mattress. "Sister, he forced himself on me. Why would I lie, for God's sake?"

Omo struggled not to cry. Adesuwa did not understand how she hurt her or how she destroyed her trust. "Did he see you with boys or not, Adesuwa?" Omo turned to face her sister, and she held her breath, her heart twisting in pain. "Answer me ehn, Adesuwa?"

"If he saw me with a boy, does that mean that I didn't get raped, sister?" she blubbered, wiping her swollen eyes with the back of her wrapper.

"How can I believe you? How do I know that it's not as Bid said?" Omo countered in a spiteful tone. "What's to say that you haven't been all over this university with every Tom, Dick, and Harry, Adesuwa, or was it the times you were giggling with Bid?" she glowered at the woman on the bed. "You've disappointed me, of all people, my husband."

"Ahh, sister," Adesuwa said, putting her hands on her head, her body aching from exhaustion. She could not believe that Omo believed everyone else except her. "Sister, God knows that I kept myself until marriage," she wailed, putting the tip of her index finger on her tongue and pointing it to the ceiling. "If I threw myself on your husband, let thunder strike me dead now. God knows."

"I'll padlock this door every night," Omo choked out a response. "You must follow me to the market daily and return to your room once we get home." She nodded to herself, her voice growing uneven as her throat clogged in tears. "Everything should be manageable until you leave," Omo muttered, keeping her eyes on her feet, unwilling to take in anything else in the suffocating room.

Adesuwa stumbled from the bed and grabbed the hem of her skirt. The wrapper Adesuwa tied across her chest fell to the floor, exposing her pink nightgown as she knelt before Omo, weeping. "Sister, please, I can't do this. Let me go home to Mama, please." She tugged on the khaki skirt in desperation, her tears staining the beige fabric, uncaring that she was a mess and smelled a mess from not showering in two days. "Please, I don't want to stay here anymore. I promise not to tell anyone. I want to go home," Adesuwa pleaded, her voice strained from crying. "Please, sister Omo, please."

Omo grimaced as her body tautened in Adesuwa's hands. She glanced at the room in mounting anger as forbidden images of her husband and sister imprinted themselves on her mind's eye. She shoved the woman at her feet with all her might.

The room vibrated with a thud, and Adesuwa yelped as pain zipped through her body. Her nightgown was geared up from the impact, and her shapely thighs were in view, supple breasts wriggling from the fall.

Omo turned cold as she examined her sister from under hooded eyelids. Bid had parted those thighs. He had groaned in pleasure between Adesuwa's legs as he had done between hers in those fruitful days of their marriage. She stepped back, nearing the sacks of food stored in the room.

"Aunty and Uncle don't want you," Omo growled, giving Adesuwa a scorching look, propelled by a need to hurt as she hurt. "Nobody wants you now. I'm stuck with you, this prostitute! Do you think Mama will take you in after you tell her what happened? Did Bid not see you with the boys? Let me see you near him this time around. I'll kill you myself."

Omo's ample breasts heaved as she released a fiery breath. "That is what we have to do," she continued in a shaking voice. "I don't want you here. I wish you'd die, disappear!" She grabbed a bag of silverware behind her and hurled it at her sister. The contents were scattered on the floor, the clanging sounds of forks and spoons making a brief orchestra of chaos.

Omo walked out of the room, slamming the door behind her.

TWENTY-NINE

The door handle twisted, followed by a more desperate attempt. It jerked three more times, paused, and then the shadow stretched from beneath the door and retreated into the unknown. Adesuwa placed her hand on her chest and released a ragged sigh.

Thank God he left. Her skin, which bristled from crippling fear, thawed into a settled tempo, and she wiped her hand over tear-stained cheeks, shifting on the mattress to peer outside the window.

The full moon shone across the blue firmament, stretching its pale veil across the quiet street and into her room. She glanced at the bedroom with disdain, her vision tainted by the memories trapped in the same room she had loved. The room, stripped of its appeal, emerged as a storage for forgotten and rejected things—an overflow of items from the kitchen and the shop. A distant owl hooted in the night, its birdsong forlorn and hopeful, stirring a deep conviction within her: She would leave this place, this hellhole.

Thank God she had pocket money saved. She would use it to travel to her friend's house in Lagos, the Center of Excellence; it had become her city of dreams.

For the first time in a long while, Adesuwa laughed, and the thought of leaving her older sister's house felt bittersweet. She closed her eyes, breathing better now that the man had gone, now that she had an escape from her predicament.

Adesuwa's laughter rumbled into weeping as she pushed down the bile rising in her throat, pushing down thoughts that threatened her fragile grip on sanity. Her Nokia phone beeped with a message from her friend, her savior, and the contents transfixed her for a long time. Adesuwa placed the phone back on her bed, swallowing a fresh wave of tears. God, if he cared enough, had mercy on her, and her earnest prayers paid off. Her friend's mother agreed to let her live with them until she went to the NYSC training camp in a few weeks.

With newfound energy, she hurried the luggage to the corner she had packed weeks ago. She pushed it to the ground, unzipping the old bag and removing her meager possessions. She could not help herself. She repacked the clothes, folding each with great care, as this time she let tears flow freely down her cheeks.

***

Present Day, 2024, Lagos, Nigeria.

She made up her mind as soon as she stepped into the office. Everything appeared the way she had left it. Rita had done an excellent job keeping the place clean. Karen sat behind the desk, her fingers gliding over the smooth surface of the mahogany table. She shifted in her chair to dispel the nagging feeling of discontent pressing upon her like an anvil in her stomach, but it had nothing to do with the table, chair, or office aesthetics. Her hesitance to return to work was more internal, as if she wore old skin, as though this place no longer existed as a part of her. Her fingers itched to reach for her prepared resignation letter.

Karen strolled to her awards on the cabinet, gleaming in the morning sun. She stood in front of them, staring. She had worked so hard for each of them; she shed blood, sweat, and tears to reach this point. Standing proudly in her office, each award proved her tenacity in a cruel world. They were proof of how far she had come, how far she had been willing to go before everything changed again. It struck her that she lived her life through a reckoning, and the pregnancy spurred her into change.

A knock rapped on the door, and Rita walked in.

"Good morning, ma."

"Good morning, Rita." Karen returned to staring at the awards as Rita waited for instructions. "Rita," Karen continued in a contemplative tone, "How long have we worked together?" She turned to the secretary, taking in the woman's black suit.

Rita hesitated. "About six years, ma"

Karen nodded.

"Have I done something wrong?" Rita's voice was laced with worry.

"No, Rita," Karen returned to her desk and retrieved her handbag. "You did everything right. You've been my support since you began working for me." She paused, with a faraway glint in her eyes, and searched her bag for the letter. "Rita, I'm leaving this company today. I think it's time."

Rita's sharp inhale echoed through the office. "But, ma," she stammered, the professional visage slipping at the weight of her boss's remark. "But, ma, why? Is there something wrong?"

"No, Rita," she said, walking from behind her desk to the door where the other woman stood. She gave Rita her car keys. "You've been an exceptional staff, and I wish you all the best. Please gather my things and put them in the trunk of my car. You can keep the furniture," she stated, her lips parting in a plaintive smile. "I only want my personal effects."

Rita accepted the keys as she gaped at Karen.

Karen walked across the hall to Majekodunmi's office, unhindered by the curious stares she received from the few people who had arrived at work. She knew they did not know how to address her or what to say if she was resentful of the results of the job promotion, but what they thought did not matter. It never did. Karen smiled as her heart soared. She had come in earlier than usual because she did not want her return to be fodder for staff gossip, but now she did not care. So Karen Ezeani held her head high, walking in powerful strides in her favorite gray pantsuit. She could hear Majekodunmi's booming voice from inside the office, and his laughter rang across the lobby as he spoke on a call. Karen approached his office door, ignoring the secretary who rushed to greet Stacy or Stephanie; for her life, she could not remember the woman's name.

Karen opened the office door and walked in; a helpless secretary stood behind her. Majekodunmi leaned back in his chair, laughing into his phone, though he frowned at the disturbance. He had made it clear that he did not like to be disturbed while his door stayed closed, but today had to be different; today, she did not care.

Karen slid her letter toward the man on his table, and he picked it up. She simmered in satisfaction, watching fleeting expressions cross her boss's face—irritation, surprise, and disconcertion.

"Let me call you back," Majekodunmi said, hanging up the phone and placing it on the desk. "Karen, Karen," he chanted as though she had not heard him the first time. He looked past her to see his secretary at the door. "Stephanie, shut the door."

Ah, that's her name, Karen thought with a small smile, as though an inside joke had made her situation amusing. The door clicked shut, and the sound of footsteps faded away.

"Karen, what's the meaning of this?" He held the stiff white paper up, his lips drawn to a thin line. "What's the meaning of this letter?"

"I'm resigning, Ayo, effective immediately."

He gestured for her to sit on one of the chairs before his desk, but she ignored him.

"Sit down," he demanded in a curt voice.

"No, thank you. I prefer to stand." She breathed. "I know this won't take long."

"So you're quitting just like that?" Majekodunmi gibed, "Because of a flimsy promotion?"

"It's not about the promotion, sir." Karen walked to the tall glass windows, staring at the road below. Vehicles drove on opposite lanes, each lane piling up at the traffic lights ahead. She smiled at the usual queue outside the bank atm stalls and wiped moist hands on her pants from a niggle of self-doubt, a reluctance to go through with her decision. Still, she pushed aside the thought, recognizing that a last sense of preservation had made her reconsider. "I wish I could say it was the promotion, but it's beyond that."

A startling silence ensued, and his questioning glare bore into her back, so Karen continued, more to herself than the man in the room. "This place is no longer right for me. Everything about it feels different; I can't explain it. I think this work served its purpose for a time in my life that has ended."

"Are you listening to yourself?"

She heard the chair creak, released from the pressure of his weight. Majekodunmi walked to the window where she stood, stopping a few feet away, but Karen's gaze remained fixed on the road as a sense of release preceded an impatience to begin a new path she had set for herself.

Majekodunmi snickered.

She turned to him, unperturbed by the disdain evident in his eyes.

"I never pegged you for a sore loser, Karen," He chortled, emitting a timbre that held his malice. "So it's because someone else took something you wanted. Look around you, Karen." He glanced across the office. "The organization won't keel because you are throwing a tantrum. We can get someone like you in a heartbeat, even better than you." He snapped his fingers. "No one is indispensable, and I'm sure you know that more than anyone here. You've seen people come and go and see how I suffer fools."

"Then find someone else," Karen responded, disappointed in her former mentor. He could be ruthless; she had seen how he dealt with people he deemed unworthy many times, but she slipped into ease with him, never envisioning that a day would come to face the cruelty she had once admired. "I said it's not about the promotion. I have other things happening in my life, Ayo."

"Like what?" Majekodunmi interrupted, putting his hands in his pants pockets. He peered outside the window and then glared at her like she was a sulking child. "Tell me like what?" He continued, propelled by her lack of response, "You and I are of the same ilk, Karen. All we have for us is work; we live and breathe for success and challenges. What are you going to do without this place?"

Karen's head started to ache. He had touched on a sore spot regarding the fear that threatened to consume her. It seemed to lurk in her room, biding its time for the moment that her guard would come down, the fear of losing Tunde and her job.

"Are you having some kind of epiphany?" Majekodunmi laughed again, this time smug, knowing he had scored a point. "Did you at least think this through, or are you suddenly taking stock of your life and having no husband with whom to grow old?"

Karen swallowed and swung her eyes out the window. Rita's figure below carried a box of items into her car. She regarded Majekodunmi with a strange sense of ease. "Ayo, I don't care about a husband or any man. You can choose to believe it or not, but my decision has nothing to do with the politics of this company."

He rolled his eyes, but she had long learned not to waste her breath convincing anyone to believe her side of the story. Karen's gaze swept across the place, taking stock of the office, for it would be her last time in the space. Her chest swelled with pride.

"Thank you for everything, Ayo," Karen muttered as she walked toward the door. She paused and pressed a hand to her throat, pushing back the sadness that washed over her. The door ahead loomed larger than life, marking the end of a significant chapter.

"Karen."

She stopped and turned to face him with one foot out the door.

"Is this it?" His lips formed a thin line on an emotionless face as he looked at her askance, as though he believed she would return.

She nodded, her throat clogged with words and emotions, as he turned away.

His back was rigid as he faced the road below, dismissing her.

She took a deep breath, determined not to let tears get the best of her, at least not here, not in this place of all places.

Karen walked back to her office, stripped bare of her, with furniture that appeared cold and impersonal like this place. She turned out the drawers and files, ensuring that nothing of hers remained. Tunde crossed her mind, but Karen forced the thought aside. Today would not be for him. It was for her.

She stood by her desk, recounting several moments with a yearning for simpler times. Karen left the office and went to the elevator, ignoring the whispers around her. She stepped into the lift, and its occupants kept mute. The strain in the air was palpable, as though she were an alien and never belonged, but it did not bother Karen; it never did.

By the time she left the building, the morning sun had given way to a fiercer heat, and her heart scorched with melancholy. More vehicles filled the parking lot; employees entered the building to start the day. It seemed funny, Karen thought, struck with sonder, as she walked to her car, that each person going into the office, each stranger on the road, also faced some complexity in their lives. They had their own stories and battles, and she was a simple cog in the enormous machinery of the earth. The sudden realization buoyed her spirits as though the ice in her heart had melted into a silent stream, giving her peace and connection with her part in the world.

She walked to Rita, who stood by her car, waiting to give Karen the keys. The woman returned the keys, lingering as if reluctant to leave.

"I realize I've never thanked you enough." Karen stuck out her hand.

Rita took her hand, and a gold wedding band glinted in the sunlight. "Thank you, madam. I know you will do wonderful things. You were good to me, very fair." She choked back tears.

Karen took note of the plain ring as they shared a firm handshake. She had never known that Rita was married; she had never bothered to learn about her secretary. Her palm felt warm afterward, and she almost laughed—it was the first time she had shaken hands with Rita.

Karen nodded, and the tears she fought to keep inside slipped out of the corner of her eye. She sniffed, grasping her car keys tighter. She watched the woman walk toward the building, her shoulders stiff in mild embarrassment. Karen smiled to herself, a genuine smile that brought an alluring twinkle to her eyes. She settled into the vehicle and grabbed a tissue, letting tears fall at Rita's parting words.

THIRTY

July 2015, Lagos, Nigeria.

His office smelled like stacks of paper.

Indeed, a tower of files stood behind his desk, and a metal filing cabinet with its first drawer half open. The outdated white desktop computer, the dull red carpet on the floor, and the grumbling air conditioner must have been as old as the man. Mr. Jakande studied her with a smirk on his large lips, his body compressed into a black leather chair, his potbelly pushing through his agbada.

"Michael said you're his girlfriend, right?" Mr. Jakande guffawed, baring yellow teeth.

"Yes," Karen responded, ignoring his leer as it slid up her exposed legs and settled on the generous swell of her breasts.

He bobbed his head and fiddled with a pen, his fingers drumming on the wooden table. A gold wedding band gleamed against his dark skin.

"You have your master's degree?"

"Yes, sir. I have an MBA in project management."

"That's good." Mr. Jakande chuckled and took the *fila* off his head, revealing a balding head.

The top of his scalp gleamed in the bright office, and she thought of an oasis surrounded by dry land in the desert as she watched his movements, noting the careless way he placed the cap on top of the documents on his desk.

"That's good, very good. I like women who work hard. That's encouraging."

"Yes, sir."

"I'll help you," he slid her a guarded gaze, leaning back in the chair, which groaned under his weight.

"Thank you, sir," Karen muttered with a curt smile. "I appreciate it."

"Ah. Wait, my dear, don't thank me yet." He threw his head back and laughed. "How can you thank me yet? A fine girl like you, see how you act as if you're not in Lagos."

She paled, and her shoulders sagged. She knew it would come to this, though she had hoped the man would admire her from afar and not make a move.

"You know you're a fine girl, *naw*," he licked his lips. "Michael is enjoying himself. He should share with us, right? See your skin glowing. How old are you again?"

She forced down the urge to gag and opened her mouth to respond, but he cut her off with a wave of his hand as he chuckled.

"Don't worry, that one is not important. Come around the table, and let me see you." Mr. Jakande grinned and leaned back, putting his hands behind his head as if daring her to walk away.

Karen's eyes narrowed, and she squirmed in her seat. The temptation to leave was not as strong as her ambition. She knew that Lagos had always been unforgiving of young women. A man was a man. His appearance did not matter; they all had the same body parts, and the process of sex made no difference, regardless of partners, if she had agreed to Mr. Jakande's less-than-subtle offer. She knew he would not tell Michael. How could he say such a thing to Michael, his godson? Karen repressed a shudder. She could walk out now, leave, and never look back.

"Are you saying no?" Mr. Jakande raised an eyebrow and clucked his teeth. "*Sisi*," he stated in Yoruba, "I have things to do today. It's because of Michael that I agreed to see you. You can see my table." He jerked his head toward the desk as he straightened. "I don't have all day."

She wanted to wipe off the smugness from his face. Karen rose from her chair, each step around the furniture heavier than the previous one as her stomach revolted. She stood before Mr. Jakande as he ogled her. Her eyes were drawn to the framed photo on top of the file cabinet; a woman and three children were smiling into the camera, and shame spiraled through her.

"*Ehen*, good girl." Mr. Jakande tittered and put his hands on her backside.

Karen bit her lip hard until it drew blood. The metallic taste spread over her tongue, and she swallowed the bloodied saliva, smarting from the cut on her lip while welcoming its distraction. He groped her, feeling and weighing to see if she met his requirements. The rest of that afternoon in Mr. Jakande's office passed as a dream, but it had changed Karen. She would never again be the starry-eyed girl from Awka.

***

Present Day, 2024, Lagos, Nigeria.

Tunde drove out of the parking lot of Karen's apartment building, his mind ticking and working in overdrive. He was worried about Karen as he left the premises, checking the rearview mirror, hoping that, by some miracle, she would materialize behind him. It was the second time he had come to find her, and there had been no response at the door.

Tunde banged the steering wheel in frustration as anguish clouded his features. He should have insisted they continue their conversation when they spoke in the office. The last time he saw her. It had been a little over a month, for heaven's sake, and no message from her, nothing; she disappeared from the face of the earth.

He steered the car toward the Victoria Island traffic with a line etched between his brows. At first, he assumed she would need time to cool off, but after two weeks of radio silence, he got frantic—calling, texting, distracted, wondering if this promotion meant so much to her that she would cut him off without giving them a chance to work things out. His face twisted into anger.

He must have been insane not to recognize how grave her selfishness was. She made it so difficult to love her; she made loving her come with grief. Stephanie had called and sent mutual friends to talk to him, but it was easier to ignore his former friend. He wished that he could ignore Karen as well.

"Why can't she be like everyone else?" he grumbled as he sped on Ozumba Mbadiwe Road. The soft music from the radio faded into a distant hum behind his thoughts. But she did not live like everyone else, rendering him helpless in how much he loved her. Still, he held on to anger; it kept him from growing desperate.

He had gone to work like a ghost, his body present, but his mind searched for Karen. He had been at it for weeks like a zombie, tired and pining for this woman. When the office announced that Karen Ezeani had resigned, his head shot up from his seat at the meeting. Resigned, someone on the team repeated, mirroring everyone else's shock; yes, Karen had vacated her office earlier in the week. The office had buzzed with gossip for days that she must have been bitter about the promotion; everyone had heard her fall out with Majekodunmi on that fateful day. Tunde listened to the voices around him, steeling himself from trembling in shock. No, not Karen. There had to be something else going on; she would never give up, and something had to have gone wrong.

The thought revived his search for her. Karen would not cower at a problem. Tunde mused that she was not the woman he knew, joining the line traffic before him with renewed strength to continue the search for his lover. He would not give up. If she wanted to end things, she would have to say it to his face. He dialed her number on his phone again, and it went to voicemail.

Tunde's face hardened at the rejection, but his mind was made up. Yes, she would have to end things to his face.

***

Karen sat in her car, peering at the club entrance and tapping her feet on the vehicle floor. She wanted to go in, but the thought of loud music and a crowd did not sound appealing when she arrived at the club gates. She became tired of being alone with her thoughts and moping around her flat since she had never been out of work in years. There was nothing to keep her mind occupied.

She took a deep breath and turned on the engine, impassive to the vehicle revving to life. The streetlights coated the buildings and cars with a yellow glow in the famous zone for Lagos nightlife. Karen made a three-point turn and headed home, navigating the speed bumps and pedestrians as they made their way to bars on both sides of the road. Her mind looped in subjects she had avoided for some time. She will have to address Omo and Tunde's issues soon. Tunde needed an explanation. At first, she had ignored his calls and texts, as a sharp pain punched her gut each time his name appeared on her screen. But one day, she opened his messages, and her heart broke anew for the anguish that shone through them, yet she could not respond before she was ready. Thoughts of Tunde felt painful and overwhelming each day.

She loved him, she knew, but she would not let anyone rush her. She needed this to figure out who she was and what she wanted. At no point in her adulthood had she prepared any plan for a baby, and she could not find fulfillment in the prospect of child-rearing, not with the baggage she carried—not until she cared for herself and focused on that.

***

They observed the other patients and their families. The ward smelled of sickness and bleach. The nurse had come to check on Omo, who was snoring quietly. Chidiogo came from school to see her mother, worried about her health, but Uloma could not answer. The girl held on to her mother's hand. They were carbon copies, but where Omo was robust, Chidiogo was slim and fairer than her mother in complexion. Uloma thought of how young Chidiogo must have been while Karen lived with them, and she wondered if the girl remembered her Aunty. Bitterness filled her mouth, and she swallowed; Chidiogo would not know how much pain her mother and father had caused.

They were still far from nearing the surgery bill, and the doctor refused to collect a deposit lower than seven hundred thousand, complaining that people often ran away from the hospital after treatment, leaving the staff to spread the bill among themselves. She had begged the nurses, who insisted they must pay the bills in full. Uloma was appalled by the inhumane conditions set before they would treat a human being, but she understood how much the government neglected hospitals. They saw it daily on the news, but no one understood it until their loved ones needed care.

Uloma glanced at the ward nurse in hopelessness as she kneaded her shoulders. There was no money after this recent admission, and she would not rush Karen. If Karen decided not to help, Uloma could not find it in her to be angry at her cousin. The woman had suffered enough, but Uloma hoped Karen would change her mind.

Omo coughed, and her eyes peeled open; she blinked, familiarizing herself with the crowded ward. Her body was shrunken, as though the illness had eaten her alive, and she smelled stale, having not showered since they arrived at the hospital. Her eyes fell on Uloma, who was staring at her with a veiled expression. She turned her face away, abashed that Uloma had judged her, yet she was indebted to her cousin for remaining by her side. The atmosphere between them had changed as the camaraderie they had shared dissolved since the night they spoke, but Omo recalled the relief she had felt from reviving a secret that had been buried for so long. She had been selfish for the sake of her marriage and children, but she did not know if she would make a different choice if they went back in time.

Uloma sat on the plastic chair beside the bed, staring at her. They had spoken all the words held back over a decade so that their bellies were empty. Omo closed her tired eyes again. For some obscure reason, Aunty Uche appeared behind her eyelids, and her aunt's somber words filtered into her mind: "This is what it means to be a woman, keeping everyone's secrets— breaking backs for husbands, children, and society." Omo disagreed in recent years that these men had their transgressions excused, and the punishment placed on women showed a tear in the societal fabric. For the umpteenth time in her hard life, she wished she had been born a man. It lingered as the last of her graying thoughts before the lull of sleep took her back to peaceful rest.

***

Tunde's eyes were glued to Karen's message, asking if he would be available to talk later that weekend. He almost did a pirouette at work. His colleagues watched him from their workstations, but Tunde ignored them. *Yes, yes,* he replied the next second as his heart fanned in anticipation. He promised himself he would get her flowers and chocolate and buy the bottle of wine she liked, and everything would be all right.

THIRTY-ONE

The Women's Group meeting ended, and Karen wiped her damp eyes as she walked to her car in a daze. She had shared her story at her third meeting, and the burden of the decade evaporated into the air, leaving her shoulders lighter. Somehow, it had become easier to talk about it after her conversation with Uloma. She needed someone to hear it, tell her she had done nothing wrong, and assure her that it could not be her fault. She closed her eyes in the vehicle, attuned to the sounds of engines purring from other vehicles and birds chirping in the tree branches above her car. She took sharp breaths in and out like the psychiatrist had taught her. Then, she started her short drive to the beach.

Karen got out of the car after arriving at the beach.

These past weeks had given her more peace than she had felt in a long time, drawing her closer to the water. The waves crashed against each other, a great tumbling of water. The seagulls' long calls and the salted breeze smell filled her senses. It was by the water that she decided to resign from her job. Karen had discovered during an earlier therapy session that she had used work to deal with the trauma. Walking out of the office building with the last of her things had been the most vulnerable part, and she drove straight to the beach afterward. It was by the water that Karen knew, for the first time in a long time, that everything would be all right from then on. She had always been a high achiever and had strived for grandiose success, anything to feel alive, to fill the space in her heart. Now, she must learn to feel alive without anything to hide behind.

The baby issue was still a dilemma. After one group meeting, a woman introduced herself as Lola—a fair-skinned, petite lady with a sing-song voice—who became her friend. Lola shared a similar experience and told Karen that she could take her to a doctor to terminate the pregnancy without fuss. Karen had been afraid, wrapping her arms to shield herself from the fear that shrouded her mind, but she agreed that it would be good to have that option if she was willing to take the risk.

Karen stood by the shore as the waves flowed around her feet. Her hand found her belly, which had not yet begun to change; she had crossed the two-month mark today, and it filled her with loneliness to experience these changes, subtle and unsubtle, within her, alone.

The support group grounded her, welcoming her to a new kind of sisterhood free of judgment. If a woman wanted to cry during her turn to speak, another woman would wrap warm arms around her; they listened with rapt attention as though they had known the person for years. It was a sisterhood that Karen never thought she would need. She had never thought women felt the same things she did. These days, Karen reflected on the past, centering her thoughts on a single question: Were the memories blocked out years ago, avoiding the pain and trauma, also a trauma response in and of itself? She had been sure she had moved past everything after leaving Awka.

Karen shivered. She longed to hear Mama call her Adesuwa and for Mama's warm embrace and earthy scent, although the last time she had seen her mother had ended in discomfiture. Karen retraced Mama's wrinkled face stretched with a smile, overcome by joy at seeing her younger daughter. However, her jubilation was short-lived, and that sad glint in Mama's eyes became more pronounced as she faced a firm rejection while trying to discuss Omo.

"Mama, please let it go," she had said to her mother.

Mama's sharp gaze stabbed her from the old settee. Karen shrank back, swathed in the dim outer banks of the candle-lit parlor.

"My daughter, please." Mama's voice quavered. "Talk to me. I didn't raise you girls to behave this way. Talk to me, my daughter; tell me what happened."

"Mama," Karen snapped, crossing her legs in the faded loveseat. Despair rang in her mind as she glanced away from Mama. Her brows crinkled, staring into the dancing fluid globe of fire.

"Adesuwa, you cut all of us off as though we're strangers. I'm your mother, or have you forgotten? The one who breastfed you and took care of you when you were sick. Is this how to treat an old woman who dreamed of seeing her children happy?"

She gave a bitter laugh and expelled a harsh breath. "Don't call me that.".

"Am I not your mother again? Can't I ask?"

Mama sniffled, and Karen peered at her with anguish. Her mother's features softened against the flame. The tangled threads of age appeared less severe, and her eyebrows fell in sorrow.

"Mama," she sighed, "please, I beg you, can't you be happy that I'm here today? We have a short time before I go back to Lagos."

"Adesuwa. That's all you'll say?" Mama folded her hands on her lap. "After begging and pleading for so many years. Ah, you, this girl, you're breaking my heart. I ask why you don't visit; you shut me up. I ask why you're not thinking of marriage, and you tell me that I should stay out of your life." Her mother hummed a sad tune as she touched her hand to her heart, swaying her body from left to right as though she sought comfort within herself. "Have I offended you in any way?"

Karen leaned back on the lumpy sofa, knocked out of energy, and left with a growing void. She fanned herself in the hot parlor, choking back tears. Her heart sank at her mother's words; she did not want to cause Mama pain, but she did not know how to act around her mother after everything that had happened. They stayed like that for a while, mother and child, in quiet contemplation, and the rest of the night was tainted with grief.

In hindsight, Karen could see how trauma shaped her life, influenced her decisions, and sank its tentacles into everything she did. Mama had given up hope that Karen would settle down. She accepted that Karen needed to quiet down, mellow, and become malleable so that men would find her endearing. Karen had given her mother an implicit ultimatum, which was her greatest regret—putting her mother between herself and her sister. She had determined that there would never be a discussion about Omo, or Mama would also be dead to her. It was a hard thing for a mother to bear.

Today, standing in the cold water with the horizon stretched out before her as endless as the possibilities she faced, she knew she still had a long way to go in this healing process. Karen shivered from the gentle wind that lapped around her.

Sometimes, she had vivid dreams of the room in Awka or Uncle Bid's tongue on her skin, and she would wake up screaming, or she would remember an intimate moment from the past, and her breathing would become short, winded gasps. It dawned on her that Adesuwa and Karen were two people becoming one, meshing memories. Her healing would be lifelong, as her psychiatrist said, prescribing medications to ease the attacks and depression. But what mattered was that she recognized and welcomed the help. Adesuwa and Karen needed help; she needed to reconcile with herself.

She spoke to Uloma more often. Uloma did not mention Omo, and she was grateful for that. Once, they talked about the first years of her relocation to Lagos, the job she resigned from, and her support group meetings these days, and sometimes they would weep a little; Uloma would say in their mother tongue, "You're safe now, Karen. You're safe now."

THIRTY-TWO

A knock on the door drew Karen out of her introspection. She checked her blurred reflection on the windowpane and headed toward the door in trepidation. The isolated clouds loomed gray outside from the continuous rain since yesterday. She had finished a call with Uloma and agreed to meet her sister. She placed a hand on her chest, calming her treacherous emotions. Uloma had been quiet, as if she needed time to understand her words, and thanked Karen with fervent prayers. She informed Karen that they were at the hospital with Omo, who was under observation for abdominal pain.

Karen stopped for a second, a hand on the cold door handle, and took a deep breath; she nibbled on her bottom lip as she recited what she hoped to say to Tunde. After another round of precise breaths, she opened the door. Karen's breath hitched at the sight of the man she loved as if she saw him with fresh eyes since Karen had accepted that she loved him.

Karen stepped aside, and he entered with a bouquet and her favorite bottle of wine in his hand. She could not help but offer him a grateful smile. She swallowed as she watched him place the items on the center table and straighten to study her, his expression sober. Guilt stabbed at her, and her courage chipped away under his scrutiny. Tunde seemed drawn and tired, and he had lost weight since the last time they saw each other. They sat on different chairs, and no one mentioned anything for a while.

"Karen."

"Tunde."

They spoke simultaneously, and their eyes widened in brief amusement. Karen cleared her throat and focused on her clasped hands on her lap.

"You go first," she stated.

Tunde took a deep breath. Her frame was slimmer and subdued but still beautiful. Swinging his gaze to the abstract painting on the wall, he processed so many emotions as soon as he saw her—excitement, love, fear, anger, joy—and then they morphed into relief.

"Karen," he started, staring at her, "I'm glad you're okay. You finally responded to my texts. I was worried. You don't know how often I came here out of concern."

"I'm sorry." Karen held his gaze as she noted his face, body, and clothes. She wanted all of him etched into her mind for as long as possible. "I had so much stuff to deal with."

"Not even a call? Is it because of the promotion?"

Karen frowned. "No, it was never about the promotion." She paused, seeing his sidelong glance. "I mean," she started again, "I wanted a promotion. I thought it was what I needed to be happy, but I don't think so anymore."

"I don't understand," Tunde's eyebrows snapped together. "Is that why you quit?" He noticed the space between them on the couch, and his smile slipped. "Can I come closer?" his words came out in a choked whisper.

"I'm sorry. Not yet, Tunde. We need to at least talk."

He scoffed and got up, walking to the spot by the balcony door she was fond of. "You're damn right. We need to talk." He fumed as bitterness suffused his features at her rejection.

"Tunde—" Karen turned to him. Her mind started to race. "Tunde, I'm pregnant." She eyed him warily, searching for any hint of an adverse reaction. It took a minute to process. She could tell the minute her statement registered in his mind. His eyes widened in shock.

Tunde's mouth hung open and closed as if unsure of what to do. "You're pregnant?" he gasped, walking beside her on the couch, examining the woman he loved, peering at her stomach, and seeing if any changes showed. "You're pregnant," he repeated. "When? How did you know?"

"The day at the office, during the meeting," Karen whispered.

He sat at the edge of the center table to face her.

"I'm sorry I didn't tell you earlier. It's just that I had so much to deal with then, and I still do." She choked, her eyes swimming in tears as his hand covered hers on her lap. "I was shocked, Tunde. I didn't know how it happened."

"Karen, I wish you had told me sooner. You don't have to figure it out alone."

"How do you feel about it? About me being pregnant?" Karen studied his expression. "I don't think I've processed things myself. I don't know what to do yet." She gulped. "Tunde, I don't want to have a baby."

His eyes widened for the second time, and he dropped her hands; straightening up, he gave her a hard look. "Are you saying …"

"Tunde, I'm not well," she rushed, desperate to ease the tension between them.

"You're sick? We can go to a doctor." Tunde muttered, trying to make sense of everything; in shock, he forgot the long speech he had prepared about how she would have to choose whether she wanted to continue seeing him. He had told himself that he would stand firm and tell her that he was more than a toy to be picked up and thrown away at will. Now all of that did not mean a thing, not a damn thing. He thought of how to tell his parents, what he would do, and how his life would change with a baby.

"What do you mean by you are sick?" he asked again as she hung her head as though there was more that the woman sitting before him had to say. "Karen," Tunde sighed and returned to the balcony door to stifle his impatience, "please tell me everything. I'm tired of having to guess. Pregnancy changes things, and we need to communicate. I must tell my family I'm not sure it's a good idea to relocate with a baby on the way. What do you want to do? Do you want to get married? I've asked you about that before. Do you want to think about it now?"

Karen put a hand up to stop him before he got carried away. "Tunde, listen. I don't know if I want to keep it."

He recoiled. "What? What do you mean? Do you want to terminate it? Is that what you're saying?"

Karen's chest stuttered at his murderous gaze.

"Karen, answer me." Tunde let out an exasperated sigh as he quivered with indignation. "Answer me, for Christ's sake, Karen. You do this every time, speaking vaguely, hiding things." He pinched his furrowed brows and dropped his hand with a huff.

"Tunde, I think it's best," Karen answered in a shaking voice. "I'm not well. I'm not emotionally well. What it means to have this baby, I don't know if I can do that. At least not right now."

"What do you mean?" he backed away when she stood as though her presence disgusted him. "Is it me? Is it because of me? You don't love me?"

Karen could not answer; she bit her lip as helpless tears escaped from the corner of her eyes.

"Answer me, Karen!" Tunde's gaze settled on the bouquet he got her; he squeezed his eyes shut and opened them. "First, you ignored me and made me feel guilty for so long. Now you say you are pregnant and, in the same breath, tell me you want to abort it. I asked you why, but you can't muster enough decency to answer me! Karen, there's only so much I can take."

Her lips trembled, and she gripped the chair at the disdain in his voice. She suspected that he might not take her news well, getting angry and hating her for considering an abortion. Karen thought she would be ready for his outcry, but the wretched look he wore seared hot, burning her resolve. "Tunde," she stammered, unsure what to say, "it's not about you. I'm dealing with things."

He shook his head. "There has never been a time you thought of someone else. It's always been about you." Tunde paused to stop the fury threatening to overwhelm him. "What things, Karen?"

She pursed her lips.

"Open your mouth and explain, dammit! Make me understand why. I love you, and I want to marry you. What else can I do to prove I want this more than anything, more than the stupid position?"

At his words, she burst into tears; he was taken aback, with his chest heaving, torn between going to comfort her and his anger. Shaken by her reaction and his confusing feelings, Tunde averted his gaze, preparing to leave.

"Karen," his voice came out with false calmness. "Do you want to be with me at all? Have I been wasting my time?"

She gave a pleading look.

He took her silence as a no, and his heart broke. Tunde wanted to shake her, kneel, and beg, but his pride would not allow it. "I don't think I can fight anymore," he said. "I'm tired."

"Tunde …"

He gave her a once-over. "It's been two years, Karen. Two years of waiting for you to decide and being in limbo. But this is too much." He walked to the door, keeping his eyes away from Karen, hoping she would try to stop him from leaving, but she did not. His eyes were glazed with water.

Karen stood in the spot and watched him walk out. The door slammed shut, and she sank into the loveseat, weeping for a long time. She had an inkling that it would come to this, but she never thought this far ahead—never planned for her reaction.

Karen fell asleep in the chair, her cheeks still moistened with tears.

***

"She's coming today, later this afternoon." Uloma watched the transient fear flitter across the woman's face on the hospital bed before being replaced by an unreadable expression. "Have you thought of what you want to say to her?"

Omo ruminated on Uloma's words. What could she say that would take away the years of hurting and hating? Omo shook her head, unable to face her cousin, and she heard the younger woman clicking her teeth in disapproval.

Uloma did not understand, but Omo thanked her. If not for this ailment, if not for Uloma, she would have made herself content to hate Adesuwa and ignore her sister for the rest of her natural life. Self-preservation made her lower herself, plead, and push aside the bitterness that festered from the hardship she had experienced since her youth. Her father thrust this crushing responsibility on her on his deathbed, telling her to act as a second mother to her sibling and to please her father; she promised him that she would. Omo fathomed how unfair it was to place such a burden on a seventeen-year-old girl, as if she were not a little more than a child, as if she did not need mothering.

Omo shut her eyes to thoughts of Papa, but she could not escape the image of his scarred back, marked by the war stories he shared with her as a little girl. Her lips quivered. Papa must have turned his back on her in disappointment as he watched over his daughters with great shame. She failed to be the first child and a sister but would keep her parents' secret. She would not fail at that; she would get that one thing right to avoid causing the family further pain. Omo watched the ceiling above her bed, her eyes heavy with moisture, lost in thoughts and regret.

***

Karen walked to the government hospital's registration desk, oblivious to the visitors and patients in the large hall. Her mind had gone numb from worrying. She had finished therapy, where they discussed her feelings about meeting her sister. Karen reminded herself that she could always turn around and leave if she did not feel strong enough for this.

The voluptuous nurse behind the large desk finished with the person in front of her and asked the purpose of her visit. She gave the nurse details, watching the older woman nod as the nurse typed in some information through smoked eyes as though she stood behind a glass, walking behind a stern nurse to the ward that held Omo. Sorrow shredded her insides, and she stalled and glanced at the hall behind her, unbeknownst to the nurse striding in front—*I could turn around now*, Karen thought, *I could turn around and put all this behind me.*

Karen forced herself to catch up with the nurse, who had turned back to frown at her. They walked into a large, busy ward, and she almost buckled at the stench of medicine and sickness. More nurses went about their work, addressing different patients and their visitors.

In contrast, other patients were asleep or sitting up, searching for something to relieve them from boredom within the stained white walls of the ward. The nurse stopped, and Karen saw her sister, Uloma, sitting in a white plastic chair beside the hospital bed. Karen heard nothing the nurse mentioned, holding the gaze of the sick woman on the bed, her ears ringing. She tried to run from this and retreat from facing the very thing she had tried for so long to forget.

THIRTY-THREE

The air around the three women thickened with tension, unnoticed by others in the ward. Karen focused on her environment to calm her quivering nerves, but the ward held no appeal. It was filled with people suffering from various ailments: a limp child sleeping on a bed, women in wrappers sitting up on their beds, showing no evidence of sickness except for their yellowed eyes and the stoic way they carried themselves. Some had relatives sitting in white plastic chairs with apprehension embedded in their postures. Splinters of sunlight from outside colored the ward through the louvered windows. Intravenous poles lined up by a few beds, with IV drips connected to the backs of patients' hands. Karen bristled at an antenatal advert hanging above another child's bed.

Uloma cleared her throat and rose from the chair, gesturing to Karen to sit. Karen declined, choosing to stand as her body trembled, too restless to sit. Her mind was out the door and in the car, but she planted her feet inches from Omo's bed.

"I'll leave you two to talk." Uloma smiled and walked toward the door.

They stayed quiet long after Uloma had gone, each woman sizing up the other, unsure of what to say or do. Omo was wrapped in a frayed blanket, her head propped on three flat pillows as she scrutinized the woman standing before her through sunken eyes. She moistened her chapped lips with her tongue, picking out lint from the blanket to keep her mind occupied.

"It's been a long time," Karen muttered. "I'm not counting Mama's funeral."

"Mama," Omo let out a mirthless laugh. "She would have been happy to see us now, like this. It was all she wanted."

Karen gave a half-shrug, biting her lip as her vision blurred.

"I'm glad you came. We need to talk. I need to explain myself; you would …" Karen's throat tightened, and she turned her body to study her sister's austere gaze. "I was in a bad place. I was always in the wrong place; you had it all—beauty, brains, favor. It felt unfair, and the one thing I tried to keep together seemed like I couldn't even do that right."

"Unfair to you?" Karen scoffed. "I don't think anything can excuse what happened. I never blamed you for being mean to me and giving me this awkward distance. It was what happened after." She pressed her fingers to her lips, and a muffled cry escaped as she struggled to push down memories. "You didn't try to protect me, Omo. You tried to protect yourself. You blamed me and still didn't let me go."

"I tried to protect you, Adesuwa!" Omo breathed hard. "I did what I could do under the circumstances."

"By purchasing a flimsy padlock and locking me in the room each night? Are you listening to yourself, Omo?" She backed away from the bed as though the force of her words had shoved her backward. "You let him come back into the house, and you refused to let me go back to Mama; you refused to give me peace. I don't understand your thoughts; what you feel could justify what you did!"

Omo's pillow was dampened from her tears. "What else could I have done? I had three children for Bid. Should I have explained what happened to Mama? What will people say?"

"How can you be worried about what people will say and not be worried about the victim?" Karen snapped. She glanced across the ward, and a few patients had formed an audience, watching the spectacle from their beds with ears perked up to catch each utterance. "Omo, do you hear yourself?" she exhaled and continued, her tone lower and trembling. "You can't protect a rapist. You are giving them more leeway to continue their depravity. Did you know he tried to come into that room after all your efforts? Did you know, Omo, did you?"

"I knew that you had NYSC in a few months, and I would happily have dropped you off at the car park and wished you well heading for Lagos at that time. I know what happened was horrible, but I did my best—I tried to protect my children and our reputation."

"You'll never get it, will you? You'll never understand. You're certain you're right, even after all these years." She raised her head to the ceiling, trapping the film of tears before they fell, and lowered them at her sister. "Mama and Papa would be turning in their graves!"

Omo gasped, her arms motionless on the blanket.

"You're a disgrace, Omo, a disgrace. I came here thinking you'd at least apologize; tell me now that you see the error in your actions." Karen bit out, her body locked up in rage. "You deserve everything that happens to you."

Tears dampened the pillow as Omo was swallowed into the imaginary black hole in the ceiling, a familiar voice she had come to know from her nights awake when she was forced to contend with her worries. This time, it gave her an escape from the woman beside her. Her parents sauntered into her mind, and the day Mama brought a baby home from the village church. The day she had promised her parents not to share the circumstances surrounding Karen's origin with a soul.

Omo let out a ragged breath—*secrets, oh, so many secrets.* She burned in humiliation worse than the day she had found out about Bid's transgression with her sister. Each word Adesuwa uttered pierced into her skin, intended to hurt.

Karen watched her sister with contempt, her chest rising and falling in rapid breaths. The woman became taciturn as though she had gone mute. Karen shook her head again. She had spewed all the hate in her stomach until nothing remained, but somehow, she felt worse, as though a great drama had ended with an underwhelming scene. Karen exited the ward, ignoring the curious looks people gave her, not caring that strangers had witnessed this intimate conversation between relatives. She walked straight to her car, unaware that Uloma followed behind.

"Karen!"

She turned to Uloma in tears, her shoulders tensed, and her cousin gathered Karen into her arms, comforting the woman like they had done when they were girls.

"She didn't understand," Karen whimpered. "She couldn't understand."

Uloma shivered, her face damp from tears of disappointment. She had dreamed of sister Omo being wiser and remorseful. She hoped that sister Omo would understand all that she had done wrong. They stood on the sidewalk, uncaring of curious strangers hurrying by.

Karen pulled away from the other woman's warm embrace, more composed, and they shared a string of words with the truth coasting beneath the surface of their mundane conversation. But it was apparent that Karen may not be back to see Omo, and Uloma shuddered inwardly as she observed her cousin through a glazed vision, ashamed and angry with Sister Omo.

***

August 1990, Ogwa Town, Nigeria.

The church sent word to Azuka and her husband. Chetachi, their neighbor's daughter, gave her the message. Azuka got up from the stool and threw the soap suds on the clay soil; the liquid made a loud splash, darkening the earth and taking the shape of an irregular tree with mobile branches. Her slippers kicked up mud as she wiped her dripping hands on the wrapper tied to her waist, leaving another basin of clothes soaked in water for rinsing.

Azuka entered the house and went straight to her daughter, who was fast asleep on the couch in her school uniform. She tapped her daughter, and the girl turned and muttered in her sleep. She tapped her daughter harder, and the girl woke with a start. "Aiferiomo. Go and rinse the clothes I left outside."

"Ma?"

"Hurry up." Azuka frowned as she crossed the living room to the room she and her husband shared. "Hurry up now before I come out of this room."

Osifo was fast asleep in a white vest and trousers. She stretched across the queen-sized bed and shook him from sleep. She paused; her devoted Christian faith took over her patience, and she shook him again with more force.

"Yes?" the tall man opened his reddened eyes, his voice hoarse from sleep.

She straightened with her hands on her hips. "Father Kelechi sent for us." Azuka turned to the row of clothes hanging on a wooden rod drilled into the wall. She laid out a shirt on the bed.

Her husband shifted to the edge of the bed, grunting as he arose. "Are you sure it's the reverend who called us?"

"Who else would it be?" she murmured, changing into a sequined blouse over the wrapper. "Chetachi delivered the message now, Papa Omo."

Osifo grunted and wore the shirt, his movements observed by his wife in a tender moment of love. He led the way out of the house, smiling as their daughter sat on a stool, bent over clothes.

"Papa, where are you going?" Aiferiomo piped up, craning her neck to see her parents until they stood before her.

"Reverend Kelechi wants to see us." Osifo smiled at his daughter again, revealing the gap where an incisor used to be. "We won't be long," he added. Before she would ask to come along, he patted her threaded hair.

"Papa Omo, let's go before it gets too dark," Azuka interrupted. Her hands rested on her jutted hip with a leather bag in the crook of her arm.

A few minutes later, they walked past mudded huts thatched and propped under rusted corrugated roofs that appeared red under the sun. Several of them had entrance doors made from cheap wood that rotted within a year or two. Three houses in Ogwa were concrete, with the third one as the government provided living quarters for the headmaster and his family. Osifo was headmaster of the single secondary school in the close-knit town of Ogwa. Most of the farmers with children knew him, and it was commonplace for people Azuka did not know to walk up to them or raise their hands in greeting.

She marched along with her husband as they talked about bits of everything. The red earth caked on their browned slippers as they went along. The occasional motorcycle plied on unpaved roads looking for customers, but most people walked to save some money. Their community was not rich; most residents did not go to school, preferring the occupation of their ancestors to the concrete walls of learning.

They passed the local beer parlor belonging to Mama Eghosa, a shack with benches outside where a few male villagers sat in the evening drinking palm wine, their brows furrowed in concentration as they played draft. The bar rocked with popular highlife music played from cassette tapes on a stereo. Often, customers would dance, moving beside their benches as their bodies swayed in sync with the tunes. As they passed, Majek Fashek's "Send Down the Rain" filtered into their ears, and Azuka hummed along to the musician's high-tremored voice.

They reached the Anglican Church, a lone white building near the village center. The Anglican diocese had converted it from a derelict town hall to a chapel. Most of the paint had turned red from particles of clay earth, and the foot of the church was the most reddened.

Azuka and Osifo stepped inside and found Reverend Kelechi sitting alone in the front row of empty pews. The chapel was small compared to those in Ekpoma, as was often the case in smaller communities than Ekpoma. The stained-glass windows on each side of the hall gave colorful reflections on the floor and benches. A wooden sanctuary stood in front, with the altar in the middle, a choir loft situated on the left side of the sanctuary, and instruments on the right. The wooden partition behind the altar had a statue of Christ on the cross, and as she had learned as a child, Azuka half-kneeled in homage to Christ.

"Reverend, good evening," she greeted as Osifo shook hands with the man.

"Thank you, Mr. and Mrs. Aigbe, for coming," his broken front tooth showcased as his lips parted in a broad smile, making his features younger in his trimmed afro. "I know it was on short notice."

"It's not a problem," Osifo returned the reverend's smile. "We're happy to help the church in any way."

The Reverend Kelechi nodded as his eyes grew severe. He clapped as if remembering that they were still in front of him. "Let's go to my office." He led the way, and they shared a curious look behind him.

"How's your daughter, Omo?"

"She's fine, Father," Azuka answered, looking around the chapel's inner chambers with interest. "She wanted to accompany us but had something to do at home."

"Please send my greetings to her."

The group walked further into the building and behind the wooden partition, dividing the hall into two unequal halves. They came into his office, the smaller of the halves, a simple space with a wooden desk containing a few documents, a rosary, a hymnal, and a Bible. A chair that seemed more like a dining chair stood behind the desk and in front of the sliding window. A metal cabinet occupied the right side of the desk, and two blue plastic chairs in front. The reverend sat down in his chair, motioning for them to sit.

He bent down behind the desk and picked up a swaddled baby from a tattered mattress on the floor. The baby opened its eyes, a striking shade of liquid brown in the orange pool of sunlight, and screamed as if on cue, revealing four incisors. Reverend Kelechi smiled at the toddler, swaying sideways to lull it back to sleep. The scene took a comic picture of a priest in his cassock rocking a wee baby to sleep, but the couple watched him with their mouths agape.

It was not uncommon for young mothers to drop their children off since the church secretary, a grandmother of nine, often watched the children.

"I can't sit down, or she'll start crying." He chuckled.

"Let me help, Father. I can rock the baby to sleep," Azuka said as she stood and extended her arms, her husband smiling at her in approval.

The reverend did not protest and handed the baby over to Azuka in relief as he sat down.

The baby opened its mouth, and its sharp cries trumpeted into her ear. She adjusted the toddler in the thin wrapper and held it against her breasts, sitting down with a measured pace and swinging her arms from left to right in unison. Azuka watched the baby, enveloped in the wrapper, unaware of the world, as it closed its eyes in sleep. The baby was beautiful, with dark, curly hair and a birthmark under her eye as though someone had painted a beauty spot on her face.

The men watched the woman and baby in wonder at how she quieted the child with practiced ease.

Reverend Kelechi coughed. "Mr. and Mrs. Aigbe," he let out a troubled sigh, "I'm in a predicament, but I know that God has a plan for us today. You see, somebody abandoned this baby in the chapel. I found her among the pews this afternoon."

The husband and wife shared a collective gasp.

"You mean someone left their child here?" Osifo shook his head as his wife mirrored his sentiments.

The priest nodded, his lips drawn in a downward curve. "Grandma watched the baby while I attended the evening service, but she can't take on another child, much less one so young. You know her children and grandchildren still live in her house."

Azuka studied the baby in her arms, and enlightenment fell upon her as to what he called them in for, but she said nothing, biding her time so Osifo would realize it on his own. She knew her husband; it was best to nudge him toward answers and not feed them at once. Azuka traced the child's long eyelashes with her fingertips and thought of her daughter, Aiferiomo, who lay cherubic in her arms many years ago.

"I just returned from the police station right before you arrived, but they said they can't do anything. They don't know what steps to take for abandoned children. Can you imagine?" Father Kelechi continued the tale after a brief stop. "My hands are full here with the chapel; I don't know when I'll be posted to another parish. We only have two workers and me, and we live on what the Lord provides." He exhaled, watching the sleeping baby. "I know it is a lot to ask, but would you be interested in helping this little one? You mentioned that you've been asking the Lord for another child?"

Osifo chewed on the information before he answered, "Reverend, we're looking for another child, but this is a bit out of the blue."

Azuka watched her husband as he spoke his confusing grammar, wondering what color had to do with the conversation.

As though Osifo knew what his wife was thinking, he interpreted, "It's a bit sudden."

"I know, Mr. Aigbe." Reverend Kelechi straightened in the chair. "We don't know what else to do, and most people have their hands full. You're in a better position in life than most of the community, don't you agree?"

Her husband hesitated before agreeing in a gruff voice, and the priest got up.

"Let me give you a moment to discuss this. At least, if you can help care for the baby for a little while until we find a home for her."

They watched the priest leave the office and turned to watch the baby as she slept.

"Papa Omo," Azuka said at length as a warm sensation like molten lava pooled within her, "let's take care of this baby. Look at her. She doesn't have anybody in this world."

Her husband shrugged.

"It's not that I'm not sympathetic, but this is a serious thing to consider," Osifo massaged the back of his neck. "Sympathetic, as in I feel sorry for her," he added so his wife would understand. He never missed an opportunity to inject his superior command of grammar, unlike Azuka, who had not gone beyond junior secondary school. "What will we tell Omo, our families?"

"We don't need to tell the family much," Azuka responded as her breath fanned the baby's hair. "They've been disturbing me for another child. This baby is another child, Osifo. You and I have been trying, and nothing is working."

"God's time is best." Osifo touched her shoulder.

"That's easy for you to say, my dear husband," Azuka's voice quavered, sliding a glance at him. "Each time we call your people, the first thing they ask me is if I'm expecting, and once I say no, I can imagine how they'd turn their noses up at me if I stood before them."

"It's okay, Azuka." Her husband squeezed her shoulder. "Am I complaining? Am I not your husband? Have I said that I'm not happy with just one child?"

"*Ehen*, I'm not happy with one child, Osifo," she interjected, bouncing her foot on the ground to simulate a rocking chair. "A tree with one fruit is almost as bad as a tree without."

The baby whimpered, and she swayed her arms, and the baby snuggled back to sleep. The church generator roared, and a fluorescent yellow bulb illuminated the room. She observed her husband beneath her eyelashes. He frowned at the window, caught in animated suspension.

She glanced outside as well, watching darkness fall. The area turned quiet except for the sounds of bleating goats and the generator. A gentle breeze swirled into the room, and Azuka tightened the wrapper around the child. They should go home soon, she thought. Omo would be waiting for them. "Let's help the child until they find a home for her. Yes, my husband, it's not difficult. We can manage it. I can manage it."

"Azuka, are you sure?" Osifo turned to his wife, the threaded plains of his face highlighted under the light as he peered at the sleeping child. "What will we name her if we take the child home?"

They sat in concentration, thinking up baby names, and Azuka studied the child.

"Adesuwa," Osifo inclined his head. "Adesuwa," he said again as if weighing the name against the child.

Azuka imagined the child, their second daughter, with them and Omo bearing such a beautiful name. "Yes, Adesuwa is a good name. What does it mean?" she asked her husband, for she was not Edo like him.

"The crown among wealth." Osifo smiled at the baby. "Has she not found wealth? The civil war displaced many children without parents, but not her." He shook his head with a forlorn appearance, remembering a dark time in Nigeria's recent history, the civil war that lasted until 1970.

The baby opened her eyes and showed her gummed teeth. He laughed, a rich rumble resounding in the office. "Let's call her Adesuwa, for she has found prosperity."

Azuka smiled at her husband, full of love. "And she's beautiful, too."

THIRTY-FOUR

Present Day, 2024, Lagos, Nigeria.

"How did you feel?"

A terse quiet proceeded, and the women watched Ezinne, their faces contorted with compassion at the frail woman speaking as she focused on her hands spread upon her thighs, at her chewed fingernails, and let out a breath.

"I felt ashamed. I blamed myself, you know? For a while, I …" Ezinne gathered herself to speak. "I still don't understand how or why it happened."

Karen bowed and sniffed, fighting to maintain her composure, her face flushed from tears threatening to fall.

The newest member of the sexual assault survivors group, The Women's Group, Karen, shared her experience with the eight women gathered around her. The women were lost in a reminiscent vacuum, each transported into their world.

Belinda spoke with a clear voice, echoing through the quiet room. "I'm sorry you went through that, Ezinne." Her gaze fell on each woman in the circle as they nodded in agreement. "It doesn't matter if you wore a miniskirt or a trailing gown covered up to your throat. Sexual assault is a crime motivated by the assailant's sense of control and power." She spoke louder so that her words resonated with them. "It's a perverted sense of entitlement one person has over another."

Ezinne snuffled, and Karen found her hand reaching out to pat Ezinne on her knee.

The girl cried harder, her face adorned with piercings, shriveling in tears. She rose from her seat and ran out of the room in tears, the plastic chair wobbling from the sudden shift before Karen steadied it, desperate for a few minutes to recalibrate as she hurried out of the circle.

Another silence fell over the room as the women digested what had happened, dissecting each piece of information and comparing it to their stories.

Belinda gave them time; healing took time. Like them, Belinda was a survivor, a fair-skinned woman, and a mother of three. She turned her life around after years of grappling with alcoholism. Knowledge and hardship shone through her eyes, and those eyes now settled on Karen; her time had come to share how she had fared since the last meeting.

Karen cleared her throat as six pairs of eyes trained on her. A niggle of shyness seared through her, and her sandaled feet suddenly became appealing, the black nail polish on her toes drawing her into their bleak pools. It behooved her to be fearless in the corporate world, and now, in this room, she sat timid and reluctant to talk about herself. Karen thought of the Trauma Workbook they received last week, a book to help with recovery. She thought of the words she had scribbled on the first page: Angry, Afraid, Sad. She took a long breath, running a hand through her cropped curls.

"I spoke to my sister." A pain gripped her chest. "I'm not sure that she understood. She said it was to protect me." Her voice trembled as she plucked at the lint on her sleeves. "I felt like I was talking to a wall."

"How did that make you feel?" Belinda asked.

"It felt strange talking to her and standing by her bedside. But I also felt angry. Very angry. After fourteen years? I couldn't believe it, and she still had nothing to say about it."

"We can't control how others think or act, but we can choose how we respond."

"But still." Morenike piped up from the corner of the room. "It's painful. It feels like we don't get closure."

Everyone regarded Morenike, some of them rolling their eyes. Morenike was fond of interrupting other people's time, though she gave salient points.

"It's Karen's turn to speak," Belinda chided with a gentle smile. "You're right, Morenike. It's painful not to have the closure we need to move on, but again, we can't depend on others to give us what we need to live a fulfilling life. We can only work at accepting the facts of our stories and move on."

"I can't go back to work. I feel empty and weak. I don't know what to do with myself; I don't know who I am," Karen cried, showing her palms. "I feel naked, exposed."

Mariam sat on the other side of her seat and held her hand while she continued.

"I don't know what I like and don't like. How do I live? For years, I blocked out the memories, and now I'm forced to figure out how to live with them, and I don't know how." She shuddered.

"Karen, you're stronger than you think." Belinda glanced at her, then at the other women. "Everyone here's stronger than they think. It took strength to admit that you needed help and another level of courage to join this support group."

Karen nodded and sniffled, drawing warmth from the hand clasped in hers.

"It's a part of the healing process. Learning how to embrace the trauma and managing your emotions daily so you can heal." Belinda's penciled brows furrowed in conviction. "Ladies, healing starts with acceptance, and after that happens, it's hard to know what to do next because you have held on to that pain, the resentment, for so long that it has become the norm."

"But now that I don't have a job, I keep second-guessing myself, wondering what has come over me," Karen whispered, releasing Mariam's hand and wrapping her arm around her stomach. "I feel like I made a hasty decision, but at the same time, it's liberating, you know?"

"Karen, do you believe that you may have hidden behind work to avoid dealing with the trauma?"

Karen frowned at the laminated flooring as the question released a flurry of unease.

"There are many ways to avoid facing painful memories, and unfortunately, society only talks about the ones that are physically evident, like alcohol and drugs."

"Sex!" Morenike interjected.

***

Tunde started on his fourth glass of wine, and Kazeem watched him with traces of sympathy. He had been surprised when Kazeem called him to catch up on old times, as close as they were—or so he liked to think.

Tunde snickered at Kazeem's joyful demeanor when he shared that he would be getting married. He did not know at which point it became a grieving session. Tunde found himself spilling out his troubles, sitting opposite his friend while he poured out his problems over the meal and wine at the Italian spot.

It may have been easier to talk to Kazeem because he was a learned person, different from their mutual friends, always with his head in a book, and a travel enthusiast. Kazeem had been more open-minded than anyone he had been around. It seemed natural that some of their friends commented that Kazeem found his missing rib in his fiancée. She was Kenyan and lived abroad, working in one of the NGOs catering to gender violence, and had weird views (as they termed it) about women today.

"I don't know, man," Tunde finished at the end of a third rant about how wicked women could be and swearing off anything to do with romance as he waited for Kazeem's input.

The man shook his head. "Look, man, the lady's going through issues. Do you want to be around that?"

Tunde's face contorted, poised to defend Karen until Kazeem continued.

"I know you love her, but there's nothing you can do if she doesn't want to be with you or, as you said, if she's not ready to be with you." He stroked his beard and continued. "I respect that she told you flat out she won't keep the baby."

"But how can she consider killing a child as though she's deciding whether or not she wants to get an outfit?" he sighed, swirling his cocktail with a straw. "Is that how much she hates me? Choosing to abort rather than figuring things out with me?"

"Terminating a pregnancy is not an easy decision for anyone, bro."

Tunde snorted.

"Who says it's about you?" Kazeem's voice was light, softening his serious expression. "Look, it's not about you. Having a child is important; some people don't want that."

Tunde nodded, sinking deeper into himself, and the evening went by until they went their separate ways, with him promising to come for his friend's wedding.

He sat in his garden, staring into the ether as it stretched black as an abyss. It had been a week since the argument at Karen's apartment. She sent him messages letting him know she had scheduled an appointment with a doctor, but he did not answer.

He grimaced. For the first time since they were together, Karen was the one who chased.

The thought sobered him up. Were they still together, or was this the end? He would never agree to kill their baby—his baby. She was behaving as though he didn't have a say. His grief morphed into anger as his pulse slammed into his neck.

Why couldn't she be normal? Did she not want marriage and a baby? Tunde buried his hands in his hair as he recalled the quizzical look Kazeem had given him when he uttered his frustration. His friend believed not wanting to have a baby or get married did not make a woman abnormal.

His hands dropped to his sides. He had been forced to reevaluate his principles and beliefs since he found out Karen was pregnant and that she intended to terminate the pregnancy. Tunde sighed. He may be a traditional man, more conventional than he thought. He wanted a traditional wife who would love to have his babies, not an overambitious woman who rivaled men.

He loved Karen, but for the first time, he wondered if that love would be enough. Would he do them dishonor by insisting that she deliver the baby? Could he insist? He had heard of hyper-independent women and had always admired Karen for her strength, but now that this strength turned against him, as though he stared down the barrel of a gun, he was not confident that he found it endearing anymore.

Tunde sighed again; worrying about the future was not the best way to go about things. He would gear his efforts toward convincing her that she would be making a big mistake. He did not think that he could be with her if she did this. He squared up his shoulders as he settled on the thought. Tunde did not know if he could forgive her because he felt betrayed, and if she went ahead with the termination, he was not sure he would look at her without resentment.

Am I wrong for wanting to settle down with her? Isn't Karen selfish, refusing to think of my needs? Tunde pondered as he rubbed his palm across his face to wipe away his sorrows. He closed his eyes, focused on his breathing, and settled into a tranquil rhythm with the sounds of crickets coming to life and horns blaring in the distance.

***

Karen got off the phone with a senior manager at the company she had applied to. After quitting Wemco, she sent out updated resumes to her network. A former colleague told her about a start-up company searching for professionals with experience in finance and project management.

It was smaller and paid less than Wemco, but the hybrid schedule gave her the flexibility to focus on herself while allowing her to focus on a new challenge. Karen promised herself that she would prioritize her health over anything else. The therapy and support group meetings were nonnegotiable. It struck Karen that the idea of downsizing to a quieter life, doing something not as grandiose as before for herself, felt good.

Sometimes, a long-suppressed part of herself—Adesuwa— emerged. That part of her, young and alive, overrode the dour outlook of her life, with endless possibilities stretched out in her mind's eye.

However, Adesuwa left as quickly as she came, as though she never existed, leaving Karen scared and alone. She grappled with thoughts of what it meant to be alone, to be without the comfort of those things that shielded her from unnamed fears, those things that had long been her bedfellows, helping her push aside the reality of her emotions. She had never been without a backbreaking job for so long; she had never been without a man to warm her bed.

She, who had been ecstatic from her call with the manager, sobered at the thought of the visit to the doctor approaching. Karen craved a bourbon as she leaned against the steel balcony railing, the still heat wrapping around her like a blanket. The Lekki-Ikoyi Bridge glittered with balls of light from vehicles, and horns chorused from the bridge like a disarranged musical piece. Still, the chaos dulled against her tumultuous recollections of the nondescript clinic in the Magodo area. The doctor had assured her that it would be a smooth procedure and that she could cancel at any time before her appointment. Her pulse had jerked in an unsteady tempo, as it did at present, teetering between terminating the pregnancy and keeping the baby. Tunde's radio silence also filled her with guilt.

She never had the urge to be married or have children. Perhaps because of women's experiences around her, she could not see herself with a baby, loving a baby, and being selfless enough to give a child the wholesome expertise they needed. She had never been bitter or hated children; that kind of family unit did not have a place in the life she envisaged, at least not now, not at a sensitive point where she tried hard to work through a troubled past, trying to heal. In her heart, Karen agreed with the psychiatrist, saying that healing could be a lifelong process. The visit to her sister at the hospital did not make the process easier; her anger had melted away, and for the first time, she pitied her sister. She pitied what life had done to Omo, that Omo would never free herself of the self-inflicted pain of blaming everyone else but never having the courage to focus inward.

Karen sighed, her breath mingling with the outside air as she gazed at the bridge. She had to see Omo again now that she knew what to expect. This time, Karen would do it to lessen the pain of looking back at memories—not for Omo, Uloma, or anyone else, but for herself. She would do it before the hospital appointment so that if she joined Mama in heaven on that hospital bed, they would know that she held no spite in her heart.

Tunde was another matter; there was a crushing anguish that things had come to this between them. He had called her the day before, pleading with her to change her mind. The plea in his voice soon hardened to resentment, and Karen wept until she woke up with a headache. Tunde had pleaded, yelled, and cursed. He threatened that he never wanted to see her again, and he had left her shaken and weak, consumed by dread, unsure, and frightened.

After a last glimpse at the starless night, Karen sighed and entered the house.

THIRTY-FIVE

"I got a job at an NGO for women trying to escape domestic violence," Morenike stated as a matter of fact. She sat by the large window with the afternoon sunlight filtering through its mesh. It cast a smattering of yellow on the floor, touching on everything and anything within its reach.

A reflective hum settled among them from the air conditioning unit. Morenike glanced across the room filled with other women. The mood was a little sad, with each woman connecting with the other's pain, bound by the survivor's story Morenike shared.

Karen did know Morenike's story since the woman had attended meetings before her, but from Lola, she heard that Morenike had suffered at the hands of her ex-husband. She endured beatings to the point that Morenike always wore long-sleeved clothes, as she did now, to hide her scars. Yet the straw that broke the camel's back was contracting HIV from him. Karen and Morenike were not close; however, observing the woman, one would never guess she carried such pain. Morenike seemed playful, never one to take life seriously, and watching her speak with a sorrowful tone was a contradiction.

"Did you know that one in four women in Nigeria experiences domestic violence at the hands of their partners?" She closed her eyes and let out a jagged breath. "I read that somewhere. What scares me the most is knowing that I'm living with this thing, this HIV, because of someone I entrusted with my body." She swallowed back tears, but they fell as she opened her eyes, shimmering in the sunlight. "I can't bring myself to trust anyone again."

Charity, a slim woman who sat beside her, squeezed her shoulders as she spoke.

"I can't forgive myself." She blubbered like a child. "I keep thinking, what made me stay? I should have left, I should have."

Belinda passed a box of tissues around, and there was a chorus of blows and sniffles.

"I'm sorry, ladies." Morenike forced a laugh. "I don't know why I get so emotional about it."

"You're allowed to," Belinda replied, and the women nodded.

"You know I watched the harrowing docuseries of this young woman raped who died. She was in her early twenties. They raped her close to a church. Can you imagine? She did everything right, according to her family and friends. She wore modest clothes, was in the choir, refused make-up and hair extensions, and all that was still insufficient." Morenike snuffled and grimaced. "They still blamed her on social media for going out at night."

Karen's eyes settled on the floor, immersed in the days she bore the name Adesuwa with pride, and shuddered. She, too, did everything right, she thought to herself, but rape had nothing to do with the victim. Her mother often quoted a jumbled proverb from their childhood: It did not matter if someone fell sick and you helped them take their medicine. They would still be sick. The proverb made more sense now than ever because it did not matter if women wrapped themselves from head to toe, for the problem lay with the perpetrators, people who thought they were entitled to take.

"Hmmn." The sound came from Simisola, a quiet woman in her fifties. Everyone turned to her to listen, although it was not her turn to speak. They allowed her because she was one of the oldest members and a maternal figure to the younger women. "I saw it too." She smoothed her skirt and continued, "As someone who works at a nonprofit for women, I know the government fails women, which continues to make it harder for victims to get some form of justice."

"Yes, I agree." Mama Nkechi glanced up at the ceiling in sober reflection. She was a victim of armed robbers who attacked her home during the 2020 pandemic. "I remember one of the many occasions we went to the police; they asked me for money to investigate, and we gave them over a hundred thousand naira.

In the end, what did they do? They asked me to move on and said that God knows best."

A woman, whose name Karen was unsure of, put her hands on her head. The other women slapped their legs together, moaning and gnashing their teeth.

"Wasn't it on the news that a woman, mother of three or so, was beaten black and blue by her husband?" Morenike remarked, her fair face twisted with disgust. "Domestic agencies intervened until the state governor's wife convinced her to reconcile with her husband."

Karen nodded, remembering the high-profile case.

"There's no point in believing in government if you'll be taken back to your abuser. Right? The worst thing you can be in this country is a woman; I've said it many times. If I had my way, I'd have left this country since." Morenike snapped her fingers.

Everyone shook their heads in a murmur of sighs. Words ceased across the room as the women chewed on this truth.

"I know it's tough," Belinda stated. "Believe me, I know how tough it is, but what can we do but keep fighting? Keep trying to survive? We must still follow due process, it's not only for us but so abusers and rapists can't win," she continued after a swallow. "I work with women and girls in these situations, and we try to sensitize them on what to do if such a thing happens, which is to go to the hospital immediately for a rape test kit."

They drew wisdom from her words.

"Morenike, would you like to stop here, or do you still have more to add?"

Morenike shook her head.

"Okay." She glanced at their faces. "I'm proud of everyone here for seeking help. It's the first step in taking back control. There's still much work, but we must do our part to ferret out these perpetrators."

"What if he's a relative?" Karen asked, so lost in old memories that it took her a moment to realize that she had spoken aloud. She cleared her throat. "My sister's husband." She plucked at the cuff of her shirt. "After everything, she still believes she did the right thing."

Everyone murmured in accord.

Morenike added, "It's prevalent among our families. Many families protect predators under the guise of not bringing shame to the family, but they don't understand that the shame isn't on them but on the perpetrator. That's who disgraced the family."

"I think many people need to understand that societal standards are not absolute," Lola spoke up, chewing a piece of gum as she crossed her legs. "Because our society alienates victims doesn't mean that's right. It shouldn't be the norm. They end up preferring to hide their trauma, you know? Nigerians must desensitize themselves to that because it protects perpetrators if we can't speak up."

The women clapped for Lola, who glowed with pride. She grinned, performing a mock bow in her seat.

"That's why I say wear your short skirt if you want to," Mama Nkechi hooted.

"Or go clubbing with friends if you want to!" Ezinne joined from the back of the room.

"Yes, wear your skirt, trousers, anything you like!" Lola laughed amid the smiling faces, and the women clapped again.

***

The line for the entrance to the beach irked her, and Karen contemplated turning the car around. She watched the vehicle in front of her move at a turtle-like speed and sighed. She had come to this beach on the recommendation of one of the women that it was an excellent place to think, and she needed space and time to think. After a brief deliberation, Karen remained on the line. The three cars in front had gone in, and she counted; she was number four. Karen's fingers thrummed on the steering wheel while wishing the ticket attendant would work faster, but Karen suspected that her behavior could be a manifestation of anxiety. She turned on the radio and turned it off again as the static screeched from a lack of signal. It got to her turn after a few minutes, which felt like hours.

She gave the attendant her money and drove onto the private beach with his approval. Karen parked under a coconut tree, drawn to its shade under the blistering August heat. She let out a breath and sat inside her car for a while, listening to the hum of her vehicle, closing her eyes to tune out the sounds and motions around her. Karen took careful inhales and exhales as Dr. Laura taught her to. Her skin prickled from the chill of the air conditioning settling on her arms, and she took another breath, concentrating on her senses. Her anxiety waned, her moist palms from earlier dried, and she opened her eyes, staring at the row of shops in front.

The appointment at the clinic drew closer in five days, and Karen could not find peace. She would go through with the procedure, but she still hesitated. Her dreams got worse and more tangible as the day drew nearer. During the night, she jolted up in bed, terrified from a dream about her miscarriage from many years ago.

The black mass in her dream had formed arms and legs, but its face remained hazy. It followed her everywhere she went: to work, eat, and sleep; it followed and passed judgment in malice. Her mother appeared after the child. She wore her favorite striped dress from Karen's childhood, but Mama sneered at her in unveiled disdain, her face pale and rotting with death.

She had gotten up with a weight pressed upon her chest and left the apartment, choosing to walk around her street. Her home had become unwelcoming, and she would oblige. Karen called a realtor once the office opened, scrutinizing her apartment with fresh eyes. The place she once loved was filled with too much of her despair, as though littered with boxes and boxes of sorrow.

With a ragged breath, Karen exited the car, ensuring that she locked the doors before walking toward the beach. She remained so wrapped up in analyzing her dreams that she did not take in the beauty of her surroundings. The white sand stretched for a great distance, and the sea breeze forced gentle waves of the blue-green ocean. A few families picnicked by the shore, dressed in swimwear as they stretched out on blankets. Colorful umbrellas of various sizes decorated the white sands of the beach. Visitors rented or bought them as protection from the sun's blaze. She approached an abandoned umbrella; a part of its canopy had come loose, so it shaded a fraction of the sand, but Karen did not mind; it pleased her to find it less busy because she was not in the mood to speak to anyone, including the beach rentals staff that patrolled the area looking for new customers.

Karen removed her shoes; the sharp, hot sand greeted her feet, and she dug them under, rewarded by its damp coolness beneath the upper layer.

Karen sat under the shaded semicircle of the broken umbrella and stared ahead. Only then did she appreciate the beauty of her surroundings. The water shimmered under the sun's brilliance, and a boat sailed a great distance from the shore; its mast stood firm and proud in the air, creating a scene one would find in picture books. She let out a sigh of contentment. Two small girls played by the shore under their father's watchful eyes, and Karen studied them for a long time. The way they laughed, splashed around, and ventured into the water a short distance from the shore, confident in the protection of their parent.

This was what Tunde wanted. Did he imagine they would have something like that? The man glanced in her direction, and Karen diverted her gaze.

The man and his children previewed the joys of parenthood, but that scenario would not sway her. Maybe before her life changed, at a time of youth and idealism, a time she read sappy love stories about princes and princesses, but this was real life. Karen closed her eyes to paint her surroundings in her mind's eye. She could not remember the last time she clamored for the traditional things: a husband and children. Success would always be her first love.

Years ago, she accepted that it made her different from most women, for an urgency existed to have a family unit. Marriage in Nigerian society was a figurative shackle to women, a transfer of parenthood from parents to husbands. The rules that women must conform to from birth never changed; they became more suffocating and not how she wanted to live her life, under the oppressive thumb of rules and expectations. Karen was unsure at what point she came to this conclusion over the years, but it freed her in a way she could not put into words. Mama once asked her what she would do in her old age without a husband, but it made no difference; she had no family, and it was almost the same as having no husband, as far as she was concerned. What would she do without her family but continue living?

Karen opened her eyes to less intense sun and new people at the beach setting up their belongings. She drew up her knees and rested them under her chin; in that moment, she felt like a girl again, safe and secure. Karen gazed at the horizon, and the waves carried her into a private world.

A man knew little to nothing about these things: childbirth and motherhood. The experiences of women and men in child-rearing were different. Karen had concluded during those same days when she made decisions that shaped her view of marriage that a child was a prize to a traditional African man, a public testament to his masculinity. For his wife, it was a duty to her husband and society. Expectations were placed upon women since girlhood had become so normalized that it was now challenging to separate the authenticity of self from the authenticity of doctrine. The two concepts merged and intertwined, shaping a woman's dreams and perceptions of herself from societal doctrines and self-reflection. Ultimately, a woman could not distinguish doctrine from her true self.

It became pertinent for Karen to choose her truth or a caricature of truth.

The boat drifted, no longer in view, but the sea retained its beauty. Karen watched the waters tumble to the edge before being pulled back by the tide, and happiness bloomed inside her. Her decision hinged on the best thing for her. It was selfish, maybe, but it was the right thing for her. No matter what it did to her relationship with Tunde, maternal love was not in her. It would not be suitable or fair to her or a child.

THIRTY-SIX

Karen called Uloma the moment she entered her flat. The phone rang for a moment before her cousin answered.

"Uloma, good afternoon"

"Good afternoon, my sister. *Kedu ka ị mere?*"

"I'm okay," Karen said, sitting on the sofa by her bookshelf. "I've been busy with things. How is she?"

The phone line went static, and Uloma's voice returned as a whisper before the line cleared to a sharper connection.

"Kedu?" Uloma asked, "I didn't hear your question."

Karen leaned back and blew out her cheeks. "I asked how she was. Omo?"

"She's doing okay," Uloma sighed. "They placed her under observation since she complained of stomach pain this morning. I just returned from the bank; our church donated some money."

She made a noncommittal hum and closed her eyes. The phone remained pressed to her ear in one hand. Karen imagined the hospital the last time she visited, the sounds of groaning from the afflicted, the smell of antiseptic and sickness, and Omo's strained expression, staring at the ceiling. At the same time, she stood over her by the bed, stewing in resentment. She snapped her eyes open before numbness infused her body.

"I'll send the money to the hospital so she can have her surgery."

"*Eh*! Karen, you would do this for your sister Omo?"

"Yeah, send me the hospital account details. I'll have my bank work the transfer now."

"God bless you," her cousin whimpered. "*Chei*! You're a good woman, Karen. You're a good woman. The things that you've endured. I don't know whether to thank you or keep quiet. I can never thank you enough." Uloma broke into a song before she said in Igbo, "You're a good woman, Karen."

Karen's tired eyes watered, and she grunted, choking back her tears while the call disconnected. Long after Uloma sent the account details, she hurdled onto the sofa, unwilling to move and lost in a world of her own making.

***

Uloma jumped to her feet from the uncomfortable plastic chair and broke into a song, shaking her hips from left to right. The patients and visitors in the ward gazed at her with interest, but she did not care; their suffering was over. Her cousin, who lay on the bed, lips sallow and white from sickness, observed her, too weak to say much. She wiped tears away from her face as she sang, ignoring Chidiogo's rapid questions. The teenager assessed her as if she had gone mad, but Chidiogo would not understand. This matter was between the three women and the spirits of old who knew the wicked secrets that brought pain between the sisters.

She sat down in a huff and, with a broad smile, turned to the girl and her cousin, ignoring the audience. "Karen just called me and said she would pay for the surgery."

"What?" Chidiogo jolted upright in surprise that a good Samaritan would choose to spend a lot of money on her mother. She broke into another song, swaying in her chair. "Everything?" she gesticulated, her eyes round as saucers.

"Yes." Uloma clapped and peered at Omo, who gazed at that point on the ceiling with an unreadable expression. "Can you imagine, sister Omo? The same Adesuwa has become your savior. The stone the laborers rejected has become the cornerstone." She referred to the Bible as a tear ran down sister Omo's pale cheeks.

"Wow, mummy, see how God works?" She also turned to her mother with a grin, showing gapped teeth.

At that moment, Uloma thought Chidiogo resembled her mother, and she wiped away her tears, smiling as Chidiogo danced in happiness, spreading the good news to other patients. Her tears of joy turned into weeping at all the family lost, and she wished Mama were here to witness this moment—so many years of sorrow came full circle.

She cried for the sisters and the loss of sisterhood; she cried for Mama, who bore some fault in how things unfolded. Mama may not have known about Karen's sexual abuse, but the weight she placed on sister Omo's shoulders must have been a heavy one to bear. Uloma did not know if she would ever unburden the little resentment toward her older cousin, but she felt satisfied that she confronted the woman and told her what must be said. In hindsight, she saw how Mama treated her younger daughter with tenderness and how the standards were more stringent for sister Omo.

A long-forgotten memory from their childhood came to mind; it seemed unremarkable if it crossed one's mind on a good day. However, under a new lens colored by despair, the memory dragged Uloma down with a certain compassion for Omo.

Sister Omo had turned sixteen or seventeen years old, and she could not recall sister Omo's exact age, while Karen was seven. She had come to live with them, still reeling from her parents' death. That day, it rained so much that it flooded seedlings in Mama's garden; it was later said that the riverbank had overflowed.

Sister Omo came home from school drenched by the rain, her cropped hair flattened on her head. She searched for Karen, whom she would pick up daily from the village's primary school.

That day, Karen disappeared as if she had not been there with them for breakfast that morning.

Mama held her hand in the rain as they knocked on doors, asking for Karen until a classmate—a wee toddler standing on crooked legs—mentioned that he saw her follow Augustina and her sister home. Mama thanked him, but the hand that held hers tightened with anger, tight and coiled as a spring. They found Karen playing at Mama Augustina's house, a reasonable distance from the school or the home. They got home, Karen followed in tow, and Uloma would never forget the painful sounds that followed.

Mama was stringent in those days. At first, she said nothing to sister Omo, who stood in a corner and watched every movement in the sitting room as though she were waiting for something terrible to happen. Not long after, Mama returned with a rubber belt folded into two; she had detached it from the industrial grain-milling machine she used for her pepper-grinding business. To this day, Omo's scar was buried underneath the folds of skin on her back.

Uloma cried harder at the memory. Other patients, tired of comforting her from their sickbeds, had retired to themselves, and she would not be consoled with Chidiogo's bewildered placations. Without a doubt, the birthright attached to first daughters lay ahead on an exhausting journey. It sat as a position with a responsibility to mother their siblings, as though they did not deserve the same token of compassion or childhood that younger children received.

Uloma quietened with the new revelation. Her shoulders sagged with grief, which had hollowed her out. All the ingredients had been evident since they were children, set up for sister Omo's failure, sister Omo's need to prove herself. If sister Omo knew that standards except hers should not measure her, maybe things would be different. Uloma turned to look at the sleeping woman beside her and let out a weary breath.

***

Tunde came to her house the night before the appointment. She sat in her living room, reading a book on a subject she had lost track of. Karen did not want to sleep, terrified of her dreams, and they grew worse now that she overworked herself with anguish. The doorbell rang; its shrill, abrupt sound broke her from worrisome thoughts. Karen glanced at the wall clock and frowned. It chimed eight, and she did not have anything planned. A light came on from her phone, and she read its simple message. It was Tunde.

Karen stood from the chair as worry gnawed at her and patted her hands on her sweatpants, buying time before the inevitable argument. Karen held her breath and opened the door.

Tunde entered in short strides. He was a wreck. The bags under his eyes were sagging and darkened.

Karen flinched as an odor of alcohol trailed behind him when he passed her by the door. They were quiet, with Tunde surveying the living room as though searching for something missing in her home.

He whirled around and pinned her gaze with his, his voice gruff. "What would it take for you to keep the baby?"

Karen backed away from him, keeping the sofa between them.

"Answer me," he said, his words a little slurred.

"Tunde, you shouldn't be here." Karen shoved her hands into her pockets. "Not like this. You are halfway drunk."

"Don't." He lifted a finger. "Don't talk to me like I'm a child. You do that every time, so stop."

"Well, you're acting like one," she crossed her arms. "This isn't the way, Tunde. We can't have a civil conversation if you are tipsy."

"And whose fault is that? I can't understand. Make me understand why you're against this." He threw his hands in the air. "What haven't I done to make this work?"

Karen breathed. She was unprepared for this battle, not at this time, not before tomorrow. She scratched her head to ease the fast-rising headache.

"Tell me," he rasped, "I can't understand what you get out of this, behaving so stubbornly."

"Why are you set on thinking this is about you, Tunde?" Karen snapped, her temper rising from stress. "You think I'd choose to terminate a pregnancy to spite you? How full of yourself can you be?"

He scoffed, staring at her in disbelief. "Wow, I was so blinded that I never realized you were always this unfeeling. Were you always this selfish?" he snarled, his face twisting with disgust.

Karen choked on her anger. It became apparent that this would not be a discussion. He had decided to be angry with her and had come to express his frustration. She felt sorry for him, but he could continue his charade elsewhere, not in her house, at this time. She turned her head away, her face set in an obstinate expression, unwilling to give him any more empathy.

"You can at least answer me!" He balled his fists, incensed by her silence. "Only you would choose not to get married and have children! You need help, Karen. No man is an island; you are not a robot! Why are you so against wanting good things?"

His words stung, and she teared up from his onslaught of words. "Tunde, I need you to leave," she muttered, giving him a frosty look.

Tunde did a double-take. "That's all I get? No explanation, nothing?"

"I said all I had to. If you can't understand, it's on you." Karen drew a breath. "I can't do this back and forth. I made up my mind."

"Then you'd lose me."

She wrapped her arms around her waist and made a half-shrug.

Tunde gave a mirthless laugh. "I can't believe I loved you." He pinched the bridge of his nose, letting out a wretched sigh. "You've done nothing but cause me pain, Karen. I can't do this anymore. This is it for me."

Karen swallowed. She walked to the door and opened it, standing aside, her face turned away from him.

He scoffed. "You'd die alone at this rate," he bit out in the coldest tone and walked out of Karen's home, out of her life.

THIRTY-SEVEN

Karen exited the beaten-up Toyota Corolla that had been converted into a taxi and pushed herself forward with no thought to her surroundings. She had been to the clinic for a consultation, and the street had not changed, but today was different—today was frightening. Karen hurried into the discreet clinic at the end of a quiet street in a residential estate. Despite the humid weather, her skin felt cold, and she wrapped her shawl tighter. She glanced around with heightened senses, imagining eyes from nearby buildings peering at her.

She breathed a sigh of relief when she crossed the gates and nodded at the security guards as they greeted her. A blast of cold air hit her from the standing air conditioner in the empty lobby, save for a young woman sitting beside an anxious man. Karen strode to the front desk, giving her name and appointment time while the smiling nurse tapped away on her computer, directing her to the row of metal chairs.

Karen sat down with a huff. She checked her phone, and the lock screen revealed no new notifications. Tunde did not call or text, and Karen knew within her that he would not, not after he came to her home drunk. He had convinced himself that she was heartless. Karen's throat thickened with sobs, and her eyes met the woman sitting at the far end of the room with the man. She mustered a hesitant smile at the woman and swung her gaze elsewhere. A nurse appeared and called out names, and the woman and her companion left with her and went into another room.

She picked up her phone again and sighed. Tunde would not call; he was too angry and hurt, but so was she—her hurt felt more profound, more suffocating. An antiseptic scent clogged her nose as her conscience clawed at her. Or should she keep this baby? Her mind wavered; maybe it was the wrong choice to do this to herself. Lord knows she had the resources to care for the baby, and Tunde would be pleased, but she could not fathom what else he would expect from her. If he asked her to marry him, Karen did not think she would say yes, as much as she loved him. She loved him, but her views on marriage were still the same. Would he understand there are other ways to approach a lasting commitment, and marriage was one of many? She would never be able to heal if she let herself be swayed into the generic life cycle, at least not now. She wanted—no, needed—to come to terms with her past and find herself.

Her name floated toward her from a distance. A nurse stood before her, and Karen apologized and rose as the woman motioned for her to follow. They entered an examination room.

"Please change," the nurse said, handing her a hospital gown. "You can change there." She pointed at a small cubicle in the corner of the room, and Karen nodded, her chest tautening as she stripped off her clothes. She took a deep breath, smoothing her frayed nerves, and came out after a few minutes.

"Please lie down. I need to take your vitals and all that." The nurse smiled.

Karen could almost hear her own heart thumping fast. She kept quiet as the nurse did the necessary preparations for the procedure.

"Do you have someone coming to meet you after?" the lady asked, her eyes bland behind her glasses.

"No," she muttered, turning her head away, afraid to find signs of disapproval on the nurse's face.

"It's okay," the nurse responded in an even tone. "It's best to do some things without people watching."

Karen gave her a fixed smile, pushing away her fear. "He may show up," her voice stumbled, but she needed to believe it. She needed to think that Tunde would be by her side when she woke up because she felt less alone when she did.

"You're all set," the nurse said, turning her swivel chair away from the computer and getting up. "Give me a moment; the anesthetist should be with you shortly."

A short, serene man dressed in a white coat opened the door.

"Ah, good afternoon, sir," the nurse chuckled. "I was about to come for you."

He smiled at the women. "Ms. Ezeani?"

"Yes," Karen answered in a tight voice as they brought more equipment.

Her eyes started closing with the chemical injected into her veins. The man's voice faded in time with the guilt that sat within her toward Tunde. The last thing she remembered was telling whoever was in the room to ask Tunde to wait for her.

***

Tunde sat opposite his friend at the dining table in Boma's house with a bottle of Guinness. From the last time he met Boma, he shared everything between him and Karen, even his brief talk with Kazeem. The man grunted and snickered at some points of the story, shaking his head at other parts. Boma wore a white vest and brown shorts, the flaps open, revealing a trail of tight curls peeking out and disappearing into the waistband of his underwear. He ate from a plate of jollof rice, and his beer was almost finished. Tunde's drink remained untouched, water droplets from condensation pooling on the glass table where the bottle stood.

"Adebiyi!" Boma called out after Tunde finished his story, ignoring Tunde's scowl. "Adebiyi!" he called out again, a grain of rice flying out of his mouth.

Adebiyi, Boma's second roommate, exited the room and stood at the door in his shorts. The house pulsed with heat, and there was no electricity or fuel to turn on the generator. Boma had lamented that the single gas station selling fuel in the area had a long queue, and none of them bothered to stand in long fuel lines. The men decided to brave the heat until electricity returned.

Adebiyi yawned. His eyes, drooping from sleep, widened as he zeroed in on the plate. He rubbed his bare stomach. "*Food dey?*"

"Forget food! Come and hear what my guy is saying," Boma shouted, angering Tunde, unwilling to share his personal life with others. Boma and Adebiyi were close, but his business did not constitute a subject for Adebiyi, an acquaintance.

"He says his madam, in the office," Boma supplied to Adebiyi in a boisterous laugh. "Madam, that's older, and he's been running on the side. She's pregnant, and she wants to abort it; my guy wants her to keep the baby, and maybe they can marry if she agrees." His friend finished positioning his fingers in the air for quotation marks.

Adebiyi tittered for a minute until he and Boma burst into laughter. Adebiyi wiped his eyes from the stray tears that formed at the humor that Tunde failed to see, whose anger evolved into embarrassment.

"Are you serious, Tunde?" Adebiyi's slim shoulders trembled with the last fragments of laughter.

"Tunde, wake up." Boma knocked on the glass table. "Wake up! Are you hearing yourself?"

Adebiyi shook his head in wonder and folded his arms across his chest as he leaned on the door frame. "Guy," his deep voice sauntered into the conversation, "don't try that. Let her go. It's good that she wants to abort *sef*. She has saved you the stress of trying to convince her."

"Thank you, my brother," his friend rested his hands on the table. "*Shey*, you've heard how another person thinks you're deceiving yourself? That's why I called Adebiyi here. If my mouth smells, maybe that's why you don't want to listen, but you'd hear from someone else."

"Is that not how Boye, too, continued 'doing love' during the period that his babe got pregnant? Only for him to find out that the child wasn't his after three years," Adebiyi hissed, scratching the back of his arm. "Fear these women, *o*. They are evil! Is your madam married?"

"No, guy," Boma answered before Tunde could speak. "She's over thirty years old."

"*Ah!*" Adebiyi put his hands on his head, exposing hairy armpits. "She wants to pin the baby on you. Run, pack your shoes, and run. How do you know that you are the father, bro?"

"She can't do that, *naw*. Karen isn't the type," Tunde muttered. "Boma, stop this. Not every woman is out to get you."

"Then why did you come to me for advice, *naw*? Go and marry your woman, *abeg*. We'll come and dance on that day. *You dey follow Kazeem talk.*" Boma rose from the chair and stepped back. "Kazeem, that guy's a fool *o*!" He turned to his Adebiyi and cackled. "Guy, you remember that weird man I told you about who always has a book as if other people are foolish?"

"Yes, guy."

"Kazeem is marrying that Kenyan girl who slept with Ofure that year!" Boma grimaced as he rolled his shoulder. "How can a man marry a woman who has slept with someone he knows? *The guy dey craze naw.*"

"*Ewoo*, bro." Adebiyi put his hands on his head.

"You better wake up and follow Stephanie, bro. That one is a good girl. Let *Kene* or *Kedu*, or whatever her name is, go. Your madam is looking for a man that she'll control."

Tunde wiped his face, eyes on an invisible point on the glass table. His temples throbbed, and the men's amusement at his expense added embarrassment to the growing list of atrocities Karen had committed. If not for her, he would not be in this position. He stared into space as the other men campaigned against women in the background. His heart twisted in resentment at the expanse of troubles Karen caused him, and rousing thoughts blurred Boma's voice as his friend went on in outrage, Adebiyi chiming in with occasional claps in wonder, encouraging the other man.

THIRTY-EIGHT

Stephanie turned off the television in her living room and glanced at the wall clock above it; it struck nine p.m. She got up from her comfortable position on the settee, heading for bed, and wrapped her robe tighter around her waist.

A knock rapped on the door, and Stephanie paused, unsure of who would be outside her door at such a time. Her phone pinged on the coffee table, and she read the notification; her mind screeched to a stop—Tunde. Tunde, who refused to speak to her weeks ago after the debacle at the office, the device vibrated, and she hesitated. Stephanie shut her mouth and opened the door. He stood in the flesh outside her metal door, a desolate expression across his features.

"Hey," Tunde gave her a slight smile. "I know it's pretty late."

Stephanie watched him for a minute and moved aside. He walked in, tall and filling up the space, and she closed the door, following the expanse of his bent shoulders. She stood some feet from him, taking in the noticeable tension lines on his face.

"Have a seat," Stephanie mumbled as Tunde took his place beside her on the couch, combusting the flutters in her chest into a blazing flare. "Do you want something to drink? Water? I have some wine left over from dinner."

"Wine would be good."

After she left, he viewed the living room. Stephanie's house differed from Karen's; Karen's was decorated with art, and Stephanie's had a calendar and family photo on the wall. The rest of the wall lay bare, coated in white paint. His chest bristled. He could not decide if it was a good idea to be here.

Tunde heard the glass clinking from the kitchen in the back of the house and recalled his conversation with Boma earlier. He took off work knowing Karen would have the procedure in the afternoon but could not bring himself to speak to or see her. He tried, indeed, he tried, but what would he do? Tunde could not stand there and pretend to be happy and support her. Instead, he visited his friend, who remained convinced that Karen was not the woman he should settle down with. As if compelled by an unknown force, he drove toward her apartment after his short hangout with Boma, who guffawed and called Kazeem a lovestruck fool.

"Why would any man want to be with such a woman? Too stubborn and believing in all the bullshit on feminism these days," Boma had yelled, his mouth curled in irritation. "That's why she's not married! Who wants to put up with that nonsense, and you want to tie yourself to her? You better prostrate yourself, kiss the ground, and thank your mother that you escaped!"

His friend's words echoed in his mind. Tunde watched Stephanie bring two glasses of wine to the center table. He murmured his thanks as she sat on the settee, leaving some space between them.

"Tunde." The red liquid swished in her glass, staining the side with a dark hue. "I'm sorry." Stephanie exhaled. "You were right. It wasn't my place to do anything about your love life."

Tunde cocked his head to the side, studying her. "It's all right. Karen and I are no longer together. You were right. It should never have happened."

Stephani's breath quickened, and she folded her hands on her lap. "Oh, Tunde," she murmured. "May I ask what happened?"

"She got pregnant and chose to abort it." He took a sip of wine to quell his sadness spiral. "She removed it today."

Tunde watched the fleeting emotions in her eyes, and silence settled between them. He thought back to Boma again, asking why he had not set his sights on Stephanie. "The babe likes you." Boma smiled with approval. "That girl is sensible, unlike all these women who want to be men by force."

He observed the woman beside him as she placed her glass to her lips. Her throat moved as the contents slid smoothly down her throat. Maybe Boma had been correct, and he had focused on the wrong person for so long.

Stephanie took a long breath. She now understood why he had come here; he needed comfort. Someone to baby him and tell him that everything would be okay. Someone to make him forget everything, even if briefly, someone to make him feel like a man, assured in himself. But she would not take responsibility for comforting him. It was not her job to babysit an adult. Watching him from the corner of her eyes, she could tell he studied her from the speculative arch between his brows. Her heart lurched, but not with love. She knew now that she may have loved him, but not enough to be used as a crutch to heal him from his relationship with another woman. For the first time, she warmed with respect for Karen, the woman who stood against societal expectations, choosing to be the master of her destiny.

Stephanie did not think that if she got pregnant with Tunde, it would cross her mind to terminate it, but today, she would take a stand, however small. She would choose her peace of mind. It would be painful today, but tomorrow, she would look back and smile, be grateful for that moment of strength.

"I don't know what I expected from Karen," he sighed. He never thought of Stephanie as pretty, but now he saw how her nose sloped gracefully into a pointed arch and the smoothness of her skin. Tunde moved closer to her, encouraged by her silence as she observed him, waiting. "I don't think we can get back to what we were after this," he said, referring to Karen.

"Why is that?" Stephanie asked, frozen as Tunde moved closer, leaving no room for ambiguity about his wants. Her flesh tingled with desire. They would be a hair's breadth away if he came closer.

He closed his eyes, and she took in his face as he closed the breadth between them and let him kiss her. Heat coursed through her veins the moment his lips touched hers. His lips were as soft as she imagined, and his mouth tasted like a mixture of beer, wine, and spice. A distant voice nudged her, saying Tunde might be drunk, but every inch of her craved his touch. She moaned, giving herself the freedom to respond as her hands roamed over his back. She allowed him to push her down, his hands slipping between the folds of her robe, let herself give in to his touch, her back arching toward him, pressing them closer. Yet, amid singing sensations, her mind nagged if this was what Stephanie would settle for: to be used as a healing patch, to be treated as an option because the man she loved had been rejected by someone else.

With great strength, Stephanie pushed at him, and he stopped, his mouth parted in lust as Tunde drew back with a questioning look in his eyes.

A sudden chill fell on the parts of her skin left exposed by his wandering hands, and she tightened the belt of her robe, setting herself back to normal. "Not like this, Tunde," she said in a quivering voice. "Not this way." This time, her tone was firmer and louder.

"Why?" Tunde gaped at her, his heart slowing to its normal tempo as the shreds of desire fell off. He thought this was what she had always wanted. He was here, with her, about to be with her in the most intimate way. What could be wrong with sharing this moment to comfort each other?

"Tunde," Stephanie started as he got up. She shuddered and put an arm across her stomach as her spirits fell. Stephanie knew what this meant; she knew they would never be friends again after this. What had happened made things awkward between them, and their friendship had been fueled by her chasing after what she could not have. "Tunde, you're hurting. That's why you're here. It's not because of me."

Tunde shook his head. He did not want to hear that he acted in pain or to know that his relationship with Karen was over.

Stephanie's throat tightened from tears. "It won't make you feel better if we do this. It only makes things between us more awkward."

"It doesn't have to be."

"But it would be. I don't know why Karen made her decisions, but I don't want to be the backup plan for what has happened between you two." She put a hand up before he spoke, her tone demure. "I deserve better, Tunde; everyone deserves better than they've received." She sighed and walked to the door. "I think it is time we call it a night."

Tunde gazed at her at length, hating that she was right. He had the grace to flush. "You're right," Tunde whispered and walked to the door to meet her, watching as her hand twisted the door handle, opening it to the black night. Tunde took a deep breath. "I'm sorry," he said quietly. "For everything."

Stephanie choked back a sob. There seemed to be nothing more to say. He stepped out into the dark outdoors, and she closed the door, denying the part of her tempted to run after him. This time, she let the tears fall, though she was proud of herself for standing firm in her resolve.

THIRTY-NINE

Lola held Karen in her arms, and Belinda ensured she had food for those days after the procedure. It had felt strange waking up alone at the clinic with no one by her bed except the staff, and that was the beginning of her downward spiral into melancholy.

Karen's legs had carried her straight to the floor-length mirror in her room the minute she got home; she stripped off her dress as though the garment had caught on fire and studied her stomach. She had pressed her stomach, feeling for any signs of life, and plunged into unexplainable sorrow. This time, Karen cried, mourning the life that had grown in her until the procedure.

She sank into a deep depression, fearful of what she had done to her baby, as shame corroded her insides for choosing to abort, choosing herself over a baby. For the first time, Karen thought of her first pregnancy, and a voice grew louder in her head, spitting at her, cursing her, reminding her that she would be alone.

For a few days, Karen waged war with her mind, countering dark thoughts, but they grew louder and bolder. She had entered a season of rebirth like a caterpillar breaking out from its cocoon into a beautiful butterfly. However, rebirth came with growing pains and disorientation from discovering a new way of life and living. No one told her that she would feel this way. She second-guessed herself, feeling these painful emotions as though Karen had not thought through her decisions enough. She would choose the same option if she had to repeat it, and the knowledge would bring no comfort.

She was a mess, thick curls tangled from lack of care into knots. She mopped around the house in sweatpants and an oversized T-shirt. Lola forced her into the shower, tired of the putrid smell of an unclean body. The sadness shattered her insides, and her bones melted into fluid. Belinda told her that having these feelings after such an experience was typical and that they were human. It was natural and did not mean that she had a problem.

She shared these thoughts with her psychiatrist, Dr. Folake, and the solemn-faced doctor listened, offering her advice and lending an empathetic ear. Karen found herself researching abortion stories on social media, shuddering at the condemning articles and posts. The words screamed at her, assuring the readers of eternal damnation, a destroyed womb for the rest of their natural life, until she threw her phone to the back of her wardrobe, to a place she could not reach, at least not now.

Standing in her favorite place in the apartment and peering at the cloudless skyline with a glass of bourbon in her hand, Karen recalled the questions she had posed more to herself than to the psychiatrist. She had soliloquized the tale of womanhood, drawing from past experiences. An infinite loop of asking why a woman would be branded selfish for choosing her happiness because it defied societal expectations. Why was a woman branded immoral for getting pregnant outside of marriage? These days, she pondered what it meant to be a woman and how tragic it was to have no peace as a woman.

"Why does society thrust these expectations on women and excuse men for their indiscretions?" Karen asked the psychiatrist. She sighed and gazed at her chapped fingertips. "It's better to be born a man in my next life if there is such a thing as reincarnation," she cried after her monologue at the psychiatrist's office.

***

Two weeks later, she met up with the realtor. He called and left messages, but she was unable to respond. She did not feel herself in those days; even now, as Lola rode beside her, she was insistent on being around so she would not slip back into old habits. The old haunting thoughts still lingered in her mind, and her dreams persisted.

Karen navigated through the light traffic on Ozumba Mbadiwe Road as she drove to the first listing the agent, Mr. Abdul, had sent. She slowed as a rickety *danfo* stopped in the middle of the road to pick up passengers, causing a buildup of cars behind. Horns blasted, piercing through the windows rolled up, and people shouted as the *danfo* remained unmoved. She glanced at Lola, engrossed in something on her phone, and smiled. She was glad her friend came with her. It made things easier. She never understood how pertinent it was to have a support system that protected women and other women she could depend on and be vulnerable to. Karen thought of her friends, Gloria and Ada, women whom she had pushed into that corner of her mind for forbidden memories.

Karen thought of them more often and wondered how they fared now—If they thought of her sometimes. She had found Ada on social media days ago with a padlock beside Ada's profile picture. Ada no longer seemed like Ada. The years had been kind to her, and Karen smiled at fond memories of her time with them.

She had thought her friend's house would be paradise when she came to Lagos over a decade ago, but as welcoming as they had been, she could not escape her demons, and a welcoming house became cold in suspicion, strangers unable to make sense of her nightmares, and her sworn silence alienated her further. She did not blame her friend; those painful memories kept her from a restful sleep. Her dreams took the form of an anchor pressed upon her chest back then, and she would jolt upright in bed with delirious eyes; once, it was in several spiders crawling on her body, and she drowned in a sea of insects, their legs dancing upon her skin, causing her to scream awake.

Pain seared through her chest from those early days in Lagos. If anything, she was at least grateful for the bittersweet experience of being far away from Omo and her family—and the struggle in Lagos taught her never to expect anything good from human beings.

A horn blasted from behind Karen's car, and the *danfo* moved along, clearing traffic, but not before the traffic light turned green. It took a few more minutes to arrive at the destination, and they heaved a sigh of relief, wincing as they stepped out of the car.

The sun stood high and proud, spreading a punishing heat over the land. Mr. Abdul, a bald man of average height with tribal marks drawn along the entire length of his cheeks from the corners of his mouth, stood in front of a house with a high fence as though he were guarding a fortress. He wore an oversized brown suit with his hands on his waist, exposing a checked shirt with a mismatched tie. He smiled at the women approaching, dabbing his forehead with a handkerchief.

He shook hands with each woman, and Karen assessed the busy street with interest. A mallam sat on a bench beside his wares in a tuck shop opposite, staring at them. Vehicles plied down the roads, some turning into strip malls further ahead.

"Mrs. Karen, thank you for coming. The landlord renovated this house." He extended a hand toward the house. "He spent a lot of money on it. You can tell from the outside," Mr. Abdul continued as they entered the gate to a large, white duplex with a sizable garden and a bell apple tree standing in the corner. "Very fine, madam, very fine."

Lola nodded as they toured the landscape, but Karen felt no connection to the property.

"So?" Mr. Abdul grinned at Karen. "Madam, what do you think? Fine, *abi*?"

"Mr. Abdul, I don't like this place." She replied, ignoring his crestfallen expression as they stood in the compound. "It's nice but not what I'm looking for."

"Ah," Mr. Abdul's arms found their way to his waist for the umpteenth time. "Are you sure, Mrs. Karen? This house is fine *o*, and very nice for children. See the big compound for children. There's a school nearby. Very nice area for children." He pointed toward an ambiguous distance.

She shook her head as Lola folded her arms beside her, jiggling her foot.

"I'm not married and don't have children, sir, so I don't need this much space."

"Oh." He floundered in embarrassment. "God will provide, my sister," his bottom lip jutted out after he muttered an *amin*, his Yoruba accent filtering into his statement. "Then you can't rent, Aunty, ma." Mr. Abdul put his hand underneath his chin for a moment. "Most landlords in Lagos want families, *shey* you understand, Aunty? You know how it is with women bringing strange men into the house. I'm not saying you're like that, Aunty, but many of these girls lack morals." He clucked his teeth.

Lola rolled her eyes.

What business had to do with a landlord who did not live on-site sounded incredible, but this was Nigeria. Karen had forgotten how brutal the housing market could be for a spinster. The condescension was not exclusive to the corporate world or real estate. It was everywhere and enraged her when she was younger, but she learned to tolerate pitying glances and prayerful gestures from strangers.

"So, there's no other property?" Lola asked.

Mr. Abdul glimpsed the sun and the ground as though the answers existed in one of them. Then, he beamed. "I have one more place, sister *mi*; it's not far from here." His exuberance returned as they left for the following location.

She offered him a ride, which he accepted, glad to be in the shade. Karen shook her head the moment Mr. Abdul pointed out the house before they got down. It was in a far lower-quality market than the first house. Rust salvaged the gates, evident in their browned wear, and a pungent smell emanated from a nearby abattoir.

Lola gasped. "Ah! Mr. Abdul, who will live here?"

Mr. Abdul winced, covering his nose with his handkerchief. "Aunty, it's fine inside. It's the outside, ma."

Karen burst out laughing as she peered at him through the rearview mirror. "I can't leave here at all."

"*Ehya* and the house inside is fine, *o*, Aunty, I won't lie to you." He muffled through the cloth. "*Shey*, we should check inside, sister?"

The women shook their heads.

"Ah, *ko buru*, *eezz* okay. The house has been on the market too long, and the landlord is a good woman, ehn."

"I'm not surprised nobody has moved in. How much is the rent, sir?" Lola covered her mouth, her expression scrunched.

"Seven hundred, ma."

The rent was too high for low-income earners, and the quality was too low for middle- and high-income earners. It was a conundrum indeed. Nevertheless, she turned it down.

The evening had settled by the time they arrived at the third location. It had been a long day, and rush-hour traffic had built up. By then, both women had lost hope and were tired. Once, Lola snapped at Mr. Abdul as he kept inserting prayers for a husband in his statements. However, Mr. Abdul, still abounding with miraculous vigor, promised that this location would be what Karen sought.

The two-bedroom bungalow was the last house on a residential street. A few cars were parked outside along two neat rows of houses. She could hear the far beeps from vehicles on the main road and generators from a few buildings; otherwise, it was quiet. It was also close to the beach. If she closed her eyes and imagined, she could feel the ocean breeze and almost taste the sea salt. They entered the property, and Karen smiled; she was home.

***

Stephanie stayed and slept at her friend's apartment for a few days. She did not want to be alone most nights, but today, she felt strong and walked into her flat. Stephanie had cried to her heart's content, but it was enough; she dried her tears that Saturday morning and told Dami she would go home. Dami hailed her, pleased that Stephanie could break free from her heartache. She left everything arranged. Stephanie glanced at her romance novels piled on the coffee table, the yellow teddy bear she had bought on a whim on the couch, and the television remote on the edge of the TV stand.

She heaved a breath and dropped her small suitcase on the living room floor, plopping onto the sofa as she recounted the last few weeks to the night Tunde came to her house.

The empty spot he had occupied taunted Stephanie, her throat closing with emotions. She was proud of herself for turning him down, though it hurt. She was prouder that she did not give in to the urge to call or text Tunde, and he made it easier by not reaching out either. It was as though nothing had happened, and they were back to being estranged. This time, he would avert his eyes on occasions when she came into his line of sight at work as though embarrassed by his behavior, and rightfully so. Now somewhat cured from pining after him, she was sure she would have been used as an emotional crutch to boost his ego because Karen was not the woman he thought he wanted.

Karen. Stephanie hugged the teddy, enjoying the feel of its furry coat on her skin. She rested her head on the settee, staring at the bare ceiling. She thought of Karen more often. That woman was a powerhouse. She had achieved impressive things, and her strength was not limited to work. In her relationship with Tunde, she stood firm in her resolve not to have children or marry him. She would never know why Karen decided against a family, but what did that matter? A woman was entitled not to want those things. She smiled at herself as pride spread through her, leaving a warm glow in its wake. Karen's strength inspired her to break free from unrequited love. Karen forced her to reevaluate how she wanted to be loved and what it meant to love on her terms.

She had watched Karen at work and listened to much gossip by the water cooler; Karen had faced resistance at Wemco Oil because she was a woman. They treated her like her job was to provide a mothering figure to subordinates, though she rubbed shoulders with senior management. But Karen never allowed herself to fall into that subtle trap. Perhaps that was why she had not been a favorite in the office.

Karen had been ruthless and methodical at her job, but the stakes must be higher for a woman than a man in leadership positions. Karen had to be more careful, work twice as hard, and think twice as fast. Stephanie accepted that she would never have Karen's backbone but would look toward a future on her terms. Yes, she would try to live a life that was true to her.

Stephanie glanced at her apartment and smiled at herself in encouragement, wondering for the nth time what could have changed in Karen's life to make her deviate from the woman Stephanie recalled her to be.

***

Karen outdid herself. She sent more than enough that the hospital moved Omo into a private ward and then some to take care of ancillary expenses. Uloma thanked her over the phone, praising her in Igbo. Karen had to beg her to stop, but Uloma refused. Karen did not know what she had done for her sister.

The paid bills made the nurses appear more approachable. The private ward was a land of milk and honey next to the general wards at the hospital. Where general wards were crammed and noisy with a particular urgency that made Uloma apprehensive, stepping into the private wing, one could almost feel the decorum. Occupied room doors were left ajar, but there was less noise, so she could hear herself think. The ward smelled clean with disinfectants, and the room made Uloma and the girls more at ease.

Uloma, Omo, and her daughters returned to the tenement building on Tuesday morning. The girls chose to skip school and help with bringing their mother back from the hospital. The building they called home stood imposing along the main road without front gates. Strangers could see inside the premises as they passed. Its navy green paint was discolored by soot and moss that grew along its walls. So when it rained, it was imperative to cover one's nose outside because the house seemed to come alive with a mephitic smell from its walls.

The sun hid behind gray clouds as they stepped out of the taxi. It rained the night before, and as usual, they scrunched up their noses, walking into their block of flats with Chidiogo and Nmesoma in tow, carrying their mother's things. A few of the neighbors going to work stopped to welcome them and fawn over Omo as she stood a little bent over with what little strength she had. They completed their slow procession to the flat, and the girls ran inside, excited to find electricity at home. The television set in the parlor came on, and Omo walked to her room, Uloma carrying the bag of medicines behind. The room smelled musty, and Uloma turned on the ceiling fan and opened the windows for good measure. Omo climbed into bed, its cheap frame creaking underneath her weight.

There was still a slight strain between them, a certain formality that did not exist until right before Omo went to the hospital. They spoke, but it was reserved, as though her cousin wanted to limit the time spent around her. Omo did not press her; she could not. She knew that her role in how things played out with her sister left her unsympathetic, although Omo could not find it in her to regret her decisions. They may have been ruthless, but she could not think of any other way to handle it. Uloma disagreed with her. That much was clear.

Through her panting that smoothed out, she watched Uloma place her medications on the wooden bedside table and turn to leave.

"Uloma," Omo panted.

Her cousin hesitated by the door, torn between ignoring Omo and answering.

"Uloma. Uloma, I know you're angry," she said in Igbo. "I want to thank you for everything."

"It's not me you should thank. You and I know that." Uloma gulped back tears, her voice rough. "The person you should thank is Karen."

Omo nodded. "I should."

"Then why haven't you done that, *ehn*, sister? I've spoken to her in front of you several times." A tear slid down her cheek as she threw her hands in the air. "How does that make us look? Like we're ungrateful. *Biko*, it's not me you should thank, so stop."

Omo expelled a deep breath. "It's not that easy."

"Sister Omo, a silent apology is like a half-handshake." Uloma's mouth parted and closed as if to say more, but she decided against it. Instead, she opened the door and left her cousin alone with troubled thoughts.

FORTY

May 2016, Awka, Nigeria.

The weather was hot on the day Omo learned that Bid had abandoned them. The sun burned so bright that they left all the doors in the house ajar, including the door to the flat. If Omo had known what would happen, she would have ensured that all the doors were bolted, maybe with padlocks, and she would have buried the key between her voluptuous breasts for good measure. It would be a day that she and her daughters would never forget.

They sat around the living room table, digging into the communal bowl of pap and the large tray of *akara* in the middle. Bid moved around the house, but Omo ignored him; she did not care that the children would know they had another fight. It was clear enough since she had moved some of her things to the other room that Adesuwa slept in.

Omo was a woman caught in the snares of a lousy marriage. She did not care anymore, though her children asked why she slept in another room, not that she gave them a precise answer, but some things were best left unsaid. Omo took another spoonful of pap and followed with a morsel of akara. Bid grumbled as he came in and out of the kitchen, making a great noise so everyone would listen to him. The children ate in measured motions, their eyes darting from father to mother, yet too afraid to leave.

He must have had enough because the bowl of pap flew out of reach, and the center table upturned from his sudden assault. The children scrambled backward, their eyes filled with terror, as Omo ran her eyes over her husband, from his bare feet to the faded khaki shorts and white singlet he wore, before settling on his snarling face.

"Nora," Omo said without glancing at her children, "take your sisters to the room."

She did not need to repeat herself, for they clambered to their room, leaving their parents in tense silence.

"What's the matter, Bid?"

"Omo, I'm warning you," Bid wagged his finger at her. "I'm warning you!"

She stood from the couch and tightened the loose wrapper around her waist, gearing up for the latest verbal confrontation that was about to take place. "Warning me for what? What did I do this time?"

"Where's my food, woman? Where's my food?"

Omo surveyed their living room with sarcasm, lifting a cushion from the couch and dropping it. "It's on the floor, my husband." In brewing annoyance, she spoke in Igbo, for words carried more weight uttered in one's native tongue.

"Woman, you're trying me," Bid cackled, shaking his head as he paced in front of the television set with his hands on his hips. His slippers kicked up some of the pap, making maps of his footsteps. "You're trying me, Aiferiomo!"

"You *nko*?" His wife asked, her chest beginning to heave and a foot tapping on the linoleum floor as she put her hands on her hips. "Bid, have you not tried me enough? All these years, have you not tried me? Because of food, you act like a delinquent, shameless man," Omo yelled, hitting her hands over her mouth and clapping at him. "See how you threw food on the floor, food you didn't buy with your money!"

"I've had it with you, woman," he shouted, his chest puffing in trepidation. "*Chineke*, and they warned me, oh, they warned me not to marry you!"

"If I had been warned. I would have focused on my future and left this man alone—" she gestured from the top of his head down to his feet. "—He has done nothing but cause me trouble!" Omo scowled at the ceiling as if Bid was not in the parlor. "I would not have married a useless man!"

"Me, Omo?" He pointed at his chest.

"Who else? Are you not a useless man? Let's call your congregation and tell them everything you have done! Let's call them now!" Omo turned around, flipping the cushions to find her phone.

A stinging pain rang in the back of her neck and then another. She turned around. Bid had never laid a hand on her. They cursed and spat at each other but never got physical until now. Today, she should have known something was different. He threw a blow at her, punching anywhere he could land a blow, rushing at Omo as she screamed and howled. Omo caught his hand flying toward her face and sank her large teeth into his skin; her husband let out a great shout.

They fought, cursed at each other, and trashed their living room, rolling and pulling. Omo made up for Bid's advantage in raw strength with her large mass. Omo did not know how long they had been at it. She did not know which of the children ran to the neighbors. All she discovered as she squinted through a swollen eye and burst lips was that strangers were in her house, pulling them apart.

***

She was allowed to return to their flat a few hours later. Nora, Chidiogo, and Nmesoma stayed behind in another neighbor's house with children their age so they would not witness their parents fighting. Omo thought it was too late; they had seen and heard too much. It did not make a difference, but she kept quiet, her throat too hoarse to waste on a few sentences.

Mama Odinaka, a widow living with her son, took her downstairs to her flat. Omo had never said more than a greeting to her, but the older woman waved it away as she tried to thank her. *Mama Odinaka is a good woman*, she thought to herself as the woman cleaned her wounds and gave her a glass of water. As though Mama Odinaka knew Omo was too embarrassed to speak to a stranger about the dysfunction within her home, Mama Odinaka did not ask questions. Instead, Mama Odinaka held her while she cried and wrapped her in her robust arms. Omo felt comforted, reminding her of Mama in the village.

***

Omo made her way back upstairs. Her left eye was swollen and shut, and her stride was hurt from the soreness in her ribs and thighs. She opened the door to her house to find Bid's family sitting in the living room. The house was the same way she had left it, except for the cushions in the place where her older in-laws sat. The knocked-around furniture littered the parlor.

She almost gasped at the sight of the television. The screen had shattered during the scuffle.

She limped to the available chair facing them while the elders watched her like hawks; they sat stiffly, three men and Ify, Bid's uncles and sister, shaking their heads, mouths downturned, and Ify tapping her foot on the floor, making disapproving noises. Bid sat on a white plastic chair, hands folded across his broad chest as he focused his gaze elsewhere. The neck of his white singlet slackened, with a tear on the side. He had a sore on his head, red from blood. It filled her with a sense of triumph that she had left a mark on him as he had on her.

Omo knew she was disheveled; her afflicted eyelids were swollen and tinged with a darker hue, but that slight injury on his skin was a small victory for her. She sobered up; his relatives' presence meant that the fight was not over, but for some reason, she did not have it in her today, so Omo started on the wrong foot, sitting down without being asked to and not greeting them as tradition demanded. There was no need. Those placations would not make a difference to these people. They came to chastise her, to help her husband rebuild his ego.

"Welcome, oh, street fighter," Ify started, raising her hands in mock salute. "Welcome, man mountain!"

"Ifunnaya, it's enough, *biko*," Amadi said, shifting forward on the sofa and glowering at his niece, who sat on a white chair at the end of the couch.

Ify hissed and kept quiet.

"*Ehen.*" He turned to Omo. "You, what's this we're hearing? A woman fighting back at her husband."

"*Tufiakwa,*" the other men chorused.

"And you sauntered in," Amadi's rugged face corrugated with a frown, "to sit down without a word to any of us. Is that how it is now, Omo? No regard for your husband's family?"

Omo knew it was her cue to apologize. "I greet you, my people," she said through tight lips, staring at her husband in defiance.

The other cronies gasped and gnashed their teeth at her behavior.

"I told you. I told you that this is how Omo is now." Bid cackled in satisfaction as if he had been proven right and the world had seen how terrible a wife she was.

"Bid, it's okay. We will deal with it; don't worry. She's a scorned woman, whether you did wrong or not; we know how emotional our wives can be."

"There's nothing new that she has done here," Oke added in an even tone as he turned to talk to his nephew. A red cap stood upright on his bald head.

"It's okay," Amadi switched to Igbo. "Every action you take has consequences. We've warned you several times over the last few years, Omo. Have we not?" Amadi raised his fingers as if counting. "If I use my fingers and teeth to count, it won't be enough to count all the trouble you've caused. Every day, it's one thing or the other."

"My elders," Omo snapped, "please ask Bid what I've done to him that he makes this house difficult for me to live in." She ignored their incredulous expression as she pointed at Bid, her words tumbling as she battled with tears. "Ask him. He's your son; he's sitting here. Why am I the one who is wrong before you have heard my side of the story?"

"*Kpuchie ọnụ!*" Pa Solomon, quiet until then, raised his voice. "I say *kpuchie ọnụ* there!" He surveyed the nodding heads in the living room. "Look at this woman. We're trying to correct you, and you sit there foaming at the mouth. How can you disrespect your husband in this manner? Other neighbors had to drag you out like a mad woman. Is that the example you want to set for your children?"

"Are they not his children also?" Omo asked the older man. "Ask him; he's sitting here, *naw*. Ask Bid to list all his examples for these girls because your son is a useless man, a very useless man. It is not by carrying the Bible; even the devil can quote the Bible front to back!"

"This woman has gone mad!" Ify unfolded her tall frame from the chair. "Yes, she has gone mad!" the woman snarled. "I told you, my fathers; I told you that she's a witch, frustrating brother Bid in his own house, meanwhile to produce a son now; she can't!"

Omo jumped to her feet and winced at the sharp pain in her ribs. "You're the witch!" she clapped at her sister-in-law. "You're the witch, Ifunnaya! I don't know how you can leave your husband's house each time there's a problem in your brother's house! Are you the only woman with a brother in Nigeria? Can't you sit down with your toothpick legs?"

The older adults held her back, forcing Omo back to her seat. Ifunnaya continued shouting, going from one point to another, beating her chest, and declaring that her relatives should leave Omo so she could teach her sister-in-law manners. Omo laughed as though she was deranged; a woman with the stature of a broom was threatening to beat her. Her frustration had overflowed since morning; she was ready to lose everything— this useless marriage.

After several insults hurled back and forth, Amadi commanded Ifunnaya to cool off in the children's room despite the women's protests. They could still hear his sister mouthing off in the room. Amadi cleared the phlegm as the other elders shook their heads, feet tapping rhythmically in dismay. Through all this, Bid sat in his chair, watching the spectacle with an arrogant ease.

Amadi released a long breath. "Omo, we've tried for you. We welcomed you to our family because Bid insisted you were a virtuous woman. But left it to us—we would have preferred he marry a daughter from our place so she would understand our ways without all this." He paused for the elders to make their sounds of acknowledgment. "As a woman, you must be patient with your husband; even if he is angry, it's your job to calm him, to know how to speak and be humble. A woman must be wise to these things, *eh*?"

Omo studied them with eyes brimming with tears. Her words had been brushed aside—no rhyme or reason with such people set in their ways and customs.

"It is well," Amadi stated in a gruff voice. "What has happened has happened, and we would have come on another day in better circumstances, but your husband has informed us that he is no longer interested in this living arrangement."

"What does that mean?" She frowned, her swollen eye aching at her expression.

Amadi coughed and glanced at Bid, unwilling to answer. The other relatives did not look at her. They inspected the walls, the floor, the broken television, and everywhere except Omo.

It was Oke who spoke. He cleared his throat, his deep voice permeating the new layer of animosity in the living room. "Omo, our Bid has been blessed with a firstborn son of his own."

"*Ehn*? What are you trying to say?"

"Our wife in Port Harcourt," Oke answered, referring to a woman she had never heard of, "has given birth to the first son in your family, and Bid needs to be with her to raise the boy."

"You mean, wait—" Omo shifted to the edge of her seat, her back erect as she scratched her head. "You mean that this man, my husband," she pointed at the man staring back at her with a hooded gaze. "You mean this Bid, my Bid, has a child somewhere outside of his daughters?"

"That's why I said it would have been better to come back another day," Amadi said to the other men, and they murmured.

Omo put her hands on her head as a dam broke within her. "*Eh*! Somebody come and save me, oh!" She slid to the floor, her wrapper unfurling to her underskirt as she wailed. "This man has killed me, *chimo*!"

FORTY-ONE

Present Day, 2024, Lagos, Nigeria.

Uloma called Karen the day she moved into her new apartment to invite her to their house. At first, she declined, but after a few minutes of pleading, which felt like hours, Karen gave in. Karen sighed in her car on her way to Festac, where they lived, recounting the day she moved out of her apartment in Ikoyi.

She had gotten out of bed earlier than usual, enthusiastic that she would leave her apartment in Ikoyi for one closer to the beach, although less prestigious. Lola had shown up a little after eleven, apologizing for running behind their planned schedule of nine sharp. Behind Lola stood her tall younger brother, who surveyed her former apartment with interest. They greeted each other and had breakfast before the real work began.

Ade, Lola's brother, carried items into the elevator while she and Lola did what they could. They all worked, boxing and arranging things into an enormous truck Ade borrowed from somewhere she could not remember. It was almost five in the evening before they arrived at the new apartment, and Ade asked, laughing, why she left such a fancy apartment building for an average place.

Karen smiled in her car, remembering how Lola had stood on tiptoe to give her brother a knock for not minding his business but missed his head by a few inches. The sight was comical indeed. Karen pressed her horn to speed past the driver in front, making a turn onto the highway.

She noted that it had rained that morning, the light showers that cooled the weather a bit. While unloading boxes and furniture into her new home, she learned that Ade was a university student who enjoyed basketball in his leisure time. They all chatted in easy rapport while they worked well into the night. She had to bribe Ade with more than a thousand naira so he could set up her bed in the main bedroom and the other in the second room for guests. Although grumbling at first, he started on his task but was rejuvenated at an unusual speed after they bargained a reasonable price for the extra service.

Karen mused as she drove past a slow trailer.

"Ade's a good boy. He would make a great entrepreneur someday with his excellent bargaining skills." Lola had remarked with a grin. That night, after they left, she took a dining chair to the compound with her mind at ease and watched the stars like cherubs in an inky void as happiness suffused her. She was home at last.

***

Karen pulled up to the front of a tenement building, parking her car as she texted Uloma. The tarred, bumpy roads added to the derelict environment. Erosion and lack of maintenance had caused the paving to split, creating hills and valleys on the ground. A public school opposite the building had most of its block fence crumbled. She could hear the noise from the school and an occasional adult sauntering along a patio in the distance. The school building was unpainted, unlike what seemed to be an administrative block across a sandy field between both structures.

It took her back to her days at a secondary school in the village, an exciting time for the children since they had preferred that to toiling away at the farm with the rest of their siblings and parents. Her thoughts were interrupted by a knock on the passenger side, and Uloma stood with a broad smile outside. Karen took deep breaths in and out, coming out of the vehicle and into her cousin's waiting arms on the other side of the car.

Uloma hugged Karen for what seemed to be a long time before she released her.

"Thank you very much for coming," she said, admiring Karen's pantsuit.

Karen smiled, for she was bereft of words. Her hands trembled as Uloma asked her about work and chatted without waiting for answers. They walked into a dilapidated block of flats, and she gagged at a putrid scent.

Uloma must have noticed because she commented on it with an embarrassed smile. "It's the walls."

Karen was careful not to stay too close to the walls or touch the rusting banisters.

"You get used to it," Uloma said quietly, to which Karen nodded.

They reached the second floor, and Karen observed the place with interest. The building seemed to be partitioned into four flats on each floor, and clothes were spread along the length of the handrail in almost all the apartments.

Sweat trickled down Karen's spine as they stepped inside the flat. She was greeted with the scent of mold, and she had to force herself not to grimace at the sight of Omo's home. The house emitted poverty. Karen almost forgot her apprehension at the sight of their living quarters. The walls were bare except for a liturgical calendar, which was still in March, four months earlier. There was an old television on a wooden stool beside the window and an antenna placed at an awkward angle on top. Two girls sat on one of the old settees placed by the window; they had been watching a movie as it played in the background while they watched her furtively. Both regarded her with reserved expressions as she stood beside Uloma.

"Chidiogo and Nmesoma, you people can't greet?"

Omo strolled out of the room, covered by a faded patterned curtain. The children got up to murmur a greeting, but Karen focused on her sister. She blinked, a headache coming on, her chest taut with pangs of unease, watching the woman as Omo watched back, taking each other in. Omo raised a hand in greeting and dragged her gaze away as she lowered herself onto the other couch, pressed against the wall adjacent to the television. Karen steadied her breath, taking in the awkwardness of it all, sisters sizing each other up, each unwilling to move into a hug.

Uloma cleared her throat. "Karen, sit here," she forced a smile as her voice filled the uncomfortable silence, nudging Karen onto the couch the girls had gotten up from.

Uloma sat beside her, and her voice came out shrill as she tried to lighten the mood, but the strain in the room was unavoidable. "What do you want to drink now that you've visited us for the first time?"

"Nothing, I'm okay." Karen gave her a feigned smile.

"Nonsense." Uloma waved dismissively and turned to the children who had migrated to the space beside their mother. "Chidiogo, Nmesoma, don't you remember your Aunty?"

The teenage girl kept her head down, fiddling with their fingers, as the smaller one observed the strange woman and shook her head.

A lump caught Karen's throat, and her heart wrenched. She crossed her legs. She had carried these girls and bathed them. She noted they resembled their mother, thankful they did not resemble that man.

"This is your Aunty! Aunty Karen." Uloma declared with candor as they gawked at their mother.

Karen pinched her hand as she held her breath, forbidding herself to cry. They did not know if their mother had siblings. They had been too young to remember.

"She took care of you when you were little," Uloma added in a quaking voice.

"Sister Nora mentioned something like that, Nmesoma. Can you remember?" Chidiogo tapped her sister as she gaped at her aunt.

Nmesoma nodded at whatever secret they shared.

Omo fixed her eyes on the floor, ashamed of the absurdity of introducing her children to their aunt as if she were playing a trick. However, that was what estrangement did: a confidant would become a stranger with each passing season.

"Don't worry, Karen." Her cousin sniffed and managed a grin.

Karen wondered how her lips had not tired from being stretched wide.

Uloma slapped her forehead. "Oh! See me, I forgot about the drink. We'll get Fanta for you. You should drink something now that you're here."

Karen opened her handbag to bring out some money, but Uloma kept her hand glaring at Omo.

"I'll pay for it," Omo mumbled, her voice dense with emotion. "It's the least I can do as a thank you." She held her younger sister's gaze for a minute, watching Karen nod. She could tell that her sister was trying not to show her chagrin, but it oozed out of her as her lips pinched in the corners. Omo sighed, sending Nmesoma to get money from her purse in the room.

Uloma declared that she would go with the girls, but neither of the sisters resisted, acknowledging that they needed to continue their conversation from the hospital. She heralded the girls, and they exited the flat.

Karen and Omo stayed quiet after the footsteps faded from the house. Nerves tightened into stringent coils, tenser with the minutes, thickening with each passing second.

It was Omo who cut through some of the tension.

"I want to thank you for coming. I know it must have been hard, especially with paying for the surgery and giving us extra to manage. I appreciate everything."

Karen gave her sister a blank expression, her insides rolled and tangled in throngs of sorrow.

"It's been a long road, but we're here now." Omo stuttered. "I'm glad you made something of yourself."

"Is that all? Thank you for everything?"

The older woman's eyes widened, and she said nothing.

"You made it very clear that you didn't feel any guilt for what happened the last time we spoke."

Omo exhaled. "Things were tough back then. I didn't know what to do."

Spurred by the rage bottled up inside her, Karen slammed her hand on the arm of the couch, unperturbed by her sister's flinch as her vision blurred with tears. "You could have at least let me return to Mama," she choked. "Do you know how it felt, every day taking blows from you? I almost think you enjoyed it, as though you blamed me for being raped and something else!"

"I don't know what else to say," Omo cried, her brows drawn together.

"You can start by understanding what you did wrong, Omo," she spat. Karen took a deep breath. "You'd never admit it. You're too scared to face what you did."

"You think I don't know what happened to you was terrible?" Omo gesticulated as she burst into tears. "What about me? Did you wonder what I was going through? Did you think I wanted that kind of man in my life, near my children?"

Karen stood up, unable to stomach her defense. "If we weren't sisters, I would have gone straight to the police. I should have let you and your foul husband rot in jail." She snarled, her frame casting a shadow looming above her older sister.

Omo's eyes spat fire, her voice hoarse from distress. "Maybe you should have. Maybe that would have been better," she sniveled. "What could I have done, Adesuwa? What else? Tell me."

Karen turned away from Omo, and her presence filled the room, giving it its own character, contrasting with the room and the woman's expensive outfit.

She continued with a tremble in her voice. "Do you know what it felt like? So many years with Bid, frustrated, trying to show the world that we were a happy family, and all I wanted was to bash his head in with a frying pan. Nobody was there for me. You had Mama. I had no one!"

"And so that excuses things?" Karen hurled in a heartbeat, choking on tears as she whirled around to snarl at Omo. "You know, I came here with no expectations. I wanted to say my piece and let you know that I'm learning to forgive you."

Omo squinted at the wall beside her, unwilling to watch the evidence of Karen's pain.

"It's hard." She shivered. "I still wake up at night, feeling his weight on me, heavy. His breath would smell in my nose, and I struggled to get him off me—" She stepped back and leaned onto the wall, flooded by a weakness that left her breathless. Karen shut her damp eyes, reliving the thing she most feared as she was sucked into the past at that vulnerable moment. "You don't know what it felt like, how I felt so dirty—"

"Stop!"

Karen snapped out of the prism of pain. She opened her eyes, tears streaming down her face, to see that Omo had covered her ears, her sister's eyes red from weeping.

Omo dropped her hands, quavering like a leaf. She did not want to look hard at her past choices; the present was enough punishment. "Stop, please. I don't want to hear it anymore."

Karen said nothing after that, tired of her anger, pain, and everything.

The sisters stayed quiet, connected by the pain from yesteryears, until the children returned. When the girls came in, they swiped their hands over their faces, but traces of evidence that could not be erased by hand lingered in the atmosphere.

"You girls should go to the room."

"*Ahan*," Nmesoma pouted.

"Go now before I smack you!" Uloma snapped in Igbo, and they moved as one unit to the room, shutting the door with a bang.

"That girl," Uloma muttered. She set the bottles drenched in ice crystals on the center table. Uloma got up and passed the sisters' tissues, and the three women sat for a long time with muffled weeping sounds.

The showers outside started in the evening, and Karen stood to leave. She clutched her handbag, staring at the wall. "I have to leave."

"Yes, yes," Uloma replied.

The women stood without speaking, watching every move the other made.

"Let me escort you," Uloma offered.

Karen declined. She gripped her handbag, infusing more strength than necessary to stop another round of tears from forming. She gave Uloma a stiff smile and walked out of the flat without saying anything to Omo.

A light rain fell on her as a gentle breeze blew on her way to the car. It sponged her hair and scattered drops of water, littering her navy blue clothing in polka dots of dampness and dryness.

Karen settled in her vehicle and glanced at the building, committing everything to memory. She closed her eyes briefly, willing herself back to tranquility, and pulled away from the block of flats.

FORTY-TWO

Karen and Lola left the theater hall after watching a dull movie. People chattered behind them as they spilled out of the theater and into a food court in the shopping mall. Karen found herself smiling as they arrived at the food court, holding back laughter, while Lola went on a tirade about struggling to hold back tears from how bland the movie was.

The food court had various vendors with louder music than the rest of the mall. A bouncy castle jiggled in a haphazard frenzy, with adults idling outside the pink balloon structure while their excited wards pranced about. People came and went, small pockets of crowds standing before food stalls while others walked past. Numerous shops had products on full display through glass windows. Their bright store signs were noticeable to visitors standing a reasonable distance away.

Lola stopped and peered at Karen as they stood outside the movie department, holding a half-eaten bag of popcorn. "Why are you smiling to yourself?"

Karen shrugged, and Lola nudged her.

"Tell me." This time, her friend smiled back in amusement, and Karen laughed.

"I was thinking how weird it is to be here." She glanced at the theater behind them, at the cashiers in red uniforms, behind a snack booth, and at movie posters placed in various spots to entice moviegoers. "I never came to the movies much, you know? So, it's crazy seeing me in the movies on a Wednesday afternoon." She examined her clothes and giggled, her amber eyes glinting in the bright hall. "And look at what me, look at what I'm wearing. I dyed my hair and dressed in skinny jeans and an anime T-shirt."

Lola took in her outfit as though seeing her for the first time that day and chuckled. She held out her hand. "I'm so happy for you, Karen," she said as the taller woman took her hand. "Isn't this fun? Not worrying about stuff that can wait for tomorrow and being a kid again!"

The women giggled like teenagers, and Karen let Lola drag her around the shopping mall to the window shop. As she followed Lola, Karen kept smiling as if she were having an out-of-body experience. Suddenly, the urge to smile shriveled into a strong desire to hide and bawl as dark moments from previous months of depression flooded into her bubble of happiness, reminding Karen of how she had wanted life to stop. She had wanted a kind of quiet that existed among the dead. Little by little, the women in her life brought her back to earth, reminding her that life must go on.

They stepped out into a vibrant sun, and Karen winced, placing her hand in the air to shield herself from the orange blurb of light. Sunrays spilled over her hands and dripped onto her arm. As though caught in a web of awe, she stretched her arm forward, her arm bathed in a sea of orange. The sun appeared so tiny that she reached out and trapped it in the palm of her hand. She opened her hand, releasing the sun, and chuckled, filled with overwhelming peace.

Lola pressed her forehead against a dirty windowpane, peering inside a clothing store. Lola had been in an abusive relationship and found the strength to walk away. Karen admired her quiet strength, flawless skin, and shocking blue hair; she was so full of life and energy that it was hard not to be drawn to Lola's light.

Although Karen did not understand why they did not enter the store, she copied the woman and closed her eyes. Her mind locked in fear for a moment, wondering if people thought they were crazy, but it was freeing to be herself, to just *be*, without worrying about strangers. Her chest warmed as though the sun hid behind her chest, and vigor coursed through her veins. The women stayed that way for a few minutes until Lola declared she was famished, and the rest of the afternoon passed in quiet reflection, each woman wrapped in her thoughts.

***

Dr. Folake sat still on the brown seat, crossing her legs under her skirt, pen in hand, poised to scribble down notes. Karen sat cross-legged on the plush gray couch, staring at the silvery swinging pendulum bulb in a triangular frame placed on the glass center table in the office. A soft glow filtered into the white office through its window and settled on her couch, emphasizing the caramel depths of her eyes.

Karen averted her gaze from the hypnotic pendulum and thought about the psychiatrist's question: How was she doing? She mulled over that question. How was she doing? Karen smiled in the sunray. Her body felt light, as though it were floating toward the sun. She felt better and ready. What she was prepared for, she did not know, but there was excitement within her, as though the next day was something she wanted to look forward to.

"Going out to the movies with Lola shifted something in me."

Dr. Folake gave her an encouraging smile, and Karen's gaze drifted to nowhere. Karen took in the pristine state of the office, bookshelves lined up against the wall.

A window air conditioner made a soft noise as it pushed out cool air, and the mental health posters on the wall were gold-framed to catch a person's attention, their captions written in bold letters. She shifted on the comfortable couch and regarded the psychiatrist, who sat patiently as though all the time in the world was Karen's.

"Lola's been such a beacon of light. She's dragged me all over Lagos." Karen's eyes twinkled as she spoke, remembering her firecracker friend. "But it's a good thing," She sighed. "It takes my mind off things, you know? I don't feel so scared to be alone while we are outside. It's like I spend my time finding pleasure in new things. Work was my life, my addiction, and I didn't want to confront the bad things that happened to me."

Dr. Folake asked, "What are you scared of when you are alone?"

"I don't know, to be honest. It's everything at once." Karen bit her lip and gazed at her pink-tipped nails, thinking of the nights she was wide awake, afraid of the invisible. "I get scared sometimes. I wonder if it's because I haven't resumed my new job, so there's nothing to keep my mind occupied."

"We don't want you slipping back into old habits, using work to avoid emotions," Dr. Folake remarked with a kind smile, her eyes bright behind her glasses. "Fear can be a good thing. It's a way our mind protects us and keeps us safe from danger, but it shouldn't hinder you from living a fulfilling life, from healthily navigating life."

"I just—" Karen's voice fell, and she breathed, unsure how to feel. She blinked back tears. "I find myself afraid and exposed, and I don't know if I'm healing or if I'm crazy?"

"No, Karen." Dr. Folake shook her head and set the notepad on her lap. "Healing doesn't happen in one day. It's not a pill we can take to feel better in thirty minutes. Healing takes time and patience—I'm sure you agree that growth isn't always evident at present but will be in the future. You must keep working on yourself, as you are doing now, and I'm proud of you for that."

Karen nodded and snuffled. In hindsight, she saw she had made strides since her breakdown. Yes, Karen struggled sometimes, but it was essential to chant positive, reinforcing facts about herself against those dark thoughts before they took root in her mind. She even suggested this method of self-assurance to the Women's Group, as Dr. Folake had taught her.

Dr. Folake let out a quiet breath and picked up the notepad. "Have you thought about Tunde lately and about your procedure?"

Karen gazed at the ceiling and sighed. The beam of sunlight upon her shifted to the space between the couches, creating a bright divide between patient and doctor, leaving her cold and alone as tendrils of sadness began to sprout. She followed the train of sunlight to the table, which gleamed in the sun, crystals of colors emanating in the air if one looked closely. Karen did, drawing from the wealth of warmth in the visible light spectrum as she thought about Tunde, whom she had placed on the back burner of her mind. "Tunde will be fine," she reassured herself and Dr. Folake.

It was as simple as that. After the termination, Karen's guilt absorbed her whole being, as though she had lost a chance at happiness. Yet it would have been an injury to her spirit to let him bamboozle her into making decisions concerning her health.

"After the termination, I was so lost, I felt like I was wandering in a black pit, no light, no end to my grief. I thought of my mother; I thought of my life." Karen said in a soft voice. "It was Lola and Belinda who helped me out of that pit. I read books on dealing with trauma, and the women in the support group led me to an author unafraid to shed light on how I felt—not Tunde; I survived on my own. The books, the women, you," she pointed. "You assured me that my feelings were valid, that I was normal."

The frightening thoughts that she had lost the only chance at happiness she would ever have seemed daunting at first, but now, as she got better and more secure, Karen learned that happiness took many forms. Being a woman did not mean that her path to a fulfilling life hinged on marriage and children. She was more than that—she was beginning to know and love herself.

Dr. Folake nodded and reminded her of the trauma-management techniques they learned each week. "Think of a happy place in your current life," she said. "It's okay to protect your mental health, to feel scared sometimes, and to be uncertain about the future." Her voice floated in the room like the sun, serene and promising, blazing and powerful. "But remember that you've grown from your first session. Continue to focus on healing each day, and tomorrow will take care of itself."

Karen closed her eyes, and images of Lola, her house, and the day she dyed her hair bright copper ignited a flame of happiness within her.

***

Karen was excited to start her job the following week. She felt rested and ready to take on a new opportunity. When she woke in the morning, she inspected her home; the wood-louvered double doors leading to the backyard were wide open in the heat, with a screen door barricading her from the outside. Karen loved the way the sunlight poured into her apartment from outside. It brightened up the space.

She walked into the living room, a sizable open-floor layout with her kitchen shaded by a bell apple tree outside. The dining table set was arranged along the wall opposite the sink, beside the refrigerator, but she loved that corner of the kitchen, where she could peer at the compound outside while washing dishes and cooking. Sometimes, small birds flew around the tree, searching for twigs and such to build a nest, she assumed. Lizards bathed in the sun, the ones with orange tops, agama lizards, nodding as they moved, lying on the concrete fence. She had taken up gardening, trying to plant corn and peppers to no avail. She recalled, fondly, how annoyed she was at the birds, realizing that the pesky creatures had eaten the kernels she had thrown on the sand that day.

The rest of the living room had her sofa and loveseat in front of the wall facing the TV, with a center table in the middle. The floor was tiled, and Karen put a rug under the table, adding more color to the living room. Ade helped set up her television on the wall, and the bookshelf stood beside it. She had bought a wooden vinyl record player and some records to go with it, which Karen now set on the platter, releasing a contented sigh as Asa's ethereal voice floated in the air. At the same time, she worked on arranging a few boxes in the guest bedroom. So many boxes remained unpacked, and Karen groaned, knowing one would face the impossible task before work. Her phone rang on the coffee table beside the couch as she reached for a box, and Uloma's name hovered on the screen. Karen took a deep breath. They had not spoken since she went to Festac.

"Good morning, sister," Uloma greeted.

"Uloma, good morning," Karen said as she went to the kitchen and leaned against the sink. She glanced at the clock and frowned; it was ten a.m. As she looked out the window, an agama lizard sauntered into her view and stopped. Its beady eyes on the side of its head fluttered as its orange head bobbed up and down in the sunlight. "Hope, no problem?"

"No, not at all, *o*. Everyone is fine. It's—" Uloma hesitated. "It's the way you left the other day. I felt sorry to see you go."

"Don't worry about it," Karen murmured. Her buoyed spirits dwindled, and she straightened, unwilling to let that fateful day spoil her morning. "Look, I'm in the middle of unpacking right now."

"Unpacking? Are you back from traveling?"

"No," she fiddled with the sponge by the tap and sighed. "I moved into a new place, and I'm trying to set things up before I return to work."

"Ah, let me come and help you, sister! I'm not going to work today."

Karen blinked at the image of her cousin in the house; she dropped the moist sponge. "No, no. There's no need to. I'm fine."

"Let me help you, Karen," Uloma pleaded in Igbo. "I'll come along to help, so don't worry. I have nothing planned for today. Please."

Karen took stock of her space and sighed. She needed help getting things done quickly. It did not seem like a bad idea, so she agreed, and Uloma told her she would be on her way after giving her the address. The call disconnected, and Karen exhaled. She was unsure how it felt to know Uloma would be in her space. No one from the family visited her except Mama once when she lived in Surulere, and that was because her mother had wailed about being treated like a leper since her daughter refused to let her see where she lived in Lagos.

Karen finished putting away the last box of shoes when Uloma arrived. She walked to the gate with mixed emotions; her hands trembled at the prospect of seeing her cousin. Uloma hugged her as soon as she opened the gate. They stepped inside, and Karen watched Uloma take in her surroundings with interest, a black polyethylene bag in her left hand.

"This compound is nice." They entered the house, and she exclaimed, "Wow, the inside is nicer!"

Karen chuckled as her cousin's eyes rounded, taking in the exquisite furniture and sunlight flooding the house.

"I bought this for you on the way." Her cousin extended the black bag to her, and she accepted it with thanks. It was a bag of mangoes. "A woman sells it in our area. They're very succulent. I picked out the mangoes with Chidiogo and Nmesoma."

"Thank you," she mumbled, taking a mango from the bag to wash and place it in a saucer. They sat at the dining table, eating mango slices from the same saucer as in their childhood. Uloma talked about many things since she came to Lagos. She spoke about her work as a cleaner and how she met a man in the church. Karen teased her cousin, who struggled not to smile. She talked about the contrast between Lagos and Awka and the culture shock of adjusting to a different lifestyle in the West.

Still, her cousin did not bring up Omo or her children, Uloma did not talk about how they felt about the contrast between Lagos and Awka, and she did not share anecdotes of their lives as she did when she spoke about Mama. Uloma concealed that part of her life, which Karen discerned with gratitude. She saw Uloma's effort to bridge the gap between them. The gesture made Karen appreciate her more, for it could not have been easy, especially since Uloma had no hand in what happened to her. Nevertheless, her cousin made an effort to smooth things out.

Within the next hour, they unpacked the rest of the boxes. Karen first showed Uloma the rest of the house, listening to her cousin gushing about the decorations she had set up. They settled in the guest bedroom, arranging spill-over clothes from Karen's wardrobe in the main bedroom. Her cousin loved an old velvet dress she bought during a trip to South Africa, and Karen gave it to her. It warmed her heart to see Uloma break into a smile, praying for her in their native tongue. The women paused for lunch after a while, chatting about random things before falling into a companionable silence and unpacking the rest of the boxes.

The day wound down, and the air was clement, the breeze gentle, while they unpacked the last box. The evening was quiet as the blue-black dusk enveloped the land. The cousins walked to the gate without saying a word, and Karen felt a little sad about saying goodbye to her. She did not know until today how much she missed her cousin. They last communed in harmony before Karen left for Awka over a decade ago. Uloma must have felt her stillness, too, because she grew quieter as they approached the gate, but moments could not be frozen. The time came to say goodbye.

"Thank you for coming," Karen whispered, pressing a bundle of money into Uloma's hand.

Uloma curled her hand around the crisp notes and gave Karen a sad smile. "Thank you for letting me see you, Karen." She crossed the gate and glanced at the isolated street.

A crescent moon illuminated the firmament with its delicate glow. Karen noted that there were no stars as her hands trembled, and she dipped them in the pockets of her sweatpants.

"Adesuwa—" Uloma quavered. "I'm sad that we lost so much time together, and I know that I can't fix your relationship with your sister to be what it once was." She raised her hand before Karen could speak, holding back a sob. "I'm glad you allowed me to spend the day with you. I think Mama would be happy if she could see you today. I can tell that you're healing."

The tarred road behind Uloma wound long and gray, and Karen shifted from one foot to the other in mild embarrassment, but she agreed she must be healing. "I'm sorry you're in the middle of this," she said after a minute, her eyes glistening in the night. "You're the best thing to happen to us, Uloma, and I'm sorry ... I'm sorry, I don't think I can revisit Omo." Her voice cracked. "I'm sorry, I don't think I can pretend."

"I'm not asking you to do so all at once," her cousin gently replied. "We'll take it step by step."

Karen nodded and gave the woman a watery smile. "I'm glad you understand."

Uloma sniffled, stretching out her arms. They hugged, prolonging the inevitable end to their story, unsure when they would see each other again. Karen watched her cousin walk down the street, a lone figure in a silver sea of phosphorescence, until she disappeared into the main road, taking with her a barrage of memories and grief, the moonlight casting a dark silhouette on her back.

EPILOGUE

Six Months Later, 2025, Lagos, Nigeria.

Karen stood in the water by the shore, letting it cool her feet. The wind blew colder than usual, and the clouds were gray from thunderous showers over the weekend. She busied herself playing with the pebbles beneath her feet. The edges were hard and blunt, and they poked into the soles of her feet, but she did not mind. Instead, she thought of the surprise message from Tunde, whom she had not heard from since their last fight.

Tunde had disappeared as though he had never been around, as though their intimate years meant nothing. By some small mercy, she had been too fatigued, although briefly, to be heartbroken that he had not come to her or called. It was unfortunate that things had turned out that way with him.

Karen expelled a careful breath to release the tightening in her chest. The smooth skin on her arms roughened at unpleasant memories or the calm wind—she was unsure which.

The curious tightening ebbed, and Karen swallowed, wading through a sea of rawness she recognized whenever the procedure came to mind. She had woken up on that hospital bed feeling raw, as though she had been given a new body—an unfamiliar body—and invaded as if a stranger had peered into her soul. It was a feeling she would never wholly shake, as though she was branded with a crest of guilt for the rest of her life. Thrust into the bleak pit of shame, she realized that before the procedure, she had felt an urgent, selfish need to protect—not the baby, but herself. She had described that need to the psychiatrist, who had listened and nodded while taking notes.

A seagull flew close to Karen, bringing her back to the beach. She watched as it pecked at the sand, searching for food scraps. Karen sighed and checked her phone. There was a message from Tunde saying that he had arrived at the beach and would find her. She scanned the area, a little anxious to see him. A few people were at the beach, some sitting on a beach chair reading a book and talking, and others walking by the oceanside barefoot. She lifted her sights, watching the sun sink lower into the horizon, and closed her eyes.

The ocean breeze swirled around Karen, ruffling the hem of her dress. She mulled over her last conversation with Uloma weeks ago, which was short and polite. They had tried to put everything behind them when she paid subsequent hospital bills and upkeep for Omo and her girls. They had invited her to their home twice, which she refused. It was not easy to pretend that all had become well, and she could not do that to herself again. Sharing her skepticism with Uloma had been a bittersweet experience, but she made peace with her decision before the words formed in her mouth.

To forgive was also bittersweet, a complicated thing; it was freeing and honest but often misunderstood. It did not mean the sisters would rebuild their closeness, nor did Karen want to. As much as Omo seemed to prefer that, she would not act as if it never happened. They could never return to their childhood or reclaim those intimate sibling moments.

Karen turned to see Tunde walking toward her in casual clothes. Her heart lurched, and she was full of love at his lone figure approaching. It hurt to reconfirm that she still loved him, though her decision changed what they shared forever; Karen had come to terms with losing Tunde from the moment she chose herself over the pregnancy. She bore her sadness well, knowing that she hurt him, but understood it would be painful for them, for everyone, if she went ahead with it. She would have done it for him, not for herself, which would never be right.

"Hi," he raised a hand in greeting, and a wistful smile spread across his face.

"Hi," Karen said with a slight wave, her inside light fluttering as the man she loved stood a foot from her.

"How are you doing?" Tunde put his hands in his jeans pockets.

"I'm fine," she glanced at the orange horizon across the sea as her voice trembled in her ears. "I've been good. I'm enjoying my job, taking things slowly."

"I'm glad to hear that." Tunde drank in her features, her relaxed frame with no trace of being on guard, her colored hair. The Karen he knew would never have done that. "You've changed," he smiled. "You're different. It suits you."

"Thank you." Karen swallowed, her amber eyes turning a darker shade of caramel in the dying sun as she turned to him. "You look good yourself," she said in all seriousness. "I want to apologize again." Karen swallowed. "For everything."

He fell quiet. The breeze whistled around them, cooling their sizzling emotions and allowing them to recalibrate their thoughts.

"Why?"

This time, Karen did not respond, meditating on his question. The sadness she repressed for months radiated in her, and her eyes gleamed with tears. Karen sniffed, tasting a tang of salt from the breeze that settled in her mouth. She wanted to tell him what happened—everything—not because Karen needed his approval. She had long accepted that he would never have been okay with her decision, regardless of whether he knew her background. She chose to tell him because she wanted final closure on what they had.

"Do you want to sit?" she gestured at a spot in the sand further from the water and a wider distance from other people.

They hunched and lowered themselves to the ground, stretching their legs. Their clothes were littered with speckles of sharp sand and tiny sea debris. Karen began her story by running a hand through the sand, sifting it between her fingers as it transported her to a world before the present.

Some time passed before either of them spoke, with Tunde staring into space. His clammy hand clasped hers at some point as he digested her words, watching her motions with the other hand in the sand. He sank deeper into Karen's past as though the sifting sand held the key to time.

"I'm not asking for forgiveness, but I wanted you to know. You deserve to know because I love you."

Tunde took a sharp breath and peered at her. He nudged her shoulder as his hand found her chin and turned her to him.

She held her breath, her eyes falling on his parted lips as he closed the gap between them and pressed his lips on hers.

"I love you, too. I think I always will."

She smiled, hearing the words she had longed to hear all these months, but sadness seeped in again. Karen knew this was not a rekindling of their romance but a goodbye. It was a last-ditch attempt to see if they still felt something for each other. Over the months, she thought long and hard about what they shared and knew that not now, or never, would she be ready to give herself to any man without inhibition. He said he loved her; maybe that was true, but Tunde was a man. They were lulled from birth into the politics of gender elitism, expecting submission as an expression of a woman's love. But women were not born to serve. They were not chattel, inanimate things prodded and poked as one liked. She continued learning to love herself daily; she continued learning what it felt like to be alone and free from external validation.

"I'm leaving Lagos," Tunde said after a minute of loving. "I'm moving to Abuja. I got a better job offer elsewhere and figured it was time. I want a fresh start." He pulled away from her. "I wanted to say goodbye."

She did not look at him as he said this, though she knew he waited for her reaction. Instead, Karen congratulated him and wished him the best. They sat a bit longer until nightfall, and Tunde said he had to leave. They shared a prolonged hug, and he kissed her temple, drawing back to examine her one last time as if ensuring that her face would always be ingrained in his memory.

Tunde promised to call her one of these days; she gave him a noncommittal nod as he got up and dusted his clothes, flecks of sand falling away. Karen watched his back, retreating in the distance, knowing that this would be the last time they would see or talk to each other. He would grieve for a while, perhaps until the very end, mourning the woman who never wholly gave herself to him, then he would find someone, someone more ready to love, and she would be a distant memory.

A small smile splayed across her lips as a silver tear trickled down her cheek. She sat, scooping a handful of sand and shaking it out of her hands, grateful that he had come to say goodbye before moving on, but struggling with a mixed bag of emotions, scared and hopeful for her tomorrow. She would lay the ghost of his presence in her life to rest and move on. Love herself more, love life more. Karen gazed at the now dark horizon, the calming blue night around her, and knew she would be okay.

ACKNOWLEDGEMENTS

The author is eternally grateful to her husband, who inspired her to "keep pushing"; her mother and grandmother, who are the strongest women she knows; her twin brother, whose music and care continue to inspire her; her closest friends, whose benevolence and support encouraged her to persevere in navigating the publishing landscape. Finally, the author is humbled by her experiences growing up in Nigeria, which have shaped her in countless ways, fueling her commitment to supporting female empowerment in her home country.

READING AND BOOK CLUB GUIDE

1. Diverse philosophies of womanhood play a significant role in this novel. For Omo, womanhood signifies a sacrifice for family and society, while Karen may hold a different belief. How does Karen's philosophy evolve through her experiences compared to Omo's perspective? What are your thoughts on womanhood?

2. Discuss the character of Tunde Awoniyi. Tunde navigates complicated relationships with Karen and Stefanie. How do his interactions with them reveal deeper themes in the novel?

3. The women in the novel navigate unique challenges shaped by their circumstances and beliefs. How do their experiences compare to women's roles, struggles, and perspectives in your community? What broader themes arise from these similarities and differences?

4. Karen's final decision regarding Tunde and her estrangement from Omo mark significant points in her journey. What aspects resonated with you, and which were challenging to empathize with? How do these decisions shape your understanding of Karen as a character?

5. Saheed's presence in the novel serves a purpose: a representation of societal issues or an embodiment of personal struggles. How do you interpret his role, and how does it reflect real-life experiences or the people you have encountered?

6. Uloma's presence in the novel serves a purpose: a representation of societal issues or an embodiment of personal struggles. How do you interpret her role, and how does it reflect real-life experiences or the people you have encountered?

7. Omo's question, "Who do I belong to?" speaks to the complexities of womanhood. How does this question reflect her journey? How does it resonate with modern women juggling personal identity and external expectations?

8. Karen's visit to the clinic in Magodo represents a pivotal moment in her journey. How does her decision reflect the

broader conversation surrounding a government's role in reproductive rights? What does her experience reveal about agency, societal expectations, and the interaction of personal and political choices?

9. Discuss the theme of power within the socio-cultural context of this novel. How do various characters interact with power in their environments? What does the story imply about power and its effects in real-life interactions?

10. Sisterhood and the role of the firstborn daughter in this novel highlight deep familial expectations. What is your perspective on how these roles shape individual identities? In what ways do these roles reflect broader societal expectations of modern women in different aspects of life

Leave a review on Goodreads, StoryGraph,
BookBub, or any platform you love!

ABOUT THE AUTHOR

Oyindamola Dosunmu is a writer and HR professional. Her debut novel, *Your Tomorrow Was Today*, was named a finalist for the Black Lawrence Press Immigrant Writing Series. She lives in North Carolina with her husband and their delightfully lazy cat, Bob Chunky Tamales.

www.oyindosunmu.com
X.com/DosunmuOyin
Instagram.com/silverdrivepress

www.ingramcontent.com/pod-product-compliance
Ingram Content Group UK Ltd.
Pitfield, Milton Keynes, MK11 3LW, UK
UKHW041108190126
467109UK00005B/23